Also by Fay Weldon

AND THE WIFE RAN AWAY
DOWN AMONG THE WOMEN
FEMALE FRIENDS
REMEMBER ME
WORDS OF ADVICE

PRAXIS

A NOVEL

FAY WELDON

Summit Books
New York

PUBLISHED BY SUMMIT BOOKS
A SIMON & SCHUSTER DIVISION OF GULF & WESTERN CORPORATION
SIMON & SCHUSTER BUILDING
1230 AVENUE OF THE AMERICAS
NEW YORK, NEW YORK 10020
DESIGNED BY IRVING PERKINS
MANUFACTURED IN THE UNITED STATES OF AMERICA
PRINTED AND BOUND BY FAIRFIELD GRAPHICS
1 2 3 4 5 6 7 8 9 10

LIBRARY OF CONGRESS CATALOGING IN PUBLICATION DATA

WELDON, FAY.
  PRAXIS : A NOVEL.

  I. TITLE.
PZ4.W444PR   [PR6073.E374]   823'.9'14   78-14376

ISBN 0-671-40061-4

PRAXIS

1

Praxis Duveen, at the age of five, sitting on the beach at Brighton, made a pretty picture for the photographer. Round angel face, yellow curls, puffed sleeves, white socks and little white shoes—one on, one off, while she tried to take a pebble from between her tiny pink toes—delightful! The photographer had hoped to include her elder sister, Hypatia, in the picture, but that sullen, sallow little girl had refused to appear on the same piece of card as her ill-shod sister.

"Of course," said their mother, apologetically, "Hypatia is the artistic one, and very sensitive. Praxis is the pretty one." She clearly valued sensitivity above prettiness.

Snap! went the photographer. Praxis beamed. Hypatia scowled. The photographer, Henry Whitechapel, had been a bombardier in the First World War, and afterwards, until too gassed, wounded and shell-shocked to continue his original profession, had taken to his present trade more in desperation than enthusiasm. But he enjoyed his summers on the coast. The sea air eased his damaged lungs, and the pickings were better than in London, and the holiday makers less likely to remember money spent in advance on photographs which then failed to turn up in the post.

"Interesting names," he observed to the little girls' mother. She was a pretty woman, and most genteel. The maid would come down to the beach at midday with a lunch basket for the little family. Henry Whitechapel, who dined off a pork pie if he was lucky, would watch with envy as she unfolded linen napkins and little grease-proof packages of sandwiches and chicken.

"They come from the Greek," she replied, as if marveling at it herself, but clearly did not want to take the matter, let alone the acquaintance, further. He wrote down her name and address, "Mrs. Lucy Duveen, of 109 Holden Road, Brighton," and even made his writing legible, just in case he was able to afford enough developing fluid to get round to these particular prints.

Praxis, Henry noticed, was easily bored. When other diversions failed she would run shrieking into the sea, still wearing her shoes and socks, to the distraction of her mother and the distaste of Hypatia, who was content to sit for hours staring at the sea and making poetry in her head.

If that young one were mine, thought Henry Whitechapel, I'd belt her one. Later he was to have the opportunity of doing so. He had never married and had no children of his own; his lungs and his concentration were not what they had been before the war; nor certainly at that time was his sexual capacity. But a romantic interest in the opposite sex remained, and Lucy Duveen, sitting on the pebbly beach with her hamper, her parasol and her two little girls, made for him a romantic image.

He took the opportunity of passing 109 Holden Road one evening in September, when only a trickle of holiday makers remained to pose before his by-now filmless camera, and he knew he would soon have to go back to London and take his chances there. He found, much as he had expected, a stout Edwardian house, sheltered by laurel bushes, with a circular drive, well-kept flower gardens and a motorcar outside the front door. All the lights in the house blazed, in apparent defiance of the electricity bill: and he heard what he took to be the noise of revelry within, but what was in fact the sound of Ben Duveen drunk, laughing and beating his wife, while the two children wailed. Benjamin Duveen had other children in other places, who wailed for the absence of their father, as these two wailed for his presence.

"Dirty Jew," shrieked Lucy Duveen at the top of her tormented lungs.

"Whore," shouted Ben Duveen, getting her in the small of the back with a hand made amazingly strong at the golf course. He was an excellent golfer; a row of silver cups on the mantelpiece bore evidence to this. Falling and stumbling from the blow, she yet managed to sweep them to the ground. Understandably. Forgivably.

The epithets hurled in the course of a domestic row, the incidental damage done to the furniture and fittings—his books, her tea set, his face, her ribs—they are all understandable, all forgivable, except of course to those involved.

Dirty Jew? Forgivable? Oh, indeed, for it was not, as Ben thought, the automatic anti-Semitism to which Lucy's race and kind were accustomed. No. Lucy was not like that. She was the odd-one-out in her own family, and identified too strongly with that then-derided race. But she suffered from his Jewishness, in a way she had not anticipated. She had thought the Christian equal to the Jew, no more nor less, but found that Ben believed differently. Ben despised her for the shiksa girl she was, lacking morality, sensitivity, history, and that profundity which constant fear can create in the individual. At the same time he worshipped her body, for the forbidden charm of its non-Jewishness. When she produced two girls, and not the son he waited for, he knew that he was right: she was tainted Christian and his guilt had found him out. She was, after all, second best. He had gone out sexual slumming, and found Lucy. She felt it. She suffered.

"Dirty Jew!" she cried, putting herself hopelessly in the wrong. Justifiably incensed, he hit her. And away went the golf cups! How she resented the time he spent at the golf course, and in the golf club, while she sat bored and miserable on the beach. Was this what she had shattered convention for; broken with her family, her friends? Everything she had ever known; doomed herself to eternal damnation, for the sake of what she had believed would be heaven on earth, and had turned out to be hell, here and now?

He was to remember Dirty Jew, and she the blow, while breath stayed in the body.

"Whore," he cried. Well, she was not his wife, yet she slept with him. She lived in sin. What else but a whore did that make her; and what did her whoredom make of Ben? They couldn't be married. Her fault, not his. She was married already. When she was seventeen she had married a young army officer. He was nineteen.

It was a year for early marriages. He'd gone off to the war and never come back. He'd deserted. He was last heard of in Holly-wood, USA, working in the movies. And that was that. The inter-national divorce laws, she told herself (and Ben), were too difficult to face. At any rate, she did nothing about a divorce. Perhaps she was afraid of being free to marry Benjamin in case he did not, after all, want to marry her. Better to live with the guilty secret than the open truth of their life together—that they were bound by the habit of illicit lust, mutual degradation. His Jewishness, her Chris-tianity.

"Drunk!" she cried, kicking him as he stooped to pick up his dented trophies. "No good, disgusting drunk!"

And indeed, Lucy's Jewish lover, her piece of exotica, had turned into as boring a drunkard as ever graced the golf courses and clubs of the twenties, frittering away in alcoholic despondency the fruits of his father's and grandfather's labours. But of course he drank to excess: it was Lucy's fault: she had dragged him down: he should be married to some nice Jewish matron and his eldest son coming up to Bar Mitzvah.

Instead of that, what?

Praxis and Hypatia, crying on the stairs!

Little non-Jewish girls, no use for anything except, when the time came, screwing: good Jewish genes lost and diluted in the great amorphous pool of barbarous humanity: even their names out of nowhere, out of a culture so far gone as to be meaningless. Ben had made sure of that.

Praxis, meaning turning point, culmination, action; orgasm; some said the Goddess herself.

Hypatia, a learned woman: stoned to death by an irate crowd for teaching mathematics when she should have stayed modestly at home.

What did he want for them, hope for them? Anything?

Crying on the stairs, while their parents savaged themselves in each other's form.

"You had to come to me; no one else would have you. Idle cow," he snarls. But who would have him? What decent Jewish family would allow a daughter to marry a drunken wastrel, with a degree in classics and a reputation for arguing with Rabbis, doubting the fundamentals of his faith, his eyes pink from alcohol, hands trembling after a night out at the gambling table, haggard from screwing barmaids and the like: no thank you. So what if he could trace his ancestry back to King David: no thank you! Drag yourself down, Benjamin, if you wish, but not our daughter, too. And you from a good Orthodox home, every privilege in the world, the best parents that ever lived, working their way over three generations from the East End to the grand suburban heights—for what? So that you could waste their hard-earned substance away?

Idle, profligate ingrate. No one decent could ever want him.

"You don't care for your family at all," she shrieked. "Look at your poor little girls—you're destroying them with these scenes."

But she makes no effort, herself, to get them back to bed. Let them witness her distress. Lucy is such a good mother: he knows she is: surely he will be aware, seeing this, that he had gone too far? No, she will not save them. She will use them as witnesses to his bad behaviour.

"Frigid bitch." He seizes her hair, pulls back her head. He is strong: she is helpless: if he wishes to rape her, he could, he would. It is in the air. The little girls fall quiet: terror silences them. Ben makes love to Lucy, these days, with hatred, not with love. The love he feels for her (and he does) weakens him, softens him, makes him impotent. He feels it. She is far from frigid: she is ashamed of her response to his violence: frightened of being out of her own control—is she not a mother? And mothers must be on duty day and night.

"Animal." She bares her teeth. She would crawl around on all fours, she would, the better to excite herself, and him. Oh, horrible!

He forces her down upon the ground. Does he force her, or does she sink?

"Get out of here," he shouts at his children, in so loud and frightening a voice that they flee, and Hypatia, much as she dislikes Praxis, allows her into her bed for the night, whereupon Praxis promptly wets the sheets and the mattress.

In the morning the mother, white-faced and wild-eyed, stripped the bed with angry movements. She did not let the maid do such things. It was her instinct to hide disgrace away.

Few visitors came to the house. Lucy did not care for Ben's loud-mouthed, hard-drinking friends. She feared he would tell them—perhaps had already told them, in drunken confidence—that they were not married, that she was a kept woman. It was one of the reasons she hated his drinking. That, and the soiled clothes, slack jaw, bleary eyes and silly talk that went with it. Animal. Except it was to this gross animal nature of his that she was so humiliatingly inclined. Little Lucy, with her prim mouth, pale face, gentle eyes and delicate wrists, born to be degraded.

As for her own friends, she had moved away from them, lost touch with them. Her own family had cast her off: she was a source of trouble and shame to them. She was in no position either to make new friends or renew old acquaintances. Imagine a tea party, or lunch on the lawn, with Ben erupting into its midst, snorting his contempt up and down his hooked, avowedly Jewish nose.

"I see you're looking at my nose," he was as like as not to shout. "You're quite right. Can't you see I'm a Jew? Why don't you spit?"

Lucy was lonely.

Lucy dressed Praxis and Hypatia in white, and pattered them off to Sunday school, and slept apart from Ben, from time to time, to punish him. Punish herself more 'like. He fell into his drunken sleep and barely noticed.

It was all too much for him. No wonder he drank too much. Within a year of Henry's overhearing of that one particular, worse than usual row, Ben had become enamoured of Ruth, the dark little waitress at the golf club (where anti-Semitic feeling ran high, but made an honourable exception for Ben, who was not only the only Jew they had ever encountered in person but was universally liked), and presently ran off with her, and married her.

Ruth was free to marry; she was the daughter of a Jewish taxi driver, made excellent beef sandwiches, and her lowly social status was sufficient to keep Ben free from sexual anxiety and mental torment. He could love her, and make love to her, all at the same time. They were happy ever after.

Lucy was, of course, unhappy ever after, and so was Hypatia, and Praxis, too.

2

Now what kind of memory is that to comfort anyone? The memory of the afflicted child one was: the knowledge of wrongs unrighted and wounds unhealed, the tearing pain of a past which cannot be altered?

Unless, of course, I remember it wrongly, and it is my present painful and unfortunate state which casts such a black shadow back over what would otherwise be a perfectly acceptable landscape of experience? But I fear not.

I, Praxis Duveen, being old and scarcely in my right mind, now bequeath you my memories. They may help you: they certainly do nothing to sustain me, let alone assist my bones to clamber out of the bath.

Last night, doing just that, I slipped on the soap and cracked my elbow. This morning the pain was such that I took the bus to the hospital, instead of to the park.

My erstwhile sisters, my former friends: I did what you wanted, and look at me now!

You have forgotten me.

Two years in prison have aged me two decades. I should not regret the new grey wiriness of my hair, the swollen veins in my

15

legs, the huddling lumpiness of my figure, the faded look in my watery eyes. But I do, I do. The eyes of the world look quickly past me, beyond me, and I am humiliated.

My fingers are stiff and sore with what I suppose to be arthritis. Writing has become painful. But I will write. I am accustomed to pain. And pain in the elbow, the fingers and, since my abortive journey to the hospital, pain in my stamped-upon toe, is nothing compared to that pain in the heart, the soul and the mind—those three majestic seats of female sorrow—which seems to be our daily lot.

I do not understand the threefold pain: but I will try. Perhaps it serves a useful purpose, if only as an indication that some natural process is being abused. I cannot believe it is a punishment: to have a certain nature is not a sin, and in any case who is there to punish us? Unless—as many do—we predicate some natural law of male dominance and female subservience, and call that God. Then what we feel is the pain of the female Lucifer, tumbling down from heaven, having dared to defy the male deity, cast out forever, but likewise never able to forget, tormented always by the memory of what she threw away. Or else, and on this supposition my mind rests most contentedly, we are in the grip of some evolutionary force which hurts as it works and which I fear has already found its fruition in that new race of young women which I encountered in the bus on the way to the hospital this morning, dewy fresh from their lovers' arms and determined to please no one but themselves. One of the New Women trod me underfoot and with her three-inch soles pulped my big toe in its plastic throw-away shoe (only I, unlike her, cannot afford to throw anything away, and am doomed to wear it forever), causing me such fresh pain that when the bus broke down and we were all to be decanted into another, I lost heart altogether, abandoned the journey and limped home.

The New Women! I could barely recognize them as being of the same sex as myself, their buttocks arrogant in tight jeans, openly inviting, breasts falling free and shameless, feeling no apparent obligation to smile, look pleasant or keep their voices low. And how they live! Just look at them to know how! If a man doesn't bring them to orgasm, they look for another who does. If by mistake they fall pregnant, they abort by vacuum aspiration. If they don't like the food, they push the plate away. If the job doesn't suit them, they hand in their notice. They are satiated by everything, hungry for nothing. They are what I wanted to be; they are what I worked for them to be: and now I see them, I hate them. They have found their own solution to the threefold pain—one I never thought of. They do not try, as we did, to understand it and get the better of it. They simply wipe out the pain by doing away with its three centres—the heart, the soul and the mind. Brilliant! Heartless, soulless, mindless—free!

Listen, I have had good times. It is only on bad days that I regret the past and hate the young. I helped to change the world. I made life what it is for those lovely, lively, trampling girls upon the bus.

Look at me, I said to you. Look at me, Praxis Duveen. Better for me to look at myself, to search out the truth, and the root of my pain, and yours, and try to determine, even now, whether it comes from inside or from outside, whether we are born with it or have it foisted upon us. Before my writing hand seizes up, my elbow rots, my toe falls off.

In the meantime, sisters, I absolve you from your neglect of me. You do what you can. So will I.

3

AFTER BEN'S DEFECTION, his mother, a stately, large-busted matron, often moved by compassion, came presently to visit her son's abandoned common-law wife. She found two little girls of whose existence she had not known. Both stared up at her with her son's sad, defiant eyes. Their hair was uncombed, their white dresses soiled, their mother distraught. The maid had left: the rent was unpaid. There was no food in the cupboard. Ben's mother left quickly, in her chauffeured Rolls-Royce.

A letter from solicitors followed, hand-delivered the next day. The rent was to be paid, the little girls provided for. If their mother was in financial or practical difficulty, she could make special application to the solicitors at any time, who would judge the merits of the case, and pay out accordingly.

Goodbye, Benjamin Duveen. Off to greener golf courses, three fine sons and Ruth, a woman who loved him for what he was, and not what he wasn't.

Lucy presently wrote to the solicitors asking if she could move away, move house, start a new life somewhere else with the girls, and still have the rent paid: but they would not hear of it. Continuity, they said, was important for the children. So Lucy perforce

18

stayed where she was, seldom leaving the house. She should have been grateful to the Duveens, and so she was. Many families would have preferred to ignore her existence altogether. She could have gone into service, to the workhouse or on the streets. The little bastards to a Barnado home.

Henry Whitechapel, arriving in the May of the following season, looked out for Mrs. Duveen on the beach, and missed her. He made his way to 109 Holden Road, and found the garden unkempt, the gravel drive full of weeds, the motorcar gone and the curtains drawn, so that he thought at first the house was empty. But Hypatia and Praxis were playing on the lawn. Or rather, Hypatia was sitting sketching a plant, and Praxis was sitting in a puddle, and her wet drawers, when she stood, hung down muddily round her knees.

"Where's your mother?" he asked.

"Crying," said Praxis.

"Shush," called out Hypatia. "You silly little girl."

"Well she is," said Praxis. "Silly girl yourself."

Hypatia sighed heavily and raised her narrow eyebrows. She had a receding chin and slightly buck teeth, yellowish, a muddy complexion and dull brown hair with a tendency to grease, but was either unaware of these deficiencies or affected unawareness. Her look was supercilious.

"And your father?"

"He's left," said Praxis.

"He's away at the moment," corrected Hypatia.

Henry took the opportunity of knocking at the door. He was not normally so bold, but his life that day seemed desperate, and the season stretched ahead, meaningless, filled with grinning, eager, silly faces, craning for a likeness; cheated and derided as they were all year, at work, and now at play, by someone of their own kind, who ought to know better. It made him feel bad but what could he do?

"Mrs. Duveen?" he enquired. "You remember me? The beach photographer? I came to check that your photographs arrived."

He thought he had never seen anyone so changed. She seemed like a little old woman, with her hair scraped back, her kimono clutched round her with a hand whose nails were none too clean.

She shook her head, vague. Then she nodded.

"If by any chance you need frames—and a photograph looks

twice as grand in a frame, I always say—I stock a special line. Very reasonable."

She did not want the frames but showed him the photograph stuck any old how on the mantelpiece in the dusty parlour.

"A big house you have here," he remarked kindly. "Difficult to keep up, for just one person, I should say."

At which she burst into tears. Her life was finished; over. Benjamin had gone. She kept her breath in her body for the sake of the girls, nothing else.

He took a room in the house. She had a male lodger! She, a woman alone. What did it matter what people said? In fact, knowing so little about her, they said nothing. Had they known more, no doubt they would have been kind: but the kindness, or lack of it, with which one regards oneself finds its echo in the outside world: and Lucy could not forgive herself. All her fault. Her lost marriage, her failed love, her bastard children, her dusty home, her condemnation to this cruel street, this unfeeling, gossiping town—all her fault. Seeking out more degradation, the seedy lodger, the false photographer, slurping milk through his moustache at her breakfast table, she began to feel better again.

Lucy curled her hair and pressed her clothes. She weeded the drive. She dressed Hypatia and Praxis in pale pink—they had somehow lost their right to white—and wrote to Butt and Son, the Duveen solicitors, for money to hire a servant, as befitted the little girls' state as descendants, albeit on the male side, of King David. Butt and Son at first demurred, but then conceded.

Benjamin's mother paid another visit, and seemed relieved by what she saw. (Henry was banished to the kitchen for the occasion.) She left the girls a signed photograph of their father; but Praxis had already forgotten what he looked like; he seemed a stranger to her, with his glowing eyes and large nose. Hypatia took the photograph, in any case, and slept with it under her pillow. Praxis set up a howl, discovering this, but Henry dealt her a sharp cuff and she soon stopped.

Lucy presently found pleasure in telling Henry what to do. He followed on her heels like a little pet dog: she scolded and chided, and soon had him fetching her bag, her book, her wrap, and so rebuilt a little world around herself, and even came down to the beach on warm days.

The girls watched their lodger take photographs, though pretending to be nothing to do with him. Nothing. A street photographer, after all. None too honest, either, with rotting lungs and bad breath; and their mother a doctor's daughter, and her daughters of the line of King David. Lucy told them so, frequently: proud of it at last. They had no concept of the notion of Jewishness: either of pogroms or Passover. Lucy was vague enough about it herself.

Hypatia and Praxis went to school and suffered with Jesus on the cross, gasped at the beauty of the Virgin Mary, drenched their souls in the blood of the lamb; were slapped if they stole or told lies, heard that they were daughters of Eve and responsible for leading men into sin and for the loss of Paradise, and must make amends forever. Praxis cleaned Henry's shoes in penance; Hypatia actually learned how to develop his prints. And he did develop them nowadays, all of them, and Lucy would send them off. His teeth never lost their blackness, but he seemed on the whole, as the years went by, less dejected. Lucy even scolded him into a vague sexual response: human beings, he perceived through her, added up to more than the tattered shreds of flesh he had observed hanging on the barbed wire of the Ypres front; the grinning faces, skin stretched over bone, which presented themselves before his camera. The world was something more than a charnel house, a human factory farm, insanely breeding flesh out of flesh as its way of cheating death.

Presently they slept together in the big brass bed: she a little brisk woman with a tight mouth, prophesying disaster even in her sleep, tossing and turning; he coughing and spluttering all night long, trying to be rid of something; both somewhat healed by virtue of the other: both older than they used to be.

Praxis and Hypatia slept soundly but woke anxious, eyes wide and stretched, forever fearful that something unexpected might happen. No one explained anything to them: where Ben had come from, where he had gone: who Henry was, and why. Why their mother cried, scolded or laughed, for no apparent reason. Who the woman in the Rolls-Royce was. If everything was inexplicable, anything might happen.

Anxiety ironed itself into their souls.

Praxis thought Hypatia might know more than she did about it

all, by virtue of the extra two and a half years to her credit, but if
Hypatia did, she said nothing. Hypatia kept herself to herself: she
was aloof, like a cat. Praxis was more like a clumsy puppy, leaping
up with muddy paws, enthusiastic but ridiculous.

4

I DO NOT WET the bed now; at least not that: though soon, I daresay, the time will come when I do. I dread the day. I do not want to be an old woman sitting in a chair, wearing nappies, nursed by the salt of the earth. It seems unjust; not what Lucy and Benjamin meant at all; rolling about in their unwed bed, year after year, moved by a force which clearly had nothing to do with common sense or anyone's quest for happiness: until, their mission apparently accomplished, they rolled apart and went their separate ways, assisted by Butt and Son, Solicitors.

I do not want to be an incontinent old lady. I would rather die. I feel today, my elbow throbbing and my toe swelling, that the time for dying will be quite soon. On Thursdays I go down to the Social Security offices, stand in a queue and draw the money which keeps me for a further week. It should be possible for a postal draft to be sent weekly and myself to cash it at the local post office, but I do not like to make the request. I am an ex-con, and the habit dies hard of not causing trouble to, let alone demanding one's rights of, those in authority.

Those in authority, at any rate, in that strange grey world of bars and keys which I have inhabited, where cause and effect work in

23

an immediate way, and the stupid are in charge of the intelligent, and each wrongdoer carries on his poor bowed shoulders the weight of a hundred of the worthy—from prison visitors to the Home Secretary—whose living is made, indirectly, out of crime, or sin, or financial failing, or criminal negligence: or, as with me, the madness of believing that I was right, and society wrong. Who did I think I was? I, Praxis Duveen.

Madness, I say. Today, certainly, it seems like madness. It's raining. I can see water seeping beneath the door, and have not the strength to fetch one of my cheap, bright, nonabsorbent towels to sop it up. Damp stains the stone floor: I feel a dark stain of wretchedness creeping up to the very edges of that part of my mind, my being, which I usually manage to keep inviolate. The part which is daily reborn with gladness, excitement and gratitude to God (or whatever you call it) because the world exists and is so full of interest and possibility: a part of me which I associate, rightly or wrongly, with the Praxis of the very early years, who would run happily into the waves with shoes and socks on to see what would happen, meet with a slap or two, and do it again the next day, unafraid.

Praxis, protected by parental love. While it lasted. Paradise was there, then snatched away.

Children who have been hurt grow up to hurt. This I know. I knew it but was helpless in the knowledge. I shouted and screamed, attempted murder or faked suicide, in my children's presence: conducted the dark side of my erotic nature beneath their startled gaze, careless of the precipice I opened up beneath their feet. I, who guarded them from the fleas of strange dogs, and nasty sights at the pictures, and brushed their hair with loving care. Yes, I did, and so did you, and you: paid back to them what mother did to you.

I remember clearly that early sense of fear and desolation of which all later fears and desolations are mere shadows. And I handed it on to them: this extreme of terror and horror; the ultimate standard by which they must judge the traumas of their own lives, and will hardly feel alive if they do not attain, and so strive to attain forever. The shrieks of generations growing louder, not softer, as the decades pass.

I am ashamed of it: as ashamed of that as of anything I have done: and bewildered as to why I feel compelled to do it. The domestic row existed, I could almost believe, in order to distress the children.

Perhaps I am dead, and this is my punishment? To believe I am still alive, and live as a useless old woman in a Western industrialized society? There cannot be much worse a punishment. Unless it be to live as a young woman in the East, and see your children die from starvation: or worse, watch them grow up sour, undersized and crippled by curable diseases.

I touch my elbow to see if I am alive. I am.

5

"I WANT TO GO TO SCHOOL," Praxis said to Hypatia when she was seven; she spoke experimentally, wondering whether it was possible, by mere words, to influence the course of events.

"Always fussing," said Hypatia. "Anyway we can't."

"Why not?"

"Just be quiet," said Hypatia, who was sensitive as to Lucy's anxieties, and knew that the matter of their going to or not going to school kept their mother awake at night. "And wipe your nose, it's dripping again."

Hypatia walked cautiously through life, fearful of disturbing stones in case she saw the insects scuttling underneath. Praxis, she felt, blundered blithely on, aiming careless kicks as she went.

Hypatia sat inside the house and sewed and embroidered with her mother. Praxis swung on the garden gate and watched the other children going to and from the council school at the end of Holden Road. Noisy, messy, muddled children, even by comparison to herself: shirts and ties awry, satchels broken, shoes dirty, trailing sweet papers as they went. They ran, shrieked, scuffled, stumbled, fell and helped each other up.

"Common children," said Lucy Duveen, "come away."

Lucy taught her daughters to read, write, add up, launder, embroider and sew. She taught them how to boil mutton, unlump a white sauce, stew cabbage and mix a plum duff.

Henry emerged from his developing room, adapted from the cupboard under the stairs. His business was thriving. He had saved almost enough to put down a deposit on a small photographic studio on the seafront. He breathed more easily, these days. He went to the pub: he had a crony or two there, although he did not tell Lucy. Her fear of gossip, of people Finding Out, was too great for her to be able to view friends with equanimity.

Lucy was worried by the matter of the children's schooling: worry made her unreasonable. She would divert her mind from its proper preoccupation and busy it with trifles: and then accord the trifles the emotional weight that better befitted the preoccupation. Anxiety, anger and a sense of injustice welled up in her at the notion of Henry's lack of breeding, and blotted out her panic at the thought of the girls' birth certificates, which would have to be produced when and if they ever enrolled at school.

Close inspection of their birth certificates would reveal the girls to be illegitimate, and their true names Hypatia Parker, and Praxis Parker; the mother's name being entered as Lucy Parker, spinster. And though in the column for father was written not the humiliating "unknown," but "Benjamin Duveen, occupation, gentleman," the disgrace of mother and daughters would become known.

"I want to go to school," said Praxis to Lucy.

"And mix with common children? Is that the kind of girl you turn out to be?" Lucy responded, with such a contorted face, and such unmaternal ferocity that her younger daughter was thereafter reluctant to present her mother with a need, let alone a want, for fear they should all tumble over the precipice into madness and despair.

"Mrs. Duveen," said Henry, "the law of the land requires that children go to school. Now the law of the land has never done anything for me except compel me to go to war and ruin my health, but nevertheless it exists, and the children must go."

"His health is a small thing for a gentleman to sacrifice for his country," replied Lucy, adding, with meaning, "I should have thought."

"I'm no gentleman," said Henry. "I thought you understood that."

"In that case," said Lucy, "perhaps you had better take your meals in the kitchen, with Judith."

"Very well," replied Henry, to Lucy's dismay. "I think I will."

He retired back under the stairs, where, half-crouching, he developed his prints. He had hoped to convert the small back bedroom to a darkroom, but Lucy thought that room much too good for photographs. The stair cupboard would do. She had begun to enjoy despising Henry.

When Henry appeared at supper, as usual, for mulligatawny soup, stewed mince (it was Wednesday) and apple tart, Lucy said, "I thought you were going to eat in the kitchen," and Henry took his plate and went. He absented himself from Lucy's bed thereafter, letting it be understood that he would not return there until she invited him back into the dining room, but she did not relent. She put out her shoes for him to clean, however, and clean them he did.

All this for Praxis was safety: waking up in the morning in the bed next to Hypatia: the dull routine of the house, of the day: Henry's comings and goings: Hypatia's moods: Judith's sulks: learning to read: going to the children's library (talking to no one as instructed: hurrying straight home); there, running parallel, was a pit, just an edge away, of violence and hatred, screams and blows, fears, illness, death. Lucy sometimes showed Praxis a face which came straight from the other side: a witch face, demoniacal, tormented. Hypatia would show that face, too, on occasion. "Let's see who can make the ugliest face," she'd say, and promptly produce a devil mask straight from the other side, which terrified Praxis so that she'd cry. "Baby," Hypatia would deride, satisfied, and Praxis would sleep with her head under the blankets, in case she woke up in the morning and caught Hypatia with her devil face, before she'd had time to remove it.

Hypatia wished her harm, Praxis accepted that. Sometimes she'd relent, and they'd play sevens against the garage wall. Throw, bounce, catch. Throw, bounce, bounce, catch. Throw, bounce, turn, catch; throw, bounce, bounce, clap, catch; on and on for a whole afternoon, or until Judith emerged shrieking that she'd hand in her notice unless the thudding stopped.

Judith was a local girl, nearly thirty, unmarried. Her breath was bad: no one else cared to employ her. Black-haired, black-browed, black-chinned, broad of face, and body: slurred of speech, coarse of hand, and sullen. That, at least, was how Lucy saw her. Pale, delicate Lucy. Judith received fifteen shillings a week, paid through Butt and Son, Solicitors. She affected a marked dislike of men, but seemed to attract sexual violence. She was propositioned by work-men, molested by strangers, became quite used to the pad-pad of unknown feet behind her, and carried a heavy handbag, which she would swing skilfully as a hand or arm appeared.

At first, Henry felt quite ill at ease, obliged to eat with Judith in the kitchen. There was little conversation. But the food in the kitchen turned out to be better than that served in the dining room. Judith would fill his own deep plate and her own from the soup tureen, place the plates carefully on the Aga stove to keep warm, then, after filling two jam jars for taking home later, would hold the tureen under the cold tap to top up the level, and take it into the dining room. He said nothing to Lucy about this practice. Why should he? His loyalties were to Judith now; below stairs, not upstairs.

The vicar came to enquire why the girls were not attending school. Lucy, watching him come up the drive, saw him as neme-sis, and greeted him with flat despair in her heart. She gave him sherry. He was a youngish man, clearly from the lower middle classes. Vicars used to be the younger sons of the landed gentry. Not what she expected:

"The girls seem so young," she fluted, ladylike, wild-eyed. "And there's such a lot of paperwork," she added, her tone altogether more sane, so, being a shrewd fellow, he took his cue from that.

"Paperwork can be very tiresome," said the vicar, "especially for a widow like yourself." He was a member of the golf course—at special rates, since he could not play on Sundays—and one of the few acquainted with Lucy—through her earlier outings with the children to the Sunday school—and her circumstances. He had assumed Benjamin had abandoned a wife: now, it seemed, he had merely left a mistress: and who was to say whose the children were, since a woman who'll live with one man, unmarried, will sleep with another.

The Reverend Allbright, nevertheless, good Christian that he was, accorded Lucy a way out. "Widow," he'd said, thereby welcoming her back into the fold, the community, the Mothers' Union. Her children would now be reckoned unfortunate, but not tainted, which was a considerable improvement.

"If you'd like," said the vicar, "to hand the children's birth certificates over to me, I'll get them registered at the school. You wish them to be called Duveen?"

"Of course." She paled. What did he know?

"Sometimes widows like to revert to their maiden names," he said, lying through his teeth. "They feel they once again have the shelter of their father's name. But you prefer to keep your husband's name alive, I see, in them. You are a brave little woman, Mrs. Duveen. I admire you and my heart goes out to you."

And so he did, and so it did, though quite why he could not have said. His own wife, Margot, was a brisk, noble and simple woman, and their sex life polite, simple and straightforward, a weekly event, with the lights out, occurring mostly on a Friday night. Saturday night, they both silently concurred, might leave the Reverend Allbright too tired for Sunday sermons, and certainly too much connected with the flesh, too little to the spirit. The Reverend and Mrs. Allbright made a sharp division between the two, assuming that the flesh existed as a trial to the spirit: and since only he enjoyed it—and thought perhaps he shouldn't—and she put up with it, for kindness' and custom's sake, they may well have assumed right. His strength and will were sapped, his vital juices drained away, when he succumbed to his sexual urges. And his wife could not recover from her sense of incongruity: the man in white dog collar and black suit, whom she had married, thus translated to pink, pounding flesh and blood. Nor, come to that, could he. Still, God had devised this means of perpetuating the race and cementing the sacrament of marriage. God said do it, so they did.

Margot Allbright was obliged to cheat, too: pushing a piece of sponge soaked in vinegar up her vagina, for fear of conceiving a fifth child. Cheating herself, God, her husband. She did it, but scarcely bore to think about it. Was sex really necessary?

Now, the Reverend Allbright, surveying the sudden softening of Lucy's sharp little face, and the gratitude dawning in her eyes, caught a glimpse of other possibilities: of the exercise of sexual power, of mastery and masochism, of an entirely different scale of sexual existence than the one he was accustomed to, lapping and overlapping emotional entanglement and physical intertwinings; and even thought wildly for a moment or so of stepping forward to embrace his unfortunate parishioner, and seeing what would happen next—

But he did not. The moment passed.

"I hope to see you at the church soon," said the Reverend Allbright. "I know your husband was of the Jewish faith, but I imagine you will want your daughters brought up as Christians?"

"Of course," said Lucy, perfectly prepared to abandon King David in the interests of respectability.

The vicar enrolled the girls at the nearest Church of England school, which was a good two miles away, and not the secular school at the end of the road.

Lucy took the girls to church and saw that they went to Sunday school, became a member of the Mothers' Union, voted for the expulsion of a young farmer's wife, mother of three, who was discovered on the desertion of her husband to have been bigamously married, although not to her knowledge at the time. Exonerating circumstances, no doubt, but not powerful enough to wipe out sin. A state of sin, especially in sexual matters, could be brought about without the sinner's knowledge. One had to be careful. Curtains must be closed lest the sun in its brilliance fade the velvet cushions. Food must be bland in case it agitated the senses: must not be too appetizing, in case gluttony, that deadly sin, eroded the spirit. Servants must not be paid too much, in case they got above themselves, forgot their place. Visitors must be discouraged, in case they found out.

Found out what? Lucy could scarcely remember. She, a decent widow, with family solicitors administering her interests, could scarcely have a guilty secret. Could she? No, she was surely too finely attuned to the lack of respectability in others: she was no hypocrite. Benjamin had said so.

"Wash the car, Henry," she'd say. He'd wash it. She'd inspect the blemishes, and complain. He'd do it again. Where had Henry come from? She began to believe he was some kind of poor relative, wounded in the war, now having to be looked after, out of charity. The odd-job man, with his hobby, his photography. His little shop on the seafront. No, not a trade. A hobby.

The money that Henry brought home from his now-prosperous business kept the household going. He slept, occasionally, with Judith; it was shared revenge upon Lucy, rather than any overwhelming desire on his part, or hers.

"I'm not a servant: not, not, not," he'd say, like a naughty child, keeping time, as in some clapping street game, with his strokes inside Judith; or vaguely inside; or at any rate round and about.

"Who does she think she is?" Judith would respond, staring up at him, unmoved. "Who's she to give herself airs? She's nobody. Rubbish!"

Judith was like some piece of wood, he thought, which ought to sprout with leafy branches in the spring, but wouldn't. Obstinate. He was reassured by her placidity, her lack of response. He could do what he liked: if he was weak, or barely roused, she did not seem to mind. He would rub himself against her, gaining such pleasure as he could: his excitement, like hers, springing from his indignation with Lucy, not Judith's hot stolid body. Active women frightened him. He'd been with a French girl once, on leave. She'd seemed to explode, as a man might. It had frightened him; sudden explosions in the trenches killed and maimed; explosions in the head, in the loins—all much of a muchness—were surely something to be feared.

"Anyway, she's a Jew," said Judith. "Dirty Jews. Everything's their fault."

There was a general feeling about, though seldom so vehemently expressed, that all social evils were the fault of the Jews. Unemployment, low wages, bad housing, depression—both national and personal—it was all due to the Jews. Few had actually ever met one: but they had heard.

Lucy was quite relieved that Benjamin was dead, and that Butt and Son, Solicitors, had such a Christian name.

"What did Father die of?" Praxis asked Hypatia, presently.

"Ask mother," said Hypatia, safe these days in the knowledge that Praxis would not. Nor did she.

Praxis liked school. The building was Gothic Victorian; it smelt of cabbage, stale urine and hot damp bodies. She loved to play and giggle and compete. The teachers were kind and complimentary. No one hid anything. Everything was open, mucky and honest. There was a separate entrance for boys and girls, and separate playgrounds, but they shared lessons. Boys sat on the side nearest

the door, girls nearest the wall. It was customary. Hypatia liked
school less. She was more responsive than Praxis to her mother's
inference that the family was different, raised above the common
herd. Though there were no more references to King David, Lucy
found figures to be proud of in her own family background: a titled
great-aunt, a great-great-uncle who had invented the steam tur-
bine. She wrote to her mother: but her mother did not reply. Why?
Had she died, gone away, moved house? Lucy did not know. Presently it seemed to her that she was an orphan, and always had
been. "My poor mother," she'd sometimes say. "My poor dead
mother."

Praxis got nits in her hair. Lucy had hysterics. Praxis' hair was
cut very short and she went to school in a scarf, along with half a
dozen others. Dirty children. Lucy wrote to Butt and Son asking if
the girls could have their fees paid at a private school. No, said the
Butts, conscious of their duty to the Duveen family finances, now
much depleted. Much of the family money had to go towards the
rescuing of obscure cousins from Hitler's Germany.

Lucy next wrote to Butt and Son asking whether the girls' sec-
ondary education could not, perhaps, be paid for by their father's
family.

No, replied Butt Senior, and was the children's mother aware
that when the younger reached sixteen, all support and maintenance would stop? In the meantime, had she considered enrolling
her daughters in a state-sponsored school for domestic training?
The girls must expect to support themselves, and in these days of
the servant problem, no girl with such a training need go short of
a job.

The letter, as were all letters from Butt and Son, was addressed
to Miss Parker. "It's because I'm a widow," she explained to the
postman: "They want to save my feelings." She believed it, but he
did not.

Lucy had not been aware that maintenance could stop. She had
envisaged it continuing forever. She asked Henry back to the dining room for meals, and he accepted her invitation. Judith crashed
and banged about the house: Lucy could not understand why.

Hypatia won a scholarship to the grammar school; Lucy was
triumphant and wrote to tell Butt and Son of her triumph. Would
they, she added, pass on the good news to the Duveen family?

"She's not going to be a nuisance, I hope," said Senior Butt to

Junior Butt, holding the scented scrawl some distance from himself the better to focus. Lucy had in fact rewritten the letter seven times in order to get grammar, spelling and presentation correct.

"You went too far," said the younger Butt, "in your earlier letter. I told you she'd respond badly to pressure. She's a real hard egg. She tried to trap the son into marriage, and now that's well and truly failed, and young Benjamin is out of her clutches, she's going to try blackmailing his unfortunate family."

"She does have his two children," demurred the elder Butt.

"That's her story," said Butt Junior. "How could one ever be sure?"

Nevertheless Butt Senior wrote back to Lucy saying how pleased he was to hear of Hypatia's success; hoping that Praxis might follow suit: and adding that the matters of rent and allowance and maintenance could be deferred until Praxis' eighteenth birthday and possibly even longer.

Lucy felt bolder and returned Henry to the kitchen. The coarse hair of his nostrils repelled her: so did the pallid trembling of his hands. She was glad when he went.

On the first day at the girls' grammar school the form mistress read out the register, while the girls murmured their presence.

"Hilda Duveen," she said.

Silence.

"When I say your name, Hilda," said the form mistress to Hypatia, "you say present. Shall we try again? Hilda Duveen?"

"Present," said Hypatia. It was her mother's doing. Lucy had never liked her children's names, and the Reverend Allbright had undertaken to talk to the grammar school headmistress about changing them. The news had been late in reaching Hypatia, that was all. When it was Praxis' turn to move on to the grammar school she found that her name was now Patricia.

6

WE CAN'T BE STRONG all the time; I comfort myself with that notion. We can't stick to our principles, act as we ought, fight for our causes, not nonstop, all our lives. We must surely be prepared to take shifts in our fight for utopia or, failing that, to hand over entirely the burden of our conscience to those who are younger, fresher and less afflicted by experience than ourselves. Then, our task done, we can sink back with a clear conscience into selfishness and apathy. Our righteousness wears out long before our bodies do.

I ought to rejoice for the girl who stood upon my toe in the bus. I ought to be glad, for her beauty, her freedom, her dignity, her pride. But I don't; I'm not. She has injured me, and I can see no further than that: my eyes are dimming with age. I ought to be thankful, and take some credit myself, for the fact that she will never have to live in such a prison of shame and hypocrisy as the one in which my mother found herself. Poor mother. Of course she should have struggled. My father's people in Germany should have struggled too. But she did not, as they did not. We see the world as we are taught to see it, not as it is. Our vision since has widened. And of course she should have kept her misery to herself, not handed it on to her children. For a time I hated her for her weakness, until I saw what I did to my children through my strength. Then I forgave her.

I am not strong at the moment. If the social worker comes knocking at my door I shall certainly let her in. I cannot hobble as far as the cooker to make so much as a cup of tea. I cannot, worse, reach the drawer which contains the painkillers. Am I Praxis or Patricia? Patricia, without a doubt. Pat, for short, for convenience. Everyone's convenience. A dismissible, neutral name, jolly at best, unerotic at worst. Others seem quite happy with it; but then they were born with it. I wasn't. The name a vengeful, if practical, mother would choose for a sensible child, the better to give orders to. Pat, fetch my bag, clear the table, weed the garden. Pat, do your homework, find Hilda's hairgrips. Poor hateful Hilda.

I called myself Pat in Holloway Prison. The social worker calls me Pat. She feels she has the right to be familiar. She does not regard me as a criminal: I wish she did. She sees me as someone half-mad, who couldn't cope, and who covered up my inadequacy by what she calls an ad hoc justification. She calls me Pat because she pities me, and her nature and training will not allow her to condemn me. To accept that I acted out of principle, and not because it was expedient, would terrify her: would open up questions and considerations she is frankly too busy doing good to consider.

I wish she would come. She could make the tea. Her name is Myra Jones. She is half my age: she has the warm light of virtue in her eye. She would never have killed as I did, coldly gritting my teeth. She would have been positive and sensible, and put the poor little half-witted thing into a home, and then set about running the home, if it didn't suit her vision of what a home for the mentally handicapped was. Would she herself have spooned slops into the adult mouth, or cleaned off the adult nappies? Yes, she would, she could, from sheer insufficiency of imagination. If she had to. Only if she had to, and until she could persuade, or train, some other slightly more high-grade half-wit to do it. I have encountered some of these latter half-wits, on the staff of mental homes, or shelters or protected communities—whatever the latest name is for these repositories for human distress: they love to be revenged upon their charges: they tease the mumbling and the twitching and the incontinent, as they themselves are teased and humiliated in the outside world. No, the seed of King David, however distorted and debased, was not to end at the mercy of such as these. Obliteration was better.

Last time Myra Jones called, I remember, I would not let her in. I did not want her poking and prying. There is something of my mother in me.

My mother, in the acuteness of her distress after my father left her, spent her nights for a time with Henry Whitechapel. Or so he told me later, and I have no reason to disbelieve him.

There was certainly no point in asking her. Mother would have denied it and believed her denial, whether she had or whether she hadn't. At a time when women's instincts were so much at a variance with the rules of society, such localized amnesias were only to be expected. But was this episode out of character; or was it that her whole life otherwise was out of character? Was my mother, from the age of thirty to the age of seventy, living out a part that did not suit her at all? I believe the latter. I concur with the vicar, the Reverend Allbright, and the younger Butt, who both avowed that a woman who'd sleep with one man, outside marriage, would sleep with another. I have friends who married as virgins, and only made love with their husbands all their lives, and wouldn't want it any other way. They seem the happiest with their lot in life. I wish it were not so, but it is. My mother tried to attain the happiness of the sexually exclusive, but had left it too late. She was polluted.

To lose one's virginity is not—as the toe trampler on the bus would no doubt have it—an insignificant event. It is tremendous, momentous, and sets the pattern for one's entire sexual life to come. I even think, sometimes, that that narrow hypocritical society was right, and that Hypatia and myself had no right to be alive: and had better have remained the outcasts we were born.

Myra Jones, where are you? I hope I have not driven you away. I need you now. I, Patricia Parker, humble murderess, who will not even argue with you about my name, need my cup of tea and painkiller.

I, Praxis Duveen. Let them carve that name upon my headstone, if I have a grave. Let them engrave it upon the urn which holds my ashes. It was the name I started with: I have changed it often enough since; and seldom for the better.

7

HILDA AND PATRICIA DUVEEN. Patricia fell in love. She wore a navy gym slip, white blouse, brown belt, black stockings and brown shoes, and fell in love with a girl similarly clad, except that she wore a yellow prefect's sash and a row of short metal bars hanging from a black tab pinned to her chest. The bars, embossed, told of one prowess or another. Louise Gaynor, Patricia's love, had bars for Athletics, Latin, English and French. She was sixteen and Patricia was twelve.

Patricia did not speak to Louise: her passion existed in her own head, and being unafflicted by reality, was the more powerful for it. She gazed, she exulted, she suffered, she all but swooned, at an imagined kind look, an imagined slight, a turning away, a coming towards, from Louise. Louise felt Patricia's eyes upon her: once or twice she smiled, or raised her eyebrows in mock wonder, but she did not speak. School rules forbade conversation between girls of different age groups: exceptions were made for sisters, or family friends. Unnatural friendships were feared, and closely watched for, and flourished.

Louise sang solo in choir: she had a gentle soprano. Patricia joined the choir, which practised on Tuesday lunchtimes, and lived for Tuesdays. The day itself seemed misty, pierced by blinking light.

> Nymphs and shepherds, come away—
> Let's sport and play—

"You have to have a crush on somebody," Elaine had instructed Patricia, at the beginning of term. Elaine was a stout, steady, competent girl who came top in everything and took Patricia under her wing. Patricia would come fourth or fifth, occasionally second or third: it amounted to competition, not rivalry, and Elaine could afford to be kind.

Elaine's father kept a corner grocery shop. Lucy did not approve of the friendship.

"You're going too far," complained Elaine, at the end of term.

Patricia became a source of half-envy, half-disapproval to her classmates. The pretence of crushes was common enough: the real swooning, genuine thing, was rare—the pallor, the trembling of the hand, the dizziness of the head, the obsessive dreams at night of a touch, a smile; the lingering in corridors, the watching of doors, and for what? For nothing. For attention from the loved object, which could only make the affliction worse, not better. No other outcome was possible. No touch, no kiss, no declaration.

Patricia started to bleed, one day. Crimson drops appeared on her legs. A scratch, a nick? No, it came from between her legs, where she never looked, or felt: from some hidden dreadful, internal wound. Patricia ran to her sister, crying.

"I don't know what it is," said Hilda, looking up from her French verbs. "It's very messy, anyway. Go and tell mother."

"Perhaps it will stop," said Patricia, hopefully. But it didn't. Patricia went to her mother.

"I don't believe it," said her mother, aghast. "Fifteen is the proper age. Now if it had been Hilda—" Lucy went to the linen cupboard, chose the most threadbare of the sheets, tore them into ten neat strips, assembled a piece of white tape into a belt, found two safety pins and handed them to Patricia.

Patricia cried all night. Five-twenty-eights of her life gone, stolen, and for no other reason than that she was a woman.

"Of course men can't know you when you're unclean," said Hilda. "It says so in the Bible. That's why it's called the curse. It's God's punishment."

"For what?"

"Giving Adam the apple, I suppose."

"He didn't have to eat it."

"Yes he did. If someone offers you food, it's only manners to take it. Why are you always so argumentative?"

A war with Germany had started, largely unnoticed by Patricia, who was too busy considering herself to pay the outside world much attention. Barbed wire covered the beaches. She could not swim if she wanted to, even on the twenty-three days allowed every four weeks by the curse. It was all clearly part of life's plan.

The signposts were turned the wrong way round to confuse German spies. Lucy stopped defending Hitler and his attitude to the Jews.

Henry's photographic studio closed. Holiday makers no longer thronged the promenade. The sellers of candy-floss and placards departed: the donkeys disappeared. Windows were shuttered, and the waterfront deserted. The pretty waves fell and retreated on barbed wire and blocks of concrete, whose purpose no one could determine. By night, the blackout was total: the streets were thronged with breathing, sighing shapes which might have been human and might not.

Henry was fortunate to find a job taking photographs of conscripts at the local recruitment centre. The hours were shorter and the money better than he was accustomed to. He bought a new suit and developed a military air—Lucy asked him back into the dining room, and started referring to him as "your cousin," and not "the lodger." He shouted at Judith if the soup was not to his liking, and the standard of food improved amazingly in spite of the shortages brought about by the war.

Judith lowered and glowered, but did not hand in her notice. No one bothered to wonder why.

Henry became something of a father to the girls: inspecting their nails for dirt and their hair for tangles before they left for school, as if they were very young children and not accustomed to caring for themselves.

Hilda's sallow plainness was gone. She was sultry, willowy and

intense, and kept her eyes cast down, fixed upon her Greek trans-
lation.

Lucy had lately seemed indifferent to the girls' behaviour and
appearance: she became secretive, hiding underwear and plates of
food about the house for no apparent reason. With Henry's return
to the upstairs part of the house, she became brighter and brisker;
even went out on occasion to bridge parties: took the girls to the
cinema on Saturday afternoons, and became quite animated and
vociferous about the lipsticked girls who hung about the army
camps.

Perhaps Henry visited her room by night: perhaps not. If he did,
by the morning she had wiped it from her memory. Perhaps he
crept to the attics and Judith's hard bed. Perhaps not.

Hilda and Patricia were instructed to come straight home after
school, for fear of licentious soldiery.

Lucy began to hoard. The cellar was full of rancid butter, flour,
rusty tins—anything. Why and how she did it no one knew.

"A brave little woman," said the vicar. "So many of our women
are now left alone." And so they were. Those who in peacetime
were expected to need male protection, in wartime were assumed
to be able to manage perfectly well. And so they did.

"Judith's a very funny shape," said Patricia to her mother. "Like
Peggy the cat when she was having kittens, only upright."

When Judith brought in the paste sandwiches for tea, Lucy
stared at her for a little and then rose and followed her to the
kitchen.

Patricia heard raised voices. After some minutes Lucy returned
and sent Patricia to fetch the vicar.

A maid ushered Patricia into the vicarage study. Mrs. Allbright
had lately died. The children had been sent to boarding school.
The house was cheerless: the vicar's study darkened—the blackout
curtains were still in place, although outside the sun blazed. The
vicar sat, as if puzzled, at his desk.

"Can you come?" asked Patricia. "Mother needs you."

"Why?"

"I don't know."

"Nobody needs me," said the vicar. Slowly, he unbuttoned his
trouser fly and watched, as if with amazement, while his penis rose
of its own volition and stood pointing towards heaven. It seemed

he did not know what to make of it: nor, indeed, did Patricia. She was still out of breath from running. Something terrible had happened at home, and something terrible was happening here. As they both watched, the strange pillar of mottled flesh decreased, shrank and wilted. Tears stood in the vicar's eyes.

"I do miss her," he said, confidingly. "You've no idea." He buttoned his fly.

"Good heavens," he said, blinking at Patricia. "I'd no idea there was anyone there."

"Vermin," said the vicar, as they walked back together to Holden Road to confront Judith's sin. "Vermin."

Nazi planes, on their way back from bombing raids, would off-load any remaining bombs over the towns of the Channel coast, and occasionally shoot up streets and playgrounds with the last of their ammunition. The rattle of ack-ack guns was constantly in their ears.

Judith was sent away. Henry left too. Lucy roamed the house. She seldom slept. Patricia found it difficult to believe in the reality of the world, so oddly was it arranged.

Only her love for Louise seemed real: and that was because it hurt.

Patricia told Elaine what she had seen in the vicar's study.

"It's a penis," said Elaine. "My little brother plays with his. He got an infection and it swelled up. Served him right if they'd had to cut it off."

Miss Mercier, the French mistress, elegant and bucktoothed, passed by and saw them whispering, heads together.

"*Pas de* whispering," said Miss Mercier, brightly, spinning them apart with red-taloned hands. She glittered with ferocity. Her home town was occupied by the Germans: she was trapped here in this barbarian land, with dough-faced, dumpy ignoramuses of English girls. "*Pas de* whispering!" Fräulein Bechter, her only friend, had been whisked off to the Isle of Man, to an internment camp. No one protested: no one seemed to even notice.

Perhaps she herself would be next. No one could tell for sure whether the French were gallant allies, or wretched traitors.

"*Pas de* whispering," said Miss Mercier, savagely, and reeled Patricia and Elaine apart, as once she'd flung a bucket of cold water over two mating dogs, who seemed unable to separate.

The effect, from the look on their faces, was as much of a shock.

Patricia had become argumentative.

"I don't see why Judith had to go," said Patricia to Hilda. "It would be lovely to have a baby in the house."

"Not that kind of baby," said Hilda. "Not a bastard."

"But it's not the child's fault."

"All kinds of things are nobody's fault, but that's not the point; like being a Jew, or blind, or deaf, or a bastard; it's just the way you're born."

"Or a woman," said Patricia. She was sweeping the floors, having sprinkled tea-leaves first, to keep the dust down. Since Judith had left, the girls shared the housework between them. Lucy seemed incapable of doing it.

"What do you mean?"

"If I was a boy I'd be allowed to get on with my homework—I wouldn't have to sweep the floors first."

The Reverend Allbright asked Lucy to take Judith back into the household. Times were hard. There was a war on. Allowances had to be made.

The vicar returned a week later with the news that Mr. Whitechapel was to marry Judith. He had persuaded him to it.

"Our best chance of happiness in this world," said Mr. Allbright, "is to do what we ought, not what we want."

Lucy took to her bed: she seemed frightened. She insisted that Hilda keep the doors locked, night and day. She would not see a doctor. No one came to the house. There was no money to buy food. Hilda brought up the hoarded food from the cellar, and they ate sardines and condensed milk for breakfast and dinner. There was no money for school dinners, so Patricia and Hilda went home at midday. They walked together, but seldom talked. They looked over their shoulders frequently, and jumped at sudden noises. Their mother's room stank like a stable. She would not let them in to clean it.

Patricia started a diary, part fact, part fantasy. She simplified the vicar's act of self-exposure into a rape; turned Miss Mercier into a German spy; and described in detail how Louise Gaynor had kissed her behind the bicycle sheds after a school concert.

Hilda went through her mother's papers, and wrote to Butt and

Son explaining her situation and asking for money. They agreed to increase the allowance, and sent an immediate postal order for thirty shillings, with which they could buy their rations.

"I think mother's gone mad," Patricia said to Hilda one day. The house was cold. Hilda and Patricia gathered driftwood from the beaches for the fires, but "Danger—Mines" signs had recently gone up, and they were more afraid of explosions than cold.

"Don't ever say that," said Hilda, leaning over and slapping Patricia's face hard, using Lucy's sharp, strange voice, so that Patricia herself felt doubly betrayed. There was little to choose, she sometimes felt, between mother and sister.

But one day Lucy got up and cleaned her room. The next day she came out into the house, and when Patricia and Hilda came home from school she was in the kitchen making tea. She had lit the fire and made sardine sandwiches. She found fault with the buttons missing from Patricia's blazer. She was so thin her ribs stuck through her dress, and she seemed unsteady on her legs, but she smiled and was brisk and seemed herself again. Patricia stopped writing in her diary. Now it was over, she described it all to Elaine.

"Why didn't you tell me?"

"It was too dreadful to talk about. Some things are."

Miss Leonard, the English teacher, asked Patricia and Elaine to tea. She gave them scones with butter (given to her by Elaine's father) and talked about love, and about how her fiancé had been killed in the First World War, and how cruel war was.

"Love is so important," she said. Patricia began to cry, for no reason that she could think of.

"What's the matter?" asked Miss Leonard, distressed. She had a soft, round, floury face and grey, soft curls and scarlet lips. But Patricia merely shook her head.

Lucy read Patricia's diary. Patricia came home to find her mother not her mother, but some glassy-eyed, violent, mad stranger. There was an elderly policeman in the room; her own diary open: and her mother hissing abuse at her, from a distance, as if to come near would be to risk pollution.

"Little Jewess, after all. Sly little lesbian. Little slut. Filthy, dirty little piece of slime. Little bastard." The policeman attempted to intercede, but failed, and presently gave up and left. There was a war on.

Lucy would only speak to Patricia through Hilda.

"Hilda, tell your sister I shall go to the headmistress tomorrow. It's no use her telling lies. It will all come out."

"All what?" Patricia beseeched. "All what?"

"Don't speak to me," said Lucy. "The gutter's where you belong. Rolling around in filth and slime." She did strange things that night: arranging the sheets of her bed into a tent at the top of the staircase: putting the teapot into the coal cellar. Hilda let Patricia into her bed to sleep. They lay together, quiet and sleepless. On the other side of the blackout curtains searchlights made moving patterns.

"Let me die tonight," prayed Patricia for the first but not the last time in her life. "Let me sleep now and never wake up." But she knew she would not be allowed to die. She could hear her mother singing, now, loudly. A tuneless, repetitive sound, as she locked and unlocked the front door; clicked the lock this way, now clicked it that way.

"What shall we do?" asked Patricia of Hilda.

"Do about what?" enquired Hilda, grimly.

In the morning Lucy was sleeping on the living room floor. Patricia and Hilda moved her onto the sofa. She weighed so little one of them could have done it on her own. For the first time it occurred to Patricia that she loved her mother: it was a love compounded with pity, anxiety and fear: but it was love. She covered her with a blanket. Her diary was still lying open. She put it in the kitchen stove and closed the door on it. Hilda watched, silently. Presently they set off for school together, in their navy gym slips, blazers and blue felt hats, picking their way through the debris which the anti-aircraft battery on the cliffs nightly showered upon the town.

"I hope the Germans do come," said Patricia.

"On top of everything else," said Hilda, "you're a traitor."

Patricia was summoned to the headmistress's office. There she found her diary, charred but still readable, on the headmistress's desk. Her mother stood and stared out of the window, and Louise Gaynor stared remotely at her fingertips.

"And what have you to say, Miss?" asked the headmistress—not unkindly.

"It wasn't meant for anyone to read," said Patricia. "It was just things I made up."

"Nevertheless, you wrote it, and to write such unhealthy nonsense shows a very sick little mind. I'm not surprised your mother's so upset. Louise assures me she's never spoken to you in her life. Is that right, Louise?"

"Yes," said Louise, to her fingertips.

"I believe you, Louise. I have great faith in the honour and decency of my prefects."

"I don't believe her," said Lucy. "I believe what's written there. There are horrible, filthy things going on in this school. Patricia's corrupt and perverted. She's the devil's spawn. I've seen it in her eyes."

The headmistress sent Louise and Patricia back to their classes.

"What did you want to go and write all that for?" asked Louise, outside in the corridor. She had a soft and slightly nasal speaking voice. Eleven words.

"I don't know," mumbled Patricia. Louise looked once or twice down the corridor, then lifted Patricia's face with her forefinger and kissed her lightly on the lips.

"Now it's not a lie," she said, "so you can stop looking so miserable."

Patricia went back to the classroom. She searched into her heart for love: for her mother, for Hilda, for Elaine, for Louise, but could find nothing now but indifference and a vague embarrassment. All events seemed much of a muchness. She pressed a pen nib hard into her hand, but it did not hurt. She was not surprised.

After school she found Hilda waiting for her. Hilda usually went on ahead.

"They've taken mother to hospital," she said.

"What's the matter with her?"

"Nothing much."

"How long for?"

"Until she's better."

"What sort of hospital?"

"Just a hospital."

"She's mad, isn't she."

Hilda turned and looked at Patricia as lately her mother had looked at her, with cold and hating eyes.

"Don't ever say that, ever."

"What about us?" asked Patricia, once they were home.

"I'm nearly eighteen; you're fifteen. They're sending the child officer round about you. In the meantime, we stay where we are. I told them I could manage. I'm in charge."

Hot coals had been flung round the kitchen. Burn marks on the linoleum were to remain for years in remembrance of that particular day. Was there not a time, Patricia wondered, some other world, some other place, when she had been happy? In her mother's bedroom she found the early photograph of herself on the beach, torn up, and in wretched pieces on the floor.

No. It had never been.

The house seemed very quiet, and the night frightening.

8

THERE, THAT'S DONE. Lived through, yet once again. Are we what our childhoods make us? I was thirty before I could even think about my past. Yes, I would say, to all enquiries, I had a happy childhood, and if pressed would give an account of prewar Brighton, with its clean pebbly beach, and long summer days in the sun, complete with candy-floss. A photographic account. Or pressed still further, forced to remember the photograph torn and on the floor, turn the whole thing into a bad joke.

Yes, I am a bastard, and a Jewess at that. My father abandoned me and my mother went mad and I was a lesbian for a time. Ha-ha.

Laugh gaily. Gayly, even.

All enquiries, I say. There were few of them. I must have carried the past with me, as an almost visible load. Why would anyone want to help me with it? They wanted me to help with theirs.

In the middle portion of my life, when I gave dinner parties by night and wrote advertisements by day, I was prepared to believe, how I wanted to believe, that I had to cure myself to cure the world. Now I believe I have to cure the world to cure myself. It is an impossible task. I am bowed down by it.

The world is ungrateful. See how I am left alone, unable to hobble to the stove? Or perhaps I just abuse the world, as my mother abused me. Call it the names I should call myself. Indifferent, ungrateful, callous.

Bastard, Jewess, slut.

I did better than my mother, or my sister. I can put such memories of joy together! Don't think I can't. Patch them together into a protective quilt of happiness to keep the cold winds of reality out. I learned how to do it. Even here, in this horrible room, hungry and in pain, helpless, abandoned by the world in general and the social worker in particular, I can feel joy, excitation and exhilaration. I changed the world a little: yes, I did. Tilted it, minutely, on its axis. I, Praxis Duveen.

The funny farm, the loony bin, the mental home. The shelter for the mentally disabled. I have visited them all, over the years. Times have got better, I will say that. The staff, medical and paramedical, the social workers, the dieticians and the researchers these days all but outnumber the patients. Each mad act now supports upon itself a whole wonderful structure of bureaucrats, commentators, observers and philosophers.

In the beginning mother was in a straitjacket, guarded by those too low, stupid and depraved to work elsewhere; her face, the only part of her allowed movement, was alive with hatred for the world in general and me in particular. She wore no quilts of exultation. No.

I did not hate her: I never did. I wanted only to be allowed to love her and help her: look after her: remove her from the distress of her life. I felt more for her pain than I ever did for my own. There could be no happiness for me, knowing that my mother was so incarcerated.

After the straitjacket days, mother was locked in. Bolts clanged before and behind. I would visit her. She seems to walk towards me forever, down long, clattery, tiled corridors, smelling of disinfectant and boiled cabbage.

Sometimes she would deign to recognize me: sometimes not. I replay the scene in my mind over and over: sending her back to the end of the corridor: walking her towards me: sometimes she deigns to recognize me, sometimes not.

Mother!

Later, when drugs took the place of locks and bars, and the patient could be imprisoned in his or her own mind (mostly her) and the outer body could be set free, and the buildings got better, and dayrooms arrived, and private sleeping cubicles, and frozen peas instead of cabbage, and well-kept gardens, and segregation of the sexes ended and there was occupational and group therapy, and patient rights, and even the occasional, though brief, visit to the psychiatrist, mother's lot was considerably better. She seemed happier. She was allowed out, for a time, on home visits.

Was she always mad, or did the world send her mad with its prudery, hypocrisy and unkindness? Or was it the likes of her that made society what it was, prudish, hypocritical and unkind? Did my father's leaving make her mad, or did he leave because she was mad? And what is madness anyway? Throwing red-hot coals about a room, hating one of your children, worrying more about a lesbian kiss than a clerical rape? Preferring to lie in bed than to get up? I suppose, had she done all these things and more, and done them cheerfully, or even drunkenly, no one would have felt obliged to lock her up.

As it was, she was miserable, anxious and showed it in her actions, and was put away.

Where did the misery come from? Women have given birth to bastards, been left by lovers, and merely laughed and carried on. Mother did not. Why not? She should have, for my sake.

9

IT WAS SOME MONTHS before the child officer called at the house. He was busy. An influx of child evacuees had arrived in Brighton and promptly had to be reevacuated, along with many of the local children. German cross-Channel guns were now shelling coastal towns, and Brighton was considered an unsafe place to be.

"Shouldn't we visit mother?" Patricia asked Hilda, in the meantime.

"It's wartime," said Hilda. "They don't allow visitors." She left the house herself, however, on Sunday afternoons, and declined to tell Patricia where she was going.

"Is mother getting better?" Patricia would ask Hilda, when Hilda received a letter from some official source or other. Hilda, by virtue of her three years' seniority, dealt with all practical matters, and had her mother's habit for secrecy.

"Of course."

"When is she coming home?"

"When she is better."

There was little to do after school except homework. That term both Patricia and Hilda earned four embossed metal bars. Hilda already had five. She walked around the house clanking. The girls

51

did not change out of school uniform when they got home. There seemed little point. School was real life: home a kind of dank limbo. They cleaned and polished rooms: then shut the door on them. They slept in their separate bedrooms, creeping up the cold, dark stairs, but otherwise spent their time in the kitchen, which could be made cosy, if not companionable.

Hilda did her duty by Patricia, but didn't like her.

So much she made obvious.

"The hospital's been evacuated," Hilda said one Sunday afternoon when Patricia asked if she were not going out.

"Where to?"

"It's a secret, in case the Nazis find out."

"Why doesn't mother write to us?"

"Because of a paper shortage."

Hilda had an answer for everything, but it was never quite the appropriate answer.

"I think Hilda's going mad, too," Patricia said to Elaine, panic getting the upper hand of reticence. But Elaine had a copy of the *National Geographic* magazine and didn't seem to hear. The magazine contained photographs of bare-breasted native girls.

"They never show white girls," observed Elaine, "only niggers. What use is that? They're probably not like us."

Since the war had closed the beaches, it was not even possible to study the human form in bathing dress. Fashions, padded shoulders, brassieres that raised, pointed and folded the breasts into a sturdy shelf effect, confused the eye of the young beholder. There was no full-length mirror anymore at 109 Holden Road—Lucy had shattered them all, on one pretext or another—and even had there been, Patricia would not have considered viewing her own body. The body, she believed, was a piece of flesh within which she lived. She could make no connection between her body and her feelings.

Patricia kept her doubts about Hilda to herself. Madness was a disgrace; better not talked about. As with cancer, there was no cure, no hope: and madness was worse than cancer, being hereditary and not merely infectious. What use to talk about it, rub people's noses in it? Something so dreadful! All you could do was pretend it hadn't happened.

In the meantime, Elaine's parents feared for their daughter's physical safety: if Patricia's mother was in the loony bin, Patricia could hardly be guiltless: might turn nasty, dangerous, any minute. It was their turn to discourage the friendship.

Patricia discovered where Henry Whitechapel lived. She waited at the terminus where the bus from the recruitment centre stopped, and then followed him to his house. He wore an old fawn raincoat: he seemed younger than her mental image of him. He was so familiar to her, and yet so strange. He was, of course, beneath her.

People, Patricia decided, dogging Henry's footsteps, unseen, were awarded merit and demerit status marks, much as merit marks were given and taken away at school.

Three points up for being a male, two down for being a lodger, three points down for being of common stock, two points up for being physically attractive, six points up for being rich, and so on. You only had to go into a room, talk to someone for a minute or two, to do the social sums required, and rate yourself and others appropriately.

Her own rating was high: she could feel it. It had lately been reduced—by her mother's madness, three demerit marks at least— but she still added up to more than, say, Elaine, or even Hilda; though why two children of the same family should get different marks she could not quite work out.

Henry's house was a semi-detached villa halfway up the hill. Washing hung from the back line—visible from the front. Three demerit points there! But roses grew up the front wall. Half a mark for overt signs of contentment.

Unfortunately, Judith, when she opened the door to Patricia, seemed insensitive to the honour done her. She carried a heavy baby boy in her arms: he bounced and butted his head into his mother's chest.

"What do you want?"

What indeed? Perhaps she hoped Henry would move back in, dilute the atmosphere somewhat.

"I just came to see you and the baby."

"Took your time about it."

"Mother's been ill."

"Yes. I heard. She always was round the bend, I suppose."

"Of course she wasn't."

"I hope she was, or there's no excuse."

"Excuse for what?"

"The way she treated me. It's not your fault. Sit down. Hold the baby. I'll make tea. Henry gets extra rations from the camp."

Patricia held the baby and marvelled at its solidity. She had always thought that babies were weak and powerless things. This one seemed king of its universe.

"It's a lovely baby."

"No one said that when it was on the way."

"Little Pattie!" said Henry, his smile warm and familiar, out of the past. "Seeking me out! Who'd have thought it? Mind you, I liked your other name. Praxis. Praxis and Hypatia. Now that had style. Patricia and Hilda! I told her not, but she wouldn't listen. We're none of us like anyone else, I'd tell her, but she was determined. Poor soul!"

"Poor soul!" derided Judith.

"We're all alone up there now," said Patricia, "just Hilda and me. Mother's hospital has been evacuated."

"Local hospital? Who said so?" He seemed surprised. He held the baby on his lap. His hands were stained, as ever, with chemicals. They seemed old, pathetic, beyond fatherhood, yet grateful for it.

"Hilda said so."

"Hilda tells lies. Always did."

"I'm sure she doesn't." Patricia was shocked.

"She's like her mother," put in Judith. "She'll say anything if it's convenient. Mind you, as pillow talk I daresay it's nice enough to hear. Lovey dovey while it lasts. The next day, who might you be, sir? You're dirtying my carpet with your muddy boots. Fetch my bag; back to the kitchen; all you're fit for."

Patricia found herself quite dizzy.

"Be quiet, Judith," said Henry. "There's no need."

"Yes there is need. What's true is true. And to see her twisting those poor girls' minds. Who was she, anyway, to turn up her nose at us? She was no better than she ought to be. Living with a man she wasn't married to, bringing children into the world with no name: passing herself off as a widow when all he'd done was walk out on her. And then when I get into my bit of trouble, carrying on as if she was the Virgin Mary. Polluting her girls! Who did the polluting, I'd like to know?"

"Hush, Judith. Don't listen to her, Pattie."

"Pattie! Friendly, aren't we? Fancy her, do you? Like her

mother, is she? At least this one's got a pair of boobs on her: Lucy was as flat as a board!"

Judith's words stopped, as if caught midair like a ball in flight.

"Sorry," she said flatly. "Sorry. You think you don't mind but you do. All those years, when she had you, and thought you dirt. Not Pattie's fault. Hope I didn't let too many cats out of the bag."

Henry walked Pattie, as she now thought of herself, to the tram stop. Pattie, Judith, Henry, all much of a muchness. Except that Pattie had a mad mother and was a bastard, too. Four embossed bars, bouncing on a nice young bosom, couldn't anywhere near counteract all that.

"Where have you been?" Hilda asked when Patricia came back. "It's nearly blackout. I got the cheese ration. We'll have Welsh rarebit. You can make it go further by adding flour and water. A Ministry of Food leaflet tells you how."

Hilda was in a good mood. Sometimes, rarely, she was. Patricia neatly disposed of her good humour.

"I've been to see Henry and Judith."

"How did you know where they were?"

"I waited for the tram from the recruiting office. Then I followed him."

"Mother wouldn't like it. They're common. Nothing. Why do you want to have anything to do with them? She's a scarlet woman; you know what she did. And under mother's own roof."

"Scarlet? She always seemed kind of black and hairy to me," said Pattie, forlornly.

"I hope you told them nothing," said Hilda sharply. "We don't want people poking and prying into our business."

"I don't think people are all that interested in us. They only think about themselves."

She was not going to tell Hilda what she knew. Not yet. Perhaps never. The way to deal with Hilda was to agree with what she said, while believing none of it and doing nothing to aggravate her. Patricia was frightened of Hilda, as she had never been, quite, of her own mother. Lucy's madness had been a deviation from maternal love: Hilda's was an intensification of sisterly hate. Pattie locked her room that night and for many to come, and sat up late at the darkened window, watching the searchlights and the pattern of distant aerial conflicts reflected on the water.

Pattie found out the whereabouts of her mother by looking up area Health Board hospitals in the post office and ringing them up in turn until one finally acknowledged having a Mrs. Lucy Duveen on its books.

She went along to the Poole General Asylum the following Sunday. She put on lipstick in an attempt to make herself look older, lest she be refused admittance. She felt wicked, so doing.

The porter at the gatehouse unlocked bars to let her in. Blank eyes followed her. Women sat isolated and remote on benches, lining corridors. All seemed old: all had thick lisle stockings, wrinkling down over slippers, as if suspender belts were unknown. Pattie was frightened. What manner of life was this?

A male nurse, keys jangling, led her to a cubicle, and there, peering through, Pattie saw Lucy, in a straitjacket.

"Mother," shrieked Pattie.

"Quiet now, quiet," said the nurse. "They don't feel as we do, in this state."

Lucy seemed quite quiet, but when she saw Pattie she began to struggle and her face contorted.

"You upset her," said the nurse. "Come away." Pattie suffered herself to be led away. Lucy, seeing her, had been animated by hate and anger, not love and despair, yet this must be some sort of comfort. Better for her mother, worse for her.

This was the manner of life, and had been for a long time.

What was good for Lucy was bad for Patricia, and vice versa.

Lucy was in bonds, so Pattie could go free.

"I went to see mother," she said to Hilda, boldly enough.

"You shouldn't have done that. It would only upset you."

"It did."

"It's bad enough for me, and she quite likes me. She hates you, though. It's her illness. The doctors said you shouldn't go. I don't know why they let you in."

"No one knew who I was, I suppose. Anyway, I don't think they have much time to think about things like that."

"They're wonderful people: don't talk against them. It's all your fault she's in there, you realize that."

"Why?"

"You were perverted, weren't you? It upsets her."

"I wasn't."

"Don't pretend. You're just disgusting. Sneaky and sly."

Hilda went to bed early, up the stairs in brown lace-up brogues, yellow prefect's sash making a sack of her navy pleated tunic. She was nineteen. Her sallowness had disappeared: her skin had a smooth yellow-to-pink glow: her waist was slender: her receding chin made her mouth pouty and provocative: her eyes were clear, steady and censorious. Her life was passed in a female world, bounded by examinations: whole weeks would pass in which she would talk only to women. Even the tram conductors were female now: the men passed in noisy clumps of uniform, vulgar, frightening, leaving a litter of gum wrapping and beer bottles behind. Soon Hilda would go to university on a scholarship, and her life would open out. People assured her it would.

Hilda did not know what was to be done with Patricia, but did not doubt the arrival of some sudden event, for good or ill, probably ill, which would make the consideration immaterial.

Hilda stopped visiting her mother, on the recommendation of the funny-farm staff. In the early days of her confinement, Lucy's rage and spite had been directed against Patricia—later it came to focus upon Hilda as well, and could be felt as uncomfortable even through the cool shell of the elder daughter's partly acquired, partly native indifference.

Pattie went to visit the Reverend Allbright. She called at the back door, as seemed natural, and not, as in earlier days, at the front. She found him in the kitchen, with his new young wife, making wine. The house smelt warm and sweet, as was his life. He had married one of his young parishioners, a girl with down-cast almond eyes, and a sensual mouth, and a devout nature. She would kneel naked by the marital bed, saying her prayers until he could bear it no longer and flung himself upon her, tumbling her over face downwards on the bed. He felt God would understand. God can be worshipped anywhere, the Reverend Allbright avowed, in Sunday sermon after Sunday sermon. In a night bomber (so long as it belonged to the Allied forces), in a submarine (likewise), in a Scouts' hall (where services were now held, since the church had been bombed out) or in the marital bed. The congregation joined in shaking their fists at a vengeful sky, from which destruction raged; they were united in love and hate. The birthrate soared.

"My mother's in a straitjacket," said Pattie, to the Allbrights.

They sat her down to help make wine. Now she too was stripping petals from dandelions; her fingers were already dyed yellowy-green. No amount of washing, even with the strong, grainy, war-time soap, would remove the discolouration: only time would help it. Pattie, yellow-fingered.

"She has to be," said the Reverend Allbright, "for her own safety, and that of other people."

"But she can't be in one forever. A person can't live in a strait-jacket."

The Reverend Allbright suspected that if the staff of the asylum had anything to do with it, she would.

"Pour soul," put in the new Mrs. Allbright, with the easy pity of the young for the old. "My husband"—and with what pride she used the term—"used to visit regularly, but his visits did seem to upset her. They said it was better for him to stay away."

Both the Allbrights were bare-armed: while Mrs. Allbright stirred the bruised dandelion petals in warm water, Mr. Allbright added golden syrup from a height, for the delight of seeing it fall. How bright-eyed they seemed: how happily arrived at the place they ought to be. Mr. Allbright's children by his first marriage were still away at boarding school. Consideration both for their safety and for his new wife's peace of mind had led him to taking this step. The eldest Allbright was barely a month younger than the new Mrs. Allbright, a fact which rendered Mr. Allbright uneasy in his daughter's presence.

"We must abide by the decision of the staff," said Mr. Allbright. "After all, they are the experts."

"I think she's in a straitjacket to save them trouble," observed Pattie.

"That's a wicked un-Christian thing to say, Patricia," said Mr. Allbright.

Mrs. Allbright laughed. "Why should she say Christian things if she's Jewish? You are ridiculous, Stephen."

"Hush," said Mr. Allbright.

"Shouldn't I have said anything? I'm sorry."

Confused and pink, she stirred the sweet, warm brew. He was angry, so she made matters worse.

"I don't see why I shouldn't say what's true," she persisted. "It can't be anything new to Pattie, after all. Is it?"

Pattie shook her head, although it was indeed new.

"Anyway," said Mrs. Allbright, "there's nothing wrong with being a Jew. I'm sorry for them, that's all, because Jehovah seems such a fierce God to have, compared to Jesus, but I don't look down at them one bit. And I know you don't, either, Stephen. You always wanted to have a Jewish quota at the golf club; you thought healthy outdoor exercise would do them good, though I can't say it seemed to help the one they did have, who ran off with the waitress."

"Hush," said Mr. Allbright, and added, "In any case it's neither here nor there since the Army has now taken over the course and the tanks are ruining the greens altogether."

But it was no use. No one was listening.

Mrs. Allbright had her pretty yellow-stained hand to her mouth.

"My father," said Pattie, flatly. "You mean my father was a Jew and ran off with a waitress?"

"Idiot," said Mr. Allbright to Mrs. Allbright. He was to say it to her many times in years to come, and she grew not only to believe him but not to mind his saying it. But this time tears sprang to her eyes. Mr. Allbright watched and marvelled. The first Mrs. Allbright had never wept; never had to. All the same, she had died young. One tear fell into the dandelion wine, and he feared lest the addition of salt might interfere with the delicate fermentation process. "He married her, according to the laws of his religion and the law of the land. He left your mother, and yourselves, provided for."

Pattie left.

"She asked for bread and you gave her stones," said Mrs. Allbright, staring at her husband, pink-eyed, red-rimmed, flushed. Wisely, he poured what was left of the golden syrup over her to cheer her up, and the resultant stickiness of both of them was the cause of much joy and marital merriment. The Reverend Allbright felt he had regained his childhood, which the first time round had not been up to much, but now was rapturous, innocent and amazing. He was obliged, if only for cleanliness and comfort's sake, and in a spirit of remorse, to suck the stickiness from her every crevice.

"You can't look after everyone in the world, I suppose," observed Mrs. Allbright, forgivingly, naked, splay-legged and golden on the floor. "Let alone, half-mad, half-Jewish, half-grown parishioners who never even go to church." He blocked her mouth, astonishingly, before she could voice any more uncharitable thoughts and thus imperil her soul.

Such acts were unthinkable, unimaginable; except they happened, and once they had happened could happen again, at any rate when imports of golden syrup allowed. The dandelion wine was excellent. Sweet and powerful, quite unharmed by Mrs. Allbright's occasional tear, and popular with parishioners young and old.

Pattie did not tell Hilda what she had found out. Perhaps, in any case, Hilda knew already. She hid the sharpest kitchen knives, however, away from Hilda, afraid of what she was not quite sure.

Her mother's madness, she now perceived, lay in her telling of the truth. But was it madness? If a mother shrieked Jewess, bastard, pervert at her own daughter, and all these things were true, then she might be accused of unmaternal conduct, but hardly madness.

Pattie lay on her bed at night, and thought of kisses, mother's, father's, Louise Gaynor's, anyone's. She lay still, hands neatly folded over her smooth midriff. Pattie had a white, clear skin.

Who will ever marry me? Pattie wondered. Who would ever want to? Jewess, bastard, pervert. Daughter of a mad mother: insanity in the blood, running strong. See it even in Hilda's eyes: in her own now, reflected back from the Reverend Allbright's.

The American servicemen were in Brighton. Local girls came in from towns along the coast to meet them. They laughed, drank, cuddled and kissed; more, even, in the bushes at the bottom of 109 Holden Road where the garden abutted the pub alley. The fence palings were so rotted that a well-shod service foot would easily collapse them, and often did. Pattie watched from her window. Knickers off, hands in, trousers down, whispers and giggles, pant and heave, in and out. Sometimes money changed hands: sometimes addresses. Sex! The force at the heart of the universe. It hardly seemed sufficiently important.

10

IT WAS NOT UNTIL SEPTEMBER that Mr. Robinson, the children's officer, arrived, knocking at the front door. The knocker was stiff with disuse—visitors seldom came to the house. The brass door furniture, so beloved by Lucy in the days of her youth and sanity, had not been cleaned since Judith's dismissal. Paint and plaster peeled and flaked; last year's leaves mouldered in the corners of steps, grubs scuttered away at the fall of Mr. Robinson's brown boots.

After the fashion of the young, Hilda and Pattie cleaned what was beneath their eyes but seldom went searching for dust or decay. They washed the dirty cups, but not the shelves where the cups were kept. They made beds, they even washed sheets; but they never turned a mattress or shook a blanket. They turned their eyes resolutely away from peripheral grime and grease, and focused on their books, their homework, or, on the good days, on the heavens and higher thoughts. Their noses had grown accustomed to the smell of the cats, which came in through the broken scullery window to get out of the cold or away from the noise of aerial warfare; and to the stale water in the flower vases, where last autumn's chrysanthemum stems had long ago rotted away to slime; and to dry rot, wet rot, woodworm, decomposing bins and decay.

Mr. Robinson's eyes and nose were fresh to such sights and smells: they made him doubt the soothing reports on the Parker sisters from both school and clergyman, which sat thick upon his clipboard and had allowed him to delay his visit.

"The girls," the headmistress wrote, "seem to do better with no parents than many do with two. Patricia is quiet, neat, well-behaved and will get a good School Certificate: Hilda is, of course, our very valuable head girl, and is much respected by the other pupils."

Pupils, it is true, certainly fell silent when Hilda approached. She seldom smiled: her eyes glittered: the black braid with its embossed metal bars now hung almost to her waist, and clanked against the buckle of her money belt: Head Girl, House Captain, the engravings read: and, descending, Hockey, Latin, English, French, Geography, Religious Knowledge, Deportment—there seemed no end to Hilda's accomplishments. She meted out punishment liberally, if erratically. She might give twenty lines or two thousand for the same offence: she invented crimes. She had designated the second peg to the left of the cloakroom door as one which for some reason must be kept free of hats and coats, and would give a detention to anyone who used it: and once compelled a third year girl, a certain Audrey Denver, to stand on her head in the playground until she fainted for the sin of having brown laces in black shoes. Then she kept the entire third year in after school until whoever had done it owned up. But done what? Nobody was quite sure: nobody owned up: and Hilda went home in the middle of the detention anyway. The staff seemed unaware of their head girl's eccentricity: on the contrary, the headmistress enthused about her capacity for keeping order and the general lack of silliness in the school since her appointment. It was as if a certain implicit insanity in the school—dressing its burgeoning female adolescents in collars, ties, boaters and blazers; having them learn classics while the walls around them collapsed, and play netball on playgrounds increasingly pitted by falling shrapnel—had become explicit in Hilda.

Since her appointment as head girl, Hilda had been unusually pale, and her eyes dark, shiny and troubled. But she had been more talkative and confiding than usual: she would keep Pattie up until the early hours, talking about the third year girls, remarking on how like rats they were, scuttling here and there, carrying diseases, secretly watching Hilda and sending each other messages concerning her. Hilda went over and over the same ground: it was as if some gramophone record in her head had stuck. Pattie almost came to believe her. Audrey Denver certainly had a sharp little face, and red eyes due (she said) to chronic conjunctivitis: it was perfectly possible that the one black shoelace and one brown was a signal of some kind and that standing her on her head would cross the connections and scramble the lines between the rat armies, before worse befell, and all was known.

Anything, Pattie thought increasingly, was possible. Mr. Robinson, standing on the doorstep, was real enough. He wore his brother's brown boots, his uncle's pin-striped suit, his deceased father's trilby, frayed along the brim and chewed by his wife's dog, but not discarded. Since clothes rationing, people had ceased to be so readily identifiable as themselves. They were an amalgam of past and present, family and friends. The identity card, carried compulsorily on the person, was almost as reassuring to the individual as it was to the State.

This is who and what I am.

Mr. Robinson made brisk arrangements for Patricia to be boarded out and for Hilda to stay where she was until it was time for her to go to Oxford. She had won her scholarship to Somerville. The school had clapped and clapped, to Hilda's distress, for all she heard was the noise of a million rat feet, scuttering, dancing, all together. Hilda was prudent and kept the rats well out of her scholarship essays. To write about them was to give them more power: to speak about them weakened them. Lucy, visited by Pattie and told of Hilda's success, merely looked blank. There were now three women in the padded cell. They sat in straitjackets, like three nodding Chinamen on a mantelpiece ornament, in a stench of urine.

"You're my grandchild, aren't you?" said Lucy to Pattie. "I am such a very old woman."

Her face, wiped of all care, seemed like that of a child.

Perhaps she was getting better?

Hilda was.

Hilda packed Pat's belongings into a damp cardboard suitcase and made a special journey to the chemist for a farewell gift of rat poison.

"They're very cunning," she said. "Do be careful."

But Hilda's colour was returning: she slept well, early and late: the sharp little teeth had stopped gnawing away in her mind. She seemed slightly bewildered by her own gift to her departing sister and subsidized it with a pound or so of ripe blackberries from the brambles which now overgrew the garden. (Butt and Son had agreed to put the house on the market, but no one came forward to buy.)

And so, in October, Pattie left 109 Holden Road, bound for the seafront and the more suitable and cheerful home the Children's Department had found her. She carried a cardboard suitcase in one hand and a paper bag of blackberries in the other. Her hair was short, ordinary and curly: her face round, ordinary and not so much innocent as expressionless. Her smile, however, was frequent, if automatic, and used both to ward off attack and to give herself time to think. She looked well bred and well brought up, as Lucy would have wished—but of course was neither. She was sixteen. She wore Lucy's old tweed coat, cut down to three-quarter length. (It was in fact the very coat in which Lucy had eloped, so disastrously, with Benjamin, but Pattie did not know that. It was merely, to her, a coat which had hung on a peg for years, and from which a cloud of moths arose when anyone brushed past, making Hilda's eyes anxious and suspicious, as if moths were part of the rats' greater plan. Hilda had attacked it first with scissors: Pattie had neatened up the jagged edges and turned up an uneven hem with bodging stitches.) Beneath the coat she wore her school uniform. Pattie seldom wore anything but her school uniform: grey blouse, striped tie, navy gym slip sponged and pressed weekly, until the pleats were paper thin and the serge shiny, black stockings, the holes darned out, and stout brown shoes. The suitcase contained her school books and papers, a single dress, spotted red and white, some underwear, rather grey and held together by safety pins and black cotton stitching, a thick flannel nightie or so, and three pairs of smart brown-and-red shoes, as used by lady golfers, donated to her by the Children's Department.

It seemed enough. Even in those early days Pattie knew that all you really need take with you anywhere is yourself: the rest is clutter, and the world will, or should, provide it. A confident and self-righteous view—if a selfish one. Hilda, on the other hand, most of her time, felt the need for possessions, liked to be surrounded by objects which reflected her self, her state of mind, however cluttered and wayward that might be. She had recently started to collect things: old birds' nests, complete with withered fledglings, awkwardly shaped stones, scraps of torn fabric, twisted driftwood from the beach—the little, meaningful objects which the world kept tossing up at her feet. She would deride Pattie for her philistinism when her lip puckered with distaste and she failed to see the significance.

"Look at the shapes, Pattie. If you have eyes to see, look at the shapes! If you have any understanding of art, then this is art. But of course you haven't; how could you?"

Sensitive Hilda, pretty Pattie; as Lucy had defined them long ago.

Now Pattie turned the corner towards the seafront, and left Hilda behind, and her spirits rose.

"Everything is meant," she thought. "Everything is planned. That was my punishment, and now it is over."

A strong wind caught the wave tops on the other side of the esplanade and beat her about with bitter foam, stinging her lips: as if to deny the sentiment. Hilda would certainly have assumed that that was the meaning of the event.

Miss Leonard taught English at Pattie's school. She lived alone above what had been a popular furniture shop but was now empty of stock and was boarded up by means of a row of assorted doors battened together with railway sleepers. Miss Leonard was comfortable and solitary up above, and refused to be driven out of her house by the exigencies of war, which she regarded as a male pastime. She had also, so far, stood out against requisitioning orders and billeting officers, until now Mr. Robinson had prevailed upon her to take in a motherless and homeless girl child.

"But you're big Pattie Duveen," protested Miss Leonard, as she opened the door. "I know you. You came fourth in English in spite of a very insensitive paper on Keats. I was expecting a little girl called Praxis Parker."

Miss Leonard looked disappointed, and was. So far the war had brought inconvenience but very little novelty. The paper bag containing Hilda's blackberries disintegrated; overripe berries tumbled out and down the pale stair-carpet, staining as they went. Praxis cried, perceiving that Hilda's influence would follow her for the rest of her life, and that her past could never in fact be forgotten, would never be over. She must be Praxis and Pattie, too, until the end of her days.

She stood limp and crying at the top of the stairs. Behind her the kettle boiled and a canary sang. Miss Leonard, perceiving a challenge, cheered up. Over a period of months she pushed Pattie there, pulled her here, patted and cosseted sense back into her: made her sweep under the beds and not just round them, hem her coat properly, hand in neat homework, take the eyes out of potatoes when she peeled them, and little by little extract from her the causes of her grief.

"Jesus was a bastard," said Miss Leonard to Praxis. "Not to mention Napoleon and Nelson. Disadvantages either make you or break you. See that yours make you."

"It's not perverted to fall in love with girls," said Miss Leonard, "if no boys are available. Freud says, in any case, that homosexuality is a normal step on the road to full sexual maturity."

"To be Jewish is no disgrace," said Miss Leonard. "On the contrary. In any case a Jewish father doesn't count. Only a Jewish mother. Sorry."

"Your mother was not trying to harm you, only to save you," said Miss Leonard. "Poor thing."

"Yes, I can well believe that your sister is mad," said Miss Leonard, "though it never occurred to me at the time. One is not accustomed to the notion of mad children. But *you're* not mad, Praxis. What did you do with the rat poison?"

Miss Leonard emptied it down the lavatory bowl, and flushed and flushed.

"Mind you," she added, "I do know what she means about the third year. They do scuttle and scamper, whisper and pry, and they seem to have very sharp, bright, sinister eyes."

But she laughed as she said it, and that day cut off the crusts of the sandwiches as a special treat—it was a practice frowned upon by the Ministry of Food—and filled them with tinned melon jam from South Africa, as opposed to the turnip pulp, flecked with wood splinters and coloured with cochineal, which did for raspberry jam.

"You're getting to be quite a pretty girl, Praxis," said Miss Leonard. Praxis' smile was less frequent, but her face becoming more expressive.

"I suppose," said Miss Leonard, with rather less certainty, "it is possible to be happy in a straitjacket. Especially if there are others in like condition to keep you company. One is usually at home in the presence of one's peers. It is if one is obliged to live with others either greater or lesser than oneself that one is so wretched—"

All the same, Miss Leonard wrote to Butt and Son, Solicitors. "It is disgraceful," she declared, "that the children of your client should have been so neglected. If you will kindly send me the father's address I will contact him personally. The mother has been driven into a breakdown by his harshness, and is in a position to sue for compensation through a third party, and I will have no hesitation in being that third party if funds are not immediately forthcoming for her transfer to a private institution."

Miss Leonard received a cheque by return of post.

"Be a carnivore," said Miss Leonard, carefully boiling the week's ration of one egg each, to make a Sunday breakfast, "not a herbivore." She wore a crimson-flowered dressing gown, and her nails were bloody red, but her slightly pop eyes were gentle and searching.

"What do you mean?" asked Praxis.

"Carnivores feed off herbivores," said Miss Leonard. "Carnivores exist to herbivores in a ratio of fifty to one. I am a herbivore. We munch away peacefully, looking wise, until suddenly snap, snap, we're gone." Miss Leonard had spent a lurid Saturday night.

Miss Leonard had lost her one true love in the First World War. First she'd slept with him: then she'd lost him. A punishment for sin, she assumed. She'd been seventeen.

"It is an honour to lose a son for one's country," observed her true love's mother, carrying on, head and chin held high, War Office telegrams mounting up on the mantelpiece, continuing with her charity fete to Beat the Boche. He was the third of her sons to die, trying to do so.

"If that's the only way you can bear it," observed Miss Leonard's mother, "call it what you like, even honour. I prefer to call it a tragedy and a wicked waste. What are my daughters going to do for husbands?"

What indeed? Miss Leonard did without one, denied any need for one, lived quite happily without one, went to Teachers Training College, and thereafter spent her time putting romantic notions into the heads of growing girls. Keats, Wordsworth, Rupert Brooke.

"If I should die, think only this of me—"

No, but there was so much else to be thought. She perceived it now: the war helped. Now the putative husbands were dying again, but this time not so willingly, Miss Leonard was glad to observe. As for sex, now that it was emerging as an easy traffic between ignoble men and willing women, it could hardly be, as she had once assumed, a matter for God's instant, personal intervention.

These days, on Saturday nights, after Praxis had gone to her early bed, Miss Leonard had taken to dressing up in black mesh stockings, high heels, yellow satin blouse, tight black crêpe de Chine skirt, swinging a white handbag and walking, unrecognizably, down the esplanade—until accosted by a man, whereupon sanity would return and she'd rush home in agreeable panic.

On this particular Saturday night, Miss Leonard had arrived home to find the lights on, and Praxis presumably awake and out of bed, and rather than be discovered so eccentrically dressed, had returned to the esplanade. This time, courteously accosted by a respectable man with an educated accent, she did not run home, but fell into step beside him. He had lost his wife, so he said, in the Coventry air-raids. Now he lived with his son. They went to bed together in a poky back bedroom, where a gas fire, fed by sixpences, spluttered and smelt. The bed creaked.

Miss Leonard's unaccustomed arms clasped thin limbs and a bony chest: she had expected more weight, more solidity. But that had been long ago: and had she been wrong then, and had it not been love she felt, but simple lust? Had she all these years regretted the loss of something not lost at all, but freely available in the bodies of all men: or had chance brought her something rare and extraordinary, something so composed of tenderness as only to be called love? Miss Leonard cried out in orgasm.

"Hush," he said, embarrassed. "Hush," and she felt ashamed. Though she sought and recognized qualities in him—such as intelligence, education and gentleness—he saw in her only an ageing tart with a swinging handbag. What else could he see? He got out of bed and went to the bathroom. When he comes back, Miss Leonard thought, I'll tell him who I really am, what I really am. Not a whore at all, but a schoolteacher, to be taken seriously, loved and appreciated. Looked after, and looking after. Forever. He'll believe me, he'll forgive me. In her mind Miss Leonard repapered the dismal room; filled it with flowers: she was his wife. One of those strange wartime marriages: but happy, how happy: happiness snatched out of loss, desolation, violence. His wife, pulped beneath falling masonry: and Miss Leonard's true love, dull dead body hanging on barbed wire, pecked at by crows, forming the comfort out of which such rare and lovely flowers grew.

When he came back and moved on top of her again, she was surprised. Surely this was the time for affection? She found his body heavy, his actions painful—and realizing it was not the father but the son—struggled and cried out.

"Did I take you by surprise?" he asked, though not desisting. "Didn't he tell you I was next? Don't worry, I'll give you extra. What's the matter? What difference can it make to you?"

He left an extra pound on the dressing table when he had finished.

"Let yourself out," he said. "No hurry."

Miss Leonard heard the lights of the house switched off, one by one, upstairs and down and all was presently silent. She dressed and let herself out, and shivered in the night air. She felt serviceable and useful, but second-rate and in need of cleaning: like some old chipped saucepan, pulled from the back of a cupboard: good enough as a receptacle but hardly for haute cuisine. Well, as one valued oneself, so one was valued. She must tell Praxis that, in the morning.

On her way home she was accosted by a drunken G.I. For ten shillings she allowed herself to be leaned against a wall, her skirt taken up, her knickers down, and herself penetrated by a member as long, pale, lean, cool and strong as the G.I. hands she had often wondered at, so unlike the tense and crooked hands of the English. She remained quite passive herself: he did not seem to notice, but walked on after the incident as if he had been merely relieving himself.

Is that what sex is? wondered Miss Leonard. Such a simple impulse, after all?

Miss Leonard arrived home, bathed, slept, boiled the breakfast eggs, and recommended that Praxis should grow up a carnivore, not a herbivore.

"You may well be one in any case," she said. "You certainly seem to be at the centre of events. A catalyst. Do you know what a catalyst is?"

"No."

"They ought at least to pretend to teach girls science," said Miss Leonard.

"Girls aren't good at science."

"Madame Curie was." It was the stock answer, unbelieving and unbelieved.

Miss Leonard presently took Patricia to visit her mother in the Seaview Nursing Home. It was a private establishment: and clean and cheerful. Lucy was sitting in the autumnal sunset, in a flowered wrap, gazing out over concrete emplacements, barbed wire and the rising and falling tides. She kept her arms rather closely to her sides, as if they rather missed their confinement, but talked charmingly to her daughter, as if to some passing stranger, about the changing moods of the seasons. She was no longer distressed, or distressing.

"What about the others?" Praxis asked Miss Leonard.

"What others?"

"The others still in straitjackets."

Miss Leonard stared at Praxis.

"Don't tell me," she said, "you're going to be the sort who cares about others." But she seemed pleased rather than otherwise.

The time for Miss Leonard's monthly period came and went, and came and went again. She thought it was the change of life and took care to wrap up well in cold winds. "Hormonal changes," she told herself when she felt sick; and "One puts on weight," when her waist band would no longer button; and "It's a difficult time" when she found herself snapping at Praxis for leaving the table uncleared, and crying instead of shouting when her pupils left their homework undone: until her shape was too characteristic of pregnancy to be denied, even to herself.

"No, I don't know the father," said Miss Leonard to the doctor. "It was rape."

"Did you go to the police?"

"No."

"Why not?"

"I felt too dirty. I couldn't even talk about it." How she lied! She who was so honest, and honourable. "Please do something for me."

"There is nothing I can do. Not even in cases of rape is abortion anything other than a criminal act."

"But I'm forty-five."

"What has that to do with it?"

"I've never had a baby! Isn't it dangerous?"

"If it is a question of your life or the baby's, it is sometimes permitted to sacrifice the baby. Not, of course, if you are a Roman Catholic. Then the newer soul takes precedence."

"You mean they'd kill me?"

"Not directly. But they'd save the baby."

"Are you a Roman Catholic?"

He was an elderly man. He shook his head. He smiled. He didn't believe her story of rape.

"No. But I know God's work when I see it. I am afraid this pregnancy is your punishment. Believe me, those who pay the penalty for their sins in this world, not in the next, are indeed blessed."

Miss Leonard went to other doctors, who declined to help. Many showed her the door, outraged at the notion that they should connive at murder. Others expressed sympathy, but did not, could not, risk imprisonment on her account.

Miss Leonard confided all to Praxis.

When Praxis had reassessed her vision of Miss Leonard, which took the best part of a week—shock modifying to surprise, surprise to disapproval, disapproval to acceptance—she observed, "It seems extraordinary to me that in a world in which men are killing each other by the million, they should strike such attitudes about an unborn foetus."

Miss Leonard, through her distraction, felt she had done well with Praxis. Praxis had joined the Peace Pledge Union. She was now a pacifist. It was not a popular thing to be, but now that she was freed from the worst of her inner preoccupations, Praxis was left with sufficient energy to strike the difficult moral attitudes suitable to her years.

"If men won't help," said Praxis, "perhaps women will."

Praxis went to visit Mrs. Allbright, that soft, honey-coloured creature.

"Tell your friend," said Mrs. Allbright, "that abortion is a wicked thing, against God's law and man's. No, of course I don't know any addresses. What your friend should do is have the baby and put it in a home, or have it adopted. There are charitable societies which will take the baby away at six weeks, and see to the whole thing for you."

"Isn't that rather hard for the mother? To wait six weeks? Why can't they take it away at birth?"

"The mother must be given every opportunity to change her mind, Pattie. She must realize exactly what she's done, and what she's giving up. No use just brushing these things under the carpet, or society will collapse into total immorality. It's only the fear of pregnancy which keeps girls on the straight and narrow."

Young Mrs. Allbright, still childless, was trying to please her husband (increasingly irritable) and seduce God (increasingly inaccessible) by adopting the views of the first Mrs. Allbright, as if by some sympathetic magic she too might be as fertile as her predecessor. She worried about Mr. Allbright's feeling for his younger daughter, now fifteen, which was increasingly displayed in huggings, strokings and kissing. A heightened sexuality, she could see, was a double-edged sword. The pleasure extracted by the body must be repaid by the mind, in the form of anxiety. Nothing was for nothing.

"I hope you're not a close friend of this particular girl, Pattie," said Mrs. Allbright. "I know that thanks to Mr. Hitler we're all jumbled up next to each other, saints and sinners, and it may even be no bad thing, but do please be careful not to get into bad company. I hope Miss Leonard keeps a strict eye on you. What news of Hilda?"

Hilda was in her second year at Somerville. She was expected to get a first. Praxis said as much.

"There's such a thing as being too clever," sighed Mrs. Allbright. "So difficult to find a suitable husband."

Praxis went to visit Judith, who by now had three small children, all with swarthy complexions and dark, watchful eyes. Her husband was in hospital with stomach pains. Judith wrote an address and handed it to Praxis.

"So you're in trouble," she said. "Like mother, like daughter."

All Judith's children were boys.

"It's not me," protested Praxis, "it's my friend."

"That's what they all say," said Judith. "You are so like your mother. A hypocrite. Well, fortunately I don't hold grudges. There's your address. It'll cost you five pounds."

"Is it safe?"

"It's done me often enough. I'm still alive."

"Does it hurt?"

"Of course it hurts."

When Miss Leonard and Praxis knocked at the suggested door, there was no reply. Dingy lace curtains were drawn over dusty windows. Dogs had been at the dustbins, and household refuse was scattered over the paths.

"Too late," said an elderly neighbour, scarf over curlers, cigarette in the mouth. "She's doing five years. One of them finally died. I'm surprised it didn't happen before. Dirt! You should have seen it. As for the inside of her dustbins—but she wouldn't listen. Dead ignorant. Good-hearted, but dead ignorant."

Miss Leonard was to have her baby. By the time she found an abortionist her condition was public knowledge, her job was lost and the baby too developed to be safely removed.

"It's your fault," she said to Praxis. "If you hadn't chosen that night to wander about, none of it would have happened."

These days Miss Leonard was childish and tearful; it was left to Praxis to be sensible and reassuring.

Mr. Robinson, the children's officer, appeared, to see if perhaps Praxis was in moral danger, and concluded it was too late to worry. In any case, where else could she go? 109 Holden Road had found no buyer. Miss Leonard swelled, and lumbered, and knitted. Praxis studied, attended to her lessons, and to the cooking. Hilda appeared, briefly, from Somerville. She was in the middle of exams, and suffering the effects of stress. She was pale, dark-eyed and certain that Miss Leonard's baby was the Immaculate Conception of the Antichrist. She wrote to Butt and Son asking them to withdraw Praxis' and Lucy's allowance—all their trouble, she maintained, could be traced back to tainted money. Praxis managed to switch envelopes so that an empty one was dispatched instead. Hilda went away.

"She doesn't really want to damage me," Praxis said to Miss Leonard, "only herself in me."

"There is such a thing," said Miss Leonard, "as being too forgiving."

Miss Leonard would sit stroking her swollen stomach. Now she had decided to keep the baby, she had grown to love it. She had high hopes for its future: of the world into which it would be born. Hitler was in retreat: the seeds of a new Jerusalem sewn thick in the churned-up soil of old England, waiting for the sun of freedom to shine, and the rain of equality to fall.

"I wonder whose it is," she would say. "The father's, the son's or the American's? I hope it was the American. He was so tall, and clean, and free. He didn't care. I would like to have a baby who didn't care. Someone to take its pleasure and move on."

Miss Leonard went into labour on the day that Praxis sat her first higher school certificate examination. English language. Praxis had worried about leaving Miss Leonard alone that morning, but had gone all the same. Her future loomed larger than Miss Leonard's present.

Miss Leonard died waiting for the ambulance to arrive: a London-aimed buzz-bomb—shot down over the Channel, but not quite in time—came down not in the sea, as had been hoped, but just inland. By the kind of miracle, half-good, half-bad, which seemed to attend bombing raids and made for memorable headlines and tales of valour and hair's-breadth escape, Miss Leonard was killed, her torso crushed, but the baby was saved. The umbilical cord was literally bitten through by a woman passer-by, who later collapsed from shock, but not before snatching the child from the mother, seconds before bed, room, dead Miss Leonard, canary, kettle and all toppled into a crater, just as the ambulance arrived. The row of battened doors, falling, made a kind of coffin lid, or so it seemed to Praxis, coming home from school.

"I told you," said Hilda. "Antichrist. A female Antichrist. Antichrists are female. Pattie, you take trouble with you wherever you go."

Pattie could see that it might well be so. She sat the rest of her examinations, but in retrospect could remember nothing about them. She did well, however, and was accepted by Exeter University. She stared and stared at the letter of acceptance, but it did not seem to mean what it should. She could feel on her face that expression of angry distaste which so characterized her sister Hilda.

Mrs. Allbright took in the baby, christened Mary, and for a time, Pattie. The first Mrs. Allbright, she felt, would have done no less.

She quickly fell pregnant.

Virtue, she was glad to observe, was thus, naturally, rewarded.

11

HOW MUCH IS FICTION, and how much is true? There can be no objective truth about our memories, so perhaps it is idle to even attempt the distinction. We are the sum of our pasts, it is true: we are altogether composed of memories: but a memory is a chancy thing, experience experienced, filtered coarse or fine according to the mood of the day, the pattern of the times, the company we happened to be keeping: the way we shrink from certain events or open our arms to embrace them.

Was my mother in a straitjacket, a real tangible, canvas straitjacket, or is this merely how I envisage her? Do I pinion her in fact as she was pinioned in her mind, prevented by circumstance and her own nature from stretching her soul and encompassing Hypatia and myself in the warmth of unconditional love? Did Hypatia really stand Audrey Denver on her head to shake the rat-thoughts out of her brain? Of course not. But she stood me on mine, metaphorically, often enough, until I doubted the truth of my own perceptions.

It is all over now: it lives only in my mind. Dead and gone, as is the reality of my mother, and Hypatia, and as I fear if things go on like this, shall be my own reality. My whole foot is swollen now: if

76

I look closely I can see a puncture on the shiny red skin near the outer edge of the nail of my big toe. This, I imagine, is where the infection entered. I should ask for help. People *do* help, I tell myself. Miss Leonard helped—and see where it landed her.

Mind you, it is pleasanter to help the young than the old. The young need crutches for a time, and then throw them away, going boldly forward of their own volition. Give the old crutches, and they use them forever, complaining of their poor quality the while.

But that is not the real reason for my hesitation: why I continue to sit here, in pain and frightened, instead of crawling out of the door and into the street, and demanding help, charity and release from passers-by.

No.

It seems to me that the wall between my own reality and theirs is so high, so formidable, as to preclude any waving or smiling over the top: let alone the touching of hands or the healing of minds: certainly not the actual calling of an ambulance. Other people's realities are nonexistent: they vanish to the touch; like my own past, they are the sorry projection of a drifting imagination. My mind may leap ahead to practical action, envisaging this course or that: my body, knowing better, simply stays where it is, and waits for the end. It prefers death. It really does.

I am alone in the reality I have created for myself. In my mind I invented old age, illness, grief, and now I am stuck with them, and serve me right.

12

"Wherever you go," Hilda whispered to Praxis, pressing a small black square into her hand, "you have to take yourself with you."

The square, unfolded, proved to be a black chiffon scarf, frayed to grey along the folds, which Lucy had worn in the old days, the good days. A small group had gathered at Brighton Station to say goodbye to Praxis, as she set off for Exeter University, a course in political science, of all things, and the world. Praxis' senses were finely tuned to the first disparate chords of the dance of Hilda's madness, and knew from the whisper, and the gift, that she was being ill-wished.

You may think you are leaving, but you are wrong. You will never be free. Childhood is never over. Thank you, Hilda, bad fairy, for this gift.

One by one the others stepped forward, good fairy godmothers, to undo the harm.

"Have a lovely time," said Mrs. Allbright. "I'm sure you deserve it." Her waist was already thickening: her eyes were bright with satisfaction. Her elder stepdaughter was back at boarding school, her husband back to normal, and life was serene. Mr. Allbright, she was sure, would find a renewal of youth in this their own new baby, and that was all that was required. Baby Mary Leonard lay in a pram at the other end of the platform and cried. "Shouldn't you pick her up?" Praxis enquired, anxiously. "Certainly not," said Mrs. Allbright. "Babies must learn discipline. It's the root of all morality." Mrs. Allbright was sorry to lose Praxis in one way, since she was useful about the house, but glad in another—for Praxis would keep picking up Baby Mary and staring into her wide, serious eyes, as if searching there for God, or the Devil, or at any rate some trace of momentous events, and spoiling her.

"Don't get in with the wrong crowd," said Mr. Allbright. "Join the Student Christian Movement: you'll meet some nice young men there." His hair was white with lime and plaster dust, and his nails horny and cracked. He had come straight to the station from the building site where he and his parishioners were rebuilding the church with their own hands. "I'm going to *study*," said Praxis, but clearly no one believed her. She only barely believed it herself.

"Be careful of the ex-servicemen," said Elaine. "Or rather don't be careful. Who wants little boys?" Elaine was off to secretarial college. While she waited for term to begin she helped in her father's shop. She had parked his bread van in the station yard, in order to say goodbye. Her parents would not let her go to university; they feared for her virtue, rightly.

"Don't worry about your mum," said Judith. "I'll go and visit." Judith had two of her nameless, swarthy children by her side. She was in mourning for her husband, and it was as if, with his death, her resentment against the Duveen family had evaporated.

"You'll write if anything happens? If she seems unhappy?" begged Praxis, as the train left.

"Nothing you can do about it if she is," called Judith after her. "You have to live your own life, not hers."

It seemed a supreme benison, leaving Hilda black, shrivelled and meaningless in the retreating station. Praxis had her head out of the window, waving, and placed the chiffon on her head to calm her hair: but the wind whipped it away and it vanished into someone's vegetable allotment.

It seemed a good omen: a further confounding of Hilda's ill wishes.

Hilda had been staying at the Allbrights', too. They were kindness and generosity itself, everyone said so. But Praxis felt uneasy.

She took care not to be alone with Mr. Allbright: he spoke sensibly but looked strangely. Mr. Allbright's elder daughter, a big bouncy bosomy girl, would sit in her father's lap after supper and nibble his ear while Mrs. Allbright played the pianola with too many stops out, and she and Hilda washed up. It had been hard work: Baby Mary to be cared for, and her nappies and clothes to be washed, for now Mrs. Allbright was pregnant and she seemed to have little strength or desire to do it herself: and, moreover, seemed to believe that even a small baby could tell the difference between right and wrong, unselfish and selfish behaviour, and should be punished accordingly.

Hilda had become obsessive about the stars. Praxis would wake in the night to find her sister staring sadly out of the window at the night sky. Perhaps she missed the searchlights, and the drama of battle. Now the war was over the sky was boring. She said as much.

"The war is never over," said Hilda. She had a gift for making such statements: meaningful in general, but in detail meaningless. It was a gift which was to stand her in good stead in later life.

"Miss Leonard is that star over there," said Hilda, pointing. "The reddish, twinkling one. She must be suffering terribly."

"That's Betelgeuse," protested Praxis. "It's a red dwarf." Praxis read books on popular astronomy.

"A dwarf? I sometimes believe you're mad," said Hilda. "Stars are souls burning in hell: that's why they flicker."

Baby Mary slept in the room with them. When she woke and cried, Hilda would wake first and get to the crib while Praxis still struggled with sleep. She would take the baby to the window, rock her in her arms and point out the stars. Hitler, Mussolini, her own father, Miss Leonard: the strange black patches in the Milky Way were spaces waiting for new arrivals. The baby would find her thumb, and suck, and stare, and stare and suck, and finally consent to be put down, and sleep again.

Praxis knew that presently she would have to rescue Baby Mary, and did not doubt that she could do it.

At college Praxis lived in a ladies' residence some half a mile from the campus. She shared a room with a large, strong, red-haired girl. The hair was wiry, mangy and curly, not the deep, smooth and sultry kind: and her complexion patchy and freckled. She seemed unaware of these misfortunes: she fell on her knees at night and thanked God for her blessings. She wore a strong white nightgown; scrubbed her face and hands at night with carbolic soap, and her smell was high but not unpleasant. She was friendly and noisy, was studying German, played a good game of hockey, ate heartily, and regarded college as a continuation of school life. Her name was Colleen; "Just call me Collie."

Praxis half-despised, half-envied her her ordinariness; taking for the person what was only the crackly shell, grown in self-defence in a world in which to be fragile and pretty was to be valued, and to be cheerful and practical the best a girl could do, if not blessed by nature. The first time Praxis heard Colleen cry in the night, she was astonished. Later, she became accustomed to it. It was years before she was to consider it.

Praxis, mind you, studying herself in the mirror (as she frequently did) saw little to indicate that she herself had been particularly blessed by nature. Two eyes, a nose, a mouth, all regularly placed. Brown, short, curly hair. A complexion rather pinker than she would have liked, but at least clear. A white, solid neck. Praxis feared that there was no distinction about her face at all; on the other hand perhaps she was merely overused to what she saw in the mirror. As for her body, other people's clothes seemed to fit it well enough, so presumably it was in no way bizarre. By virtue of clothes rationing and shortage of money—Praxis lived on a local authority scholarship grant of 120 pounds a year, paying 105 pounds of that to the ladies' residence—she wore mostly second-hand clothes.

The pride of her wardrobe was Miss Leonard's leopardskin coat, blown into the street when the bomb fell. Praxis had also salvaged a string of bold metal beads which Miss Leonard so often wore, taken from her dead body by rescue workers and placed in a canvas bag with other bits and pieces for the family to go through at their leisure. Waste not, want not: it was the motto of the war: and Praxis was sure, besides, that Miss Leonard would not mind. She had taken two of Lucy's dresses and three of Lucy's skirts, one black wool, one brown rayon, one green silk, which she had found at the back of a wardrobe at home, and which more or less fitted, although still smelling strongly of mothballs. Hilda had given her two spotted blue-and-white blouses, which were too large for her: and she had a great quantity of the first Mrs. Allbright's underwear—stout white cambric knickers and brassieres, woollen vests and beige lisle stockings—which the second Mrs. Allbright had given her. Washing and drying the latter took a long time. On her feet, Praxis wore the black court shoes which Judith had bought to go to her husband's funeral; but bought too small, her judgment clouded by her distress. They fitted Praxis very well.

Praxis did feel that there was perhaps something odd about her appearance: a feeling made more pronounced by the existence in the next room of a girl called Irma Henry, who would wander idly down the corridors towards the bathroom—while others scurried, if immodestly dressed—naked beneath a clinging wrap made out of parachute silk: the shape of her breasts, and even her nipples, clearly visible. She had no parents, but a guardian, and some distant cousins in Sussex: she had been to Roedean, a girls' public school, and spoke the language of the privileged. She painted her nails scarlet, studied French and made long-distance telephone calls from the booth outside the dining room, while the other girls waited about for the toad-in-the-hole to be served. When it arrived, she would push aside the soggy batter—the best part—and disdainfully eat a morsel or so of the sausage. She was pretty, in a hollow-eyed, bad-tempered kind of way. No one liked her: everyone admired her. For some reason she made a friend of Praxis, shaking her head in wonderment over the white cambric knickers.

Irma dressed and undressed in front of Praxis, who was relieved to find that other girls too had a triangle of hair where their legs started. Praxis' body seemed as much of a mystery to her as ever. She bled once a month, regularly, but barely knew why, and had ceased to wonder. She neither felt nor investigated the area between her legs, and certainly never took up a mirror to look, imagining that an area so soft, private and forbidden was better left alone. Irma seemed to have no such inhibitions.

Irma was accustomed to going to the weekly students' dance, and asked Praxis to go with her. Colleen advised against it.

"The ex-servicemen will be there," said Colleen.

"They're like animals," said Colleen; "they're men, not boys anymore, and they've seen and done terrible things. They go to the dances and just lie in wait for nice girls."

"They can't do any harm," said Praxis. "What harm could one come to?"

"But they've been abroad," said Colleen, "and their passions have been inflamed by hot climates and spicy foods. Don't you *understand*, Praxis? Men like that can't control themselves. They're like animals. If you dance with them you're just asking for trouble.

"If you're interested in boys," said Colleen, "they have nice socials at the Student Christian Movement, with free coffee and cakes."

Praxis went to the dance with Irma. Nothing would stop her. She wore Lucy's cerise satin dress and hoped that no one would notice how unevenly the hem had dropped. Over the dress she wore the leopardskin coat. "You'd do better to go in your ordinary clothes," said Irma, but Praxis couldn't agree. Irma abandoned her at the door.

Irma wore a low-cut black sweater and a full pink skirt; her hair was swept up in a pony-tail, one of the first to be seen in the West. Irma danced all evening, abandoning one partner, choosing another. She was all candid eyes, laughing mouth and pressing breasts.

"Cock-tease," someone muttered in her ear, and did not mean it pleasantly. Irma had heard it often enough before; she took no notice.

Praxis danced the first dance; then her partner took her to the bar. She had learned dancing at school. This felt different. He gave her gin and lime. She was unused to drink.

"That's a funny dress," he said. "Is it very fashionable?" She did not care for her partner, or his opinion. He was no taller than she: he wore no tie: his hair needed cutting: his chin needed shaving. His face was flat and shiny and seemed a matter of planes and angles, like a piece of cut glass. His eyes were small but bright behind thick spectacles: his arms were hairy: his cuffs were frayed: he wore ex-army boots. His hand upon her arm trembled with nervous energy. His name was Willie. He was, he told her, doing political science and economics.

"So am I," said Praxis.

"It's a men's option," he said, surprised.

"They thought I was a man," said Praxis. "I have an odd name. But once they accepted me they could hardly throw me out. They tried, but I wrote a letter."

He wasn't listening. His eyes were on her breasts. Her dress was without straps: it kept up by virtue of whalebones, which had escaped their padding and now dug into her flesh. It was, perhaps, too large for her. She became aware that anyone taller than she, looking down, could see more than he ought.

Fortunately, Willie was not tall: and, besides, she reckoned, his opinion of her hardly counted. She accepted another drink and then another. It seemed preferable to dancing. She did not like the feel of his arm round her waist. It seemed very familiar. At school girls had danced with girls.

"Why do you look so odd?" he asked. "Is it policy, or accident? I look odd, but then I mean to. I don't believe in washing, for one thing. It reduces the body's natural defences against disease; soap is a needless expense. I'm very mean, I warn you. I got in here tonight through the back door. It's very easy. All you have to do is just walk in: there's no one to stop you."

His eye had strayed further down, contemplatively. His trousers, she observed, were held up by string.

"Why wear a belt when string will do?" he remarked. "Belts are a waste of money, if you come to think of it."

"Don't you care what people think?" she asked.

"Depends who," he said. "I saw a lot of people die. I was in D-Day. I don't like to waste my time, my money or my life. Am I wasting my time with you? Or my money?"

She was not quite sure what he meant. His breath was sweet: it smelt of slightly fermented honey.

She shook her head.

He bought her two more gin and limes, counting the change carefully.

He was joined by his friend, who was tall, clean-cut with a soft voice and wide, innocent eyes. His skin was as clear and soft as Baby Mary's, and his hair the same fine silver yellow colour. He stared and stared, as speculatively as Willie did. His mouth was full, pink and curved. Praxis fell in love at once. His name was Phillip. He drank a good deal of beer: but his shirt was crisp and white and his tie stayed straight.

"Does she have a shape under that dress?" he asked.

"I believe so," said Willie. "You're drunk."

"Never," said Phillip, staggering. "Is she willing?"

"Of course she is," said Willie.

"But how do you know?"

"I have a fine instinct for these things. On the other hand, she's in our department. It might be complicated."

"Not science?"

"No."

"I could have sworn she was in science," said Phillip. "They're so easy to lose."

He bought the next round of drinks. Presently they all went out onto the downs. Praxis left her mother's handbag behind, and all her money, her comb and her orange lipstick, but didn't care.

"It's going to be a good term," said Phillip. "I can feel it in my bones. A good year for available girls." He took off his shoes. Willie took off his boots. He wore no socks and his toes were dirty.

"If you loved me," said Willie, sadly, "you'd wash my toes."

Praxis wouldn't. Phillip said she shouldn't, in any case. If Willie was too mean to buy soap, he must put up with the consequences. Praxis was no substitute for soap.

"What is she then?" enquired Willie. Phillip studied Praxis, contemplatively.

"You can't tell, in that dress," said Phillip.

Ceremoniously they removed the dress: one on each side they raised her arms to study the marks left by the whalebones.

"I suppose," said Willie, "it's an engineering problem."

"I was in the sappers," said Phillip. "It would be nothing to me." He ran his finger over the weals and round her breasts.

"You take your hands off her," said Willie. "She's an object lesson, not a body."

"She's better without the dress," said Phillip. "Her face isn't so green." He stood back and offered Praxis a swig from his beer bottle, which she accepted. She was beginning to feel sick. Phillip offered to sell Willie a swig for a shilling. Willie argued that friendship entitled him to two swigs for sixpence.

Phillip pointed at Praxis' white bloomers and asked her what they were. She told them: they listened with reverence.

"Poor lady," said Phillip. "This is no place for a dead clergyman's wife."

"A clergyman's dead wife," said Willie. "Take them off." Praxis took them off.

"It's not respectful to the church," said Phillip. "My father was a clergyman."

Phillip kissed the elastic marks round Praxis' thighs. Lower down he found the marks left by her suspenders, and helped her take those off too, and then her stockings.

His lips were fresh and moist, as he helped heal her various wounds. She felt he was very kind, and simple.

Willie, on the other hand, seemed unreasonably sober.

"She'll only catch cold," he said. "You're drunk. I met her first. Do go away."

"But I love her," said Phillip. "If anyone's to go, you should. Though it doesn't seem necessary to me. It's all quite friendly. See! Nothing hidden."

"She doesn't know what she's doing," said Willie.

"Yes she does," said Phillip. "She loves me."

"Yes, I do," said Praxis, as distinctly as she could.

Phillip's mouth moved upwards and settled in what she felt to be a strange and woolly place. His arms were placed warmly and comfortably round her waist, and both steadied her—which she needed, being never quite sure whether it was she who was rocking, or the ground—and warmed her. The wind, she was remotely aware, was cold. Her arms were goose-pimpled, rough to her own touch: she kept them clasped round her bosom with some remnant of modesty.

Phillip bore her down upon the ground. The grass was damp and chilly, but his body was warm and welcome. His belt and buttons scratched her. As if in the interests of her comfort, he removed the belt and undid his trousers, scarcely rising from his prone position; unaware that his shirt buttons were making severe indentations on her right breast. As fast as he assuaged one wound, it seemed he created another. His knee came between hers, forcing them apart.

Never mind. Only Willie seemed to mind, and who cared about him?

Praxis had a clear vision of the Reverend Allbright, on the occasion when she had gone running to him with news of Judith's pregnancy: and of his member, rising from the dark grave of his clerical trousers, to new life. This was that, brought eventually to fruition, via the first Mrs. Allbright's stout knickers. Pregnancy!

The thought alarmed her. Perhaps she should have kept them on? Perhaps they were the talisman, meant to preserve her? Weren't men supposed to wear something? Why was Phillip not?

She struggled.

"I think I'd better go," said Praxis as best she could. "I think I'd better get back."

She had a vision of Colleen's strong, disapproving face.

"Let her go, for God's sake," said Willie. "She's drunk and so are you. Supposing she gets pregnant? She's in our department."

"Never met her before in my life," said Phillip, entering secret, undisclosed places. Praxis, her head turning from side to side, saw Willie leave, staggering over the turfy hillocks. The night was moonlit; Willie's body was silhouetted for a moment against a starry sky. The souls of the damned burned; and Willie seemed to sink down into nothingness, and was gone. She was conscious of the sound of her own quickened breath, and Phillip's harsh panting. Without Willie she was frightened: no element of choice remained. Phillip's body was powered by a force she could not understand. It occupied, moreover, a space she had always considered her own, but which apparently total strangers could enter with impunity.

He cried out: he seemed to have finished, whatever he was doing: he had lost interest. He lay on top of her and fell asleep. Presently his weight became unbearable; she rolled him off her. Nothing of him now remained behind: he had slipped out of her easily: some moist foreign body, inadvertently inside her own, now back in its own place. He lay where she had pushed him. He snored. She tried to shake him awake; but still he slept. She wandered the hillocks, finding stocking here, dress there, Mrs. Allbright's knickers yet beyond. She dressed unsteadily, and went back to the hostel, and there, to her relief, for it was long past curfew time, found a little group of locked-out girls, scaling the walls via each other's shoulders, and joined them and got back to her room, and bed, and slept.

"I didn't hear you come in," said Colleen, suspiciously, in the morning, but Praxis could only groan. Gin and beer combined to make her ill as she could never remember having been ill before— staggering between washbasin and lavatory bowl, wishing for death.

"Serve you right," said Colleen, nevertheless folding away Praxis' clothes, wiping Praxis' brow, cleaning up Praxis' vomit.

In the afternoon Praxis felt better: the bruises on breast and thigh pleased her. She was getting a cold in the nose.

"Your brother wants to see you," said Colleen, presently. "He was here this morning but I didn't let him in. He doesn't look like your brother."

Men visitors were only allowed in the hostel if they described themselves as close male relatives. Popular girls had many brothers. Praxis was gratified to find she had one. She had hoped for Phillip, but Willie came.

"I came to apologize," said Willie. "Phillip can't even remember leaving the dance. It's very embarrassing. I should have looked after you better."

"You mean if I met him in the street," asked Praxis, "he'd think I was a perfect stranger?"

"I suppose that's so," said Willie. What yesterday had seemed unshaven stubble, today seemed rather more like a beard; it gave him an almost patriarchal air. Since she was lying down and he was standing, Willie no longer seemed so short. He was, in fact, altogether less negligible than she had originally supposed. Or was she just becoming accustomed to the scale of his existence?

"Well, you know what drink is," he added.

"I don't," said Praxis. "Beyond a glass of sherry at Christmas."

He seemed taken aback.

"Or sex?" he asked, more nervously still. "I suppose you were familiar with that."

"No," said Praxis, and cried, from sentiment more than distress, at the notion of how very unshared an experience the loss of her virginity had been.

Willie got into bed beside her, to comfort her; cold, white-skinned, hairy-limbed. His body was bony, strong and wiry. His muscles vibrated, as if he were some kind of taut string which she plucked, alive with pent-up energy. Praxis was conscious of physical pleasure, as she had not been with Phillip, but also that Willie was in some way distasteful to her. She feared that he was laying claim to her, impaling her for further investigation, marking out some kind of territorial boundary inside her, which he would from now on feel entitled to occupy and defend. He did not take off his glasses: he watched her expression carefully, and with a dispassion which did not fit with the urgency of his body. His nails, none too clean, dug into her upper arms: she would have bruises there to-morrow. So long as the skin was not broken she supposed she would be safe from germs.

Germs. Lucy had feared germs, the contamination of sin. Praxis, her body impaled, found her mind agreeably free to wander. She thought it perhaps ought not to be so. Moreover, was there not some danger of pregnancy? Remember what had happened to Miss Leonard. Last night had been bad enough: this was doubling the risk. But how could she give voice to her fears without insulting Willie, and indicating her failure to be carried away by desire, love, gratitude, or whatever it was he expected of her?

The impalation ceased. His struggles continued. He cried aloud, a haunted, eerie cry. She was amazed. It seemed to mean a great deal to him.

"Coitus interruptus," he said, eventually: breathless. "It does terrible damage." His body was hot now, not cold.

"I hope you didn't worry," he said, kindly. "I'll look after you." He liked to look after people. She settled for that. He lived out of college: he shared a room with Phillip: a dirty basement room. But it was Phillip she wanted to see, and be near, not Willie.

When she cooked Willie's meal—mostly sausages and mash—she cooked for Phillip too. It was enough. She could not wash Willie's socks, for he had none, but she could, and did, wash Phillip's shirts, although he protested that he could do them himself. She smuggled soap out of the hostel for Willie's use, and induced him to use it, and Phillip was amused. Phillip smiled at her in a vague and friendly and totally unlustful way, and talked around her, to Willie, about Beowulf and Kant. He was engaged to a doctor's daughter in London, Willie said. He would marry her when he had his degree. Only occasionally did he drink too much beer: and then he always forgot what had happened.

"He wants to be pure for his virgin bride," said Willie, marvelling more at the ambition than the self-deception.

Willie and Praxis went to bed together between lectures: that, at any rate, was how they described it. They seldom actually reached the bed. No sooner were they inside the door than he would bear down upon her, pressing her onto floor, table, chair, anywhere, in his urgency. The sheets of the bed were filthy, in any case: the dusty, greasy floor, the littered table, the ripped chair were really no worse. He liked the dirt: he took pleasure in it, and dissuaded her from too much cleaning. There were better things to do with life, he told her. Phillip did not seem to notice the dirt. He merely bathed a good deal, and moved in an aura of soap, reminding Praxis, rather painfully, of Baby Mary. She tried not to think and worry about anything: about Baby Mary, Hilda or her mother. Willie helped.

At a quarter to seven in the evening Praxis would return to the ladies' residence and to Colleen, moodily cleaning sports shoes, or polishing medallions, or pressing the pimples which now erupted between her freckles; and to Irma, painting her toenails, shaving her legs, complaining of the predatory nature of men; and to supper. Praxis did not eat with Willie: since her year's board at the residence had been paid for in advance, to do so would clearly be a waste of money. Willie urged Praxis to eat as much as she could, to be sure of getting her money's worth. The staple residence diet, toad-in-the-hole, baked in nameless grease in slow ovens, and cabbage, put on to simmer at midday by the morning staff, strained, compacted and cut into wedges by the evening staff, sickened her but did not seem strange to her.

Willie told Praxis about the war: how he had been called up at eighteen, seen two years active service in Burma, then spent a year rounding up the Japanese in Siam, clearing the dams formed by, at best, human bones, at worst, dead bodies, which stopped the flow of rivers in those parts and held up the return of the countryside to normal agricultural life. He had four expensive wristwatches and five gold fountain pens in a secret place, which Praxis felt privileged to be shown. He fingered them with mixed honour and pride.

"I couldn't just leave them to rot, could I? There was no identification on the bodies. Mostly parts of bodies. If it was an American watch, it was probably on a Japanese, anyway, and vice versa. I hate waste. I really hate waste."

Praxis told Willie about Brighton, and school, and Hilda, and her mother, and Miss Leonard, and her horror of madness. He listened attentively and she felt, with him, the same kind of relief that had attended her conversations with Miss Leonard. She almost, likewise, came to expect his sudden death—half dreading it, half hoping for it—as a relief from the drudgery, sometimes six or seven times a day, of politely, kindly and affectionately responding to his sexual needs.

"Thank you," he would say: and he was fond of her and she of him: the nakedness of his need touched her: but neither he nor she herself seemed to expect a female response in the least equivalent to the male. She never cried out, or thought she should, or knew that women did, or why they would.

She typed Willie's essays though, and found books for him in the library, getting there early so as to be first in the queue when work was set. After Willie's essays were completed and typed, she would then begin on her own. She typed slowly, using only two fingers. It was assumed by both of them that this was the proper distribution of their joint energies. He got A's and she got C's.

"Well and truly snapped up," said Irma, "more fool you. It's war, you know. They lose and you win, or vice versa. It's vice versa for you. Mind you, they're all like that in the Humanities Department. They talk virtue and practice vice." Irma often got A's, but always pretended she got C's. To look at her, as Colleen remarked, you wouldn't think she had a brain in her head, and that was the way Irma wanted it. Irma was looking for a husband. She'd tried to get into Oxford and had failed—there were few places available for women—and so had missed out, she felt, on her chances of marrying a future prime minister. She was, perforce, now prepared to settle for an embryo famous novelist, atomic scientist or Nobel prize winner, of the kind who could presumably be found at the lesser provincial universities. Provided, of course, one could spot a winner. Irma was certain she could.

Skirts were narrow and calf-length and split up the back. Irma wiggled her bottom, pouted her orangey-red lips and wriggled out of goodnight kisses and away from groping, futureless hands.

"If you want to waste your time at college," said Colleen to Praxis, "that's up to you. If you want to be soiled and second-hand, so you'll never find a husband, just carry on the way you are." But Colleen dyed her white Aertex shirt bright red, and bravely went to the weekly students' dance, unescorted. No one asked her to dance. She didn't go again: and the next week was penalized for cracking the ankle of a Cardiff College left wing with her hockey stick, and grew another crop of spots. Sometimes, Praxis, stiff and sore about the thighs, trying to sleep in the airless room, strong with Colleen's body odours, would hear her friend crying in the night. Colleen cried from loneliness and bewilderment, and the sense of life slipping by, of time already running out, her own negligible place in the world so suddenly and disappointingly marked out.

One week Praxis got an A for her essay, on political establishments in the USA in the eighteenth century, and Willie got a C for his on the same theme. Praxis could not understand why he was so cross, or why he felt obliged to hurt her. But he certainly did. He claimed that Phillip had remembered the Night of the Downs in every sordid detail, but had been so unenthusiastic about her sexual attractiveness that they had agreed to toss a coin as to who should have her, for her domestic and secretarial services. Willie had won, gone to the hostel to stake out his claim and now wished he hadn't. Praxis, said Willie, was a neurotic, a bore, a rotten cook and a slow typist.

Praxis reeled, at the sudden presentation of the malice which underlies love; the resentment which interleaves affection between the sexes, of which she had until that moment no notion. She was shocked; she would not cry. Willie looked at her with Lucy's eyes. As with Lucy, they hated: they feared: they wanted to hurt: they had learned how, and all too well. Now Willie, too. Praxis went home to the hostel.

"What did you say to him in return?" Irma enquired, briskly. "Did you tell him he was a dwarf, a sex maniac; that he smells? That he's a looter of dead bodies?"

"Of course not."

"Well, he is, he does, he did."

"I'd never say so to his face."

"But you've thought it. You must have. He just said the things he thought about you in his worst moments. I don't suppose he means them. They're not nearly as awful as the things you've thought about him."

She could be very kind. Praxis, relieved, cried herself to sleep in a rather comforting and comforted way.

"If you behave like a whore," said Colleen, "you get treated like a whore. Would you like to borrow my red shirt?"

"No thank you." Praxis' clothes had become more orthodox. Willie picked her out garments from church sales, excellent bargains all, and more in keeping with the times, albeit somewhat washed out.

The next day Willie came round and apologized, and even bought her a half of shandy and paid for it himself. She was vastly relieved. Her main fear had been that she would presently find Willie in the student's bar investing in the gin and lime which would buy him his next term's sex, comfort, company and secretarial services.

Praxis made sure that her next essay was poorly executed and badly presented, and she inserted a few good extra paragraphs of her own composition into Willie's essay while typing it out for him; this time he got a straight A and she a C minus and a sorrowful note from her tutor.

The earlier A had been a flash in the pan, her tutor could only suppose. One of the tantalizing little flashes girls in higher education would occasionally display: for the most part flickering dimly and then going out, extinguished by the basic, domestic nature of the female sex, altogether quenched by desire to serve the male. Indeed, the consensus of the college authorities was, not surprisingly, that girls seldom lived up to early promise; were rarely capable of intellectual excellence; seemed to somehow go rotten and fall off before ripening, like plums in a bad season. The extension of equal educational facilities to girls had been a hopeful, and perhaps an inevitable, undertaking, but was scarcely justifiable by results. He had hoped it was not true, but was beginning to believe it was.

For Praxis, Willie's A's and her own C's seemed a small price to pay for Willie's protection, Willie's interest, Willie's concern; for the status of having a steady boyfriend.

Red-lipped Irma, red-haired Colleen, had to do without. Irma through choice, Colleen by necessity.

Praxis, in the meantime, with Willie around, about and into her body, loved Phillip with her head. She had secret knowledge of him: she dreamed of him: of the mature male that lurked behind the childish eyes and boyish lips: the soft voice that murmured easy endearments over the telephone to his virgin, distant love. She saw the look of distracted boredom on his face as he replaced the receiver: before the permanent half-smile returned. Praxis *knew*: Praxis knew what his boring fiancée did not, the harsh grip of his hands on her shoulders, male and digging, the savagery in his eyes, the obscenities from his mouth. She remembered.

If she had known how to seduce: she would have. But she had no conception of herself as temptation. She was a slice of bread and butter on the table, not a cream eclair just out of reach; and Phillip was clearly not hungry for bread and butter, or thought he wasn't. He found it easier to yearn romantically after the unavailable: lick his lips over imaginary scented cream.

Praxis hated being alone with Phillip. She did not know what to say to him: nor, she suspected, did he know what to say to her. It did not stop her loving him. It was almost as if she associated love with embarrassment.

Christmas was coming. Hilda wrote to say she would be staying at Holden Road for the vacation: that Butt and Son had written to offer the freehold of the house as final settlement of their (purely voluntary) obligations to Miss Parker's family; that Lucy had accepted the offer, and so was now back in a National Health Service hospital, but a very nice one, with modern equipment; that the Holden Road house was in a very bad state, riddled with woodworm, charred by the stars (what did that mean? Praxis shuddered); that Baby Mary had developed pneumonia as a result of Mrs. Allbright's habit of leaving her out under the night sky; and would Praxis please come home at Christmas to help clear up the house—why should everything be left to Hilda?

"What does modern equipment mean?" Willie asked. Praxis shook her head, unable to speak, afraid to think. There were tears of shock in her eyes.

"A new form of straitjacket, I daresay," said Phillip, blithely. "What a superb film could be made inside a mental asylum. Do you think they'd let me in? If only cameras were smaller, I could go in as your brother and no one would be the wiser. What a scoop it would be."

Phillip had started a film club. He had a cine-camera. He seemed to think only of films. He would form his two hands into squares and look at the world through them: first this way, then that. Sometimes he looked at Praxis, framing her with his hands. It made her uneasy. Sometimes, nowadays, he would come home between lectures and surprise Willie and Praxis on the floor, or against the cooker, or wherever, and would appear surprised, which surely by now he couldn't be, and take his time to leave. Her breasts would tingle at the thought of his observation: the back of her mouth go dry: her eyes blacken: her buttocks tighten; the centre of her body shrink, oddly, away from him, not towards, as if desiring yet fearful of too overwhelming an experience. Her body acquiesced to Willie: yet crept round him, through some darkening of vision, some fusing of matter into magic, reaching out to Phillip.

But he was nothing, nothing. Something trivial in herself called out to the trivial in him: she knew it was no more than that. Listening to him speak now, using the griefs of the world as if they were bucketfuls of oats to be fed to some lively horse he was determined to mount and spur on to personal victory, with the sound of popular applause ringing in his ears, she knew that he was not really to be taken seriously. It was an intuition she would have done well to recall, in later years.

Willie kicked Phillip. She saw it and was grateful. Willie at least recognized personal pain when he saw it. Phillip, who did not, looked puzzled, as people do when they are woken from hypnosis and are obliged to travel from early childhood to maturity in the space of seconds.

"Not if it upsets you, of course, Praxis," Phillip said, politely. "But the more people can be persuaded to turn private grief into public good the better. Film is the way ahead. Photographic images of recorded time. We must hold up a mirror to the world, so it can see itself, and reform itself. Everything else has failed. Religion, literature, art, war, mass education and political systems. Film is what we need."

Photographs!

Lucy had relegated the beach photographer, her lover, to the cupboard under the stairs: had sent him there from her bed. Years later, when clearing out the cupboard, Praxis was to come across an envelope of nude photographs, showing her mother, Lucy, in her prime, posing for the camera, oddly coy, with one hand over her breasts, the other one over her crotch, head thrown back, enticing. The white of her eyes showed unnaturally. And why was that? Was it from madness, lust, embarrassment or despair? And why had she destroyed the innocent photograph of Hypatia and

Praxis on the beach, but not these? Was there a significance in it? Had it been a struggle between decency and indecency, the maternal nature and the erotic, that had in the end destroyed poor Lucy? Or none of these: just the piling up of chance on chance, episode on incident; the wrong enzymes in the brain; a faulty heredity; the accumulation of loss, trouble and social humiliation, which had sent her storming so angrily and destructively back into the inner refuge where she huddled for the rest of her days, safe from reality.

"No one's going to take pictures of my mother," said Praxis unduly bold, out of instinct, if not knowledge. "It won't do her any good."

"It might do society good," Phillip persisted. His eyes were soft and large. He rarely spoke to Praxis directly.

"Anyway," said Praxis, "I'm not going back home for Christmas."

Baby Mary would have to look after herself, suffer from starlight as she might.

Praxis spent Christmas with Willie and Willie's mother, sleeping in the spare room for appearance' sake, waylaid by Willie in pantry and corridor. Willie's mother was a slight, nervous, tidy woman who spoke only of practicalities, and then only briefly, and hid behind spectacles even thicker than Willie's own. She walked about her chilly, spotless house, reading books on philosophy, politics or economics: anything so long as it was removed from the day-to-day actualities of life, which she found boring. Sometimes she would stumble, so engrossed in her book would she be, and cry out, but rejected help or comfort. Her husband had died of lung cancer when Willie was twelve: it seemed to her, thereafter, that life was something which had to be got through, rather than enjoyed, whilst observing the proper formalities. Or so Willie related it.

Willie had been a mere accident: an afterthought: a by-product of the marriage. His mother was polite to him, even interested in his welfare and progress, but still surprised by his existence. So Willie said.

Praxis saw Willie's eyes, large behind his thick glasses, dilated with hurt, and believed him.

Praxis found her arms creeping round Willie (as they had never used to) as he penetrated her, in the greenhouse, or the bathroom, or wherever, her own bottom cold against the shiny Christmas surfaces of his mother's house, trying to warm him, and make up for what he had never had.

Christmas dinner was served formally in the unheated dining room. A pair of candles were lit, placed in saucers to catch the drips. There was roast chicken: a sliver each. The remainder was served cold on Boxing Day, as a fricassee the day after, and the carcass boiled for soup the day after that. There was an agreeable sense of ceremony, properly and frugally performed.

Willie's mother smiled, as she pecked Praxis goodbye. Praxis went to London and was fitted with a contraceptive device at the Marie Stopes clinic. It was a rubber cap which fitted over her cervix. Willie was relieved of the conflict between his dislike of coitus interruptus and his reluctance to spend good money on French letters.

The new term started. Willie was in his final year at Exeter, Praxis in her first: part of his course and hers overlapped. Willie had a plan for Praxis' future. After he had taken his final examinations he meant to do statistical research at London University. If his degree was good enough he could get a grant: otherwise, he could scrape together only a certain amount by way of bursaries, but if Praxis was earning, and they lived simply and economically enough, there should be no difficulty in his managing. He did not mention marriage, and Praxis did not presume to do so.

"You're mad," said Irma, "to even think of it."

Irma had temporarily settled for a young man with a future, or so she predicted, in back-bench politics. His name was Peter; he belonged to the Young Conservatives; he bought her flowers and chocolates and she kissed him goodnight on the doorstep, regulating the length and passion of the kiss according to the value of the gifts he had bought her that evening and the quality of the attention he offered. (Willie and Praxis seldom kissed. There seemed no need.)

"You have to send your life in the direction you want it to go," said Irma. "You can't just let things happen. You can't just live with men because they're there. You know Willie's there because he *smells*."

Praxis didn't speak to Irma for a good week. If Willie smelt, she had long since ceased to notice it.

"You've got to make him marry you," said Colleen.

Colleen's life had changed, along with the fashions. Skirts had become full, waists nipped, shoulders dropped, hair softened. Colleen had abandoned sport and taken to sex. She frequented the cafe where the rugger set hung out, and on a Saturday, after closing hours, could be seen making for the downs, laughing heartily and noisily in the company of one or other of the brave, who clearly deserved the fair. In her New Look Saturday dress, Colleen at last felt herself one of the fair. She serviced Irma's Peter once a month or so, secretly, when the balls ache, as he described it, brought on when Irma's doorstep goodnights became too much for him to bear. Colleen suffered badly from guilt on this account: and still cried herself to sleep at nights, though nowadays for a different reason; she lived in constant fear of being pregnant. Victory and beer made the rugger boys fearless: defeat and beer made them invite disaster: French letters were expensive, embarrassing to procure, and tended to be kept back for special occasions, special girls. Not just Colleen on a Saturday night. Peter was of course always gentlemanly, and withdrew, politely, turning away to use a handkerchief. Colleen loved him. Irma didn't. It hardly seemed fair.

"It's different for you," said Praxis to Colleen. "You've got a home. You don't understand. I've got nothing, no one. Only Willie."

"I wish I had nothing and no one," said Colleen, gloomily. She'd had a letter from her mother. Her father, a parish councillor and church warden, had, for many years, been on the verge of leaving her mother for a gentle spinster lady who arranged flowers on the altar for Sunday services. The affair had finally become public knowledge. Colleen's mother, jolly and stoical to the end, threw the information out in a paragraph and expressed the hope that her daughter would be bringing home a really magnificent show of sports trophies to join her own array of cups and shields, won in the good old premarriage days. Colleen was her mother's hope and consolation; Colleen's mother made that clear. All else had failed her.

"What can I possibly take home now? I'm out of all the teams," moaned Colleen.

"A baby and V.D.," said Praxis. "Give her something to think about. It's the kindest thing."

Colleen barely spoke to Praxis for a week. They were hard-hearted with each other. A sense of desperation seemed to afflict them: as if whatever path they took, whatever new avenue opened up, it would narrow and block, and they would be turned round once again, to face their own natures.

13

WOMEN OF CHILD-BEARING AGE have it easy: if all else fails they can always give birth to another human being, who will love them, at least for a time.

Watch a baby at the breast: blankly studying its mother, eyes dewy with love. Whoever else ever looked at her like that?

I have a cat: I had a cat: a raggedy white tom. When I went to prison a neighbour took it in. When I came out my raggedy tom was a plump white neuter, with calm, kind eyes. The vet had recommended it, the neighbour said, uneasily. But I think she found the cat's maleness too naked and too smelly. Well, it was her right. I had left her in charge. Did the cat remember me? He settled back with me easily enough. He shared my Social Security money without guilt: coming and going through the dirty window, himself yet not himself, as I was.

He would lie along the back of the dirty armchair, staring at me as I paced and muttered, cried and ranted, without comment, accepting me.

He came to the window just now and found it closed. I can't walk. I tried, I really did: my leg would not let me. I got out of the chair somehow, and began to crawl, but I think I lost consciousness: when I realized again who and where I was, the window sill was empty. The cat was gone. Perhaps he will never come back? I wouldn't, if I was him, and betrayed.

It was not his fault, or mine. But I feel I should have done better.

Listen, I am going to die: murdered by a thoughtless girl on a bus, but never mind all that. There isn't much time. I must offer you what I can.

Watch Praxis. Watch her carefully. Look, listen, learn.

Then safely, as they say to children, cross over.

14

"I won't decide until the end of the year," said Praxis to Willie, with a fine show of self-determination. "Until you have your results. If you do get a first, then I'll stay on and get my own degree."

"Can I trust you to be faithful?"

"Of course," said Praxis, believing it to be so.

"But if I don't? The examiners are fools. They wouldn't be examiners if they weren't."

"Then I'll leave, and get some kind of job; it won't bring in much because there's nothing I can do; except scrub or cook or baby-mind, I suppose. But it will get the rent paid and if we live frugally we'll manage. It'll be such fun. And we'll be really together." She added the last two sentences as conventional afterthoughts, rather than because they sprang naturally together. Living with Willie, supporting Willie through his further degree, could not be anticipated as exactly fun. Companionable, perhaps. Intimate certainly.

"I suppose we'll have to leave it like that," he conceded. "But I'm always much happier if I know exactly what's going to happen. I hate uncertainty."

It was a good term. Willie was particularly kind and attentive, as if trying to prove to her that she could not possibly live without him. He allowed her to clean up the flat, and put out the old milk bottles twenty at a time, and even defied the milkman, who declined to take them away in case they contaminated his vehicle.

"It is your statutory duty to remove them," said Willie. "Why should we be obliged to live with the property of your company against our will?"

"You've lived with them long enough," said the milkman. But he took them.

Praxis cleaned the windows and a little sunlight filtered down into the gloom.

"The trouble with you, Praxis," said Willie, "is that you're a born housewife. The tax-payer's wasting his money on you." Praxis feared that it was so. Occasionally, when she forgot, she got a B. Once a B plus. Once an A minus, but she kept quiet about it.

Easter approached, and six weeks' vacation.

"Praxis," said Willie, "you have a perfectly good house at Brighton."

"It's not perfectly good. It's horrid. I hate it. The nearer I get to it the lower my spirits sink."

"Nevertheless, you can live in it rent-free. So can I. We could let this place and accumulate a little money. We're going to need every penny we can get."

"What about rail fares?" She was struggling against common sense. The victory was his already. He had known it would be.

"We'll hitch-hike."

"Who'd ever rent this place, except you?"

"You can clean it up a little, if that's what you want."

Praxis did so.

Two American exchange students paid 37/6 a week for six weeks, for the privilege of living in the two rooms. Willie and Phillip continued to pay 25/— a week to the landlord. The transaction had already been arranged when Willie and Praxis had their conversation.

"You'll have to clean it up a bit," they'd said.

"The dirt's its charm," Willie had said.

"Not to us."

"Very well," Willie had conceded.

"I'd love to do an exchange to the States," said Praxis. "Shall I apply?"

"You wouldn't get to first base," said Willie. "They're not interested in housewives." She had rubber gloves on at the time, and was scraping out mouse dirt from under the cooker. She saw his point.

They hitch-hiked down to Holden Road. Willie found a nice pair of high-heeled shoes for Praxis at a church bazaar, for 2/6, and she wore them for hitch-hiking, instead of her usual sensible lace-ups. She sat on a rucksack by the side of the road with her legs showing to above the knee. Willie hid behind a tree. When a car stopped he would step out and there they would be, the pair of them, and the car driver left with little option but to take them both.

Praxis felt uneasy about such tactics, but could not quite find the words to express what she felt. Willie's eyes were bright with pleasure and victory when it worked, and she did not wish to dampen his animation. He showed it seldom enough.

Hilda was home for the holidays, wild-eyed, high-coloured, beautiful and talkative. She was very thin. She put her arms round Willie and kissed him: she took to him at once.

"What a good rat-catcher he'll be," she said. "You're just like a ferret. I love ferrets. I shall call you mannikin, and you shall be our pet."

Willie kissed her back, not seeming to object to this nonsense. Praxis felt jealous: and dull, plodding and dreary. It seemed to her that, for these particular holidays, Hilda had cast herself as Mary, and Praxis as Martha.

"Don't you mind?" she asked, later, safer, in the damp double bed with its broken springs, beneath the heavy weight of rancid blankets.

"Mind what?"

"Hilda being mad?"

But Willie didn't, it seemed.

"It's a different view of reality," he said. "You must learn not to be frightened by it. Go along with it."

"If I go along with it," said Praxis, "I'll be like her. You don't understand."

He laughed at her. He enjoyed the dirt and decay of the house.

"Don't bother," he'd say to Praxis as she fought her way into caked corners with scrubbing brush and soapy water. "Just don't bother. The more immune we get to germs the better."

Hilda took off her clothes one night and danced naked in the garden under the stars. Willie took off his and danced, too, prancing about, all white and sinewy, in full view of any passer-by who chose to peer through the broken palings. He beckoned and begged Praxis to join them, but she wouldn't. She was horrified.

Hilda changed her mind in the middle of a pas de deux about whatever it was she intended, and stomped off to bed, locking the back door against Willie and Praxis so that they had to break in through a skylight window.

Willie wasn't angry. Willie had looked, Praxis thought, rather regretfully after Hilda.

"She's got a lovely body," he said. "Longer in the waist than you; and longer legs. Your face is prettier, mind you. She doesn't have enough chin. And unpredictability could be difficult to live with."

Praxis had the same feeling of nightmare as had so often afflicted her in youth. She visited her mother in the new State Institution for the Mentally Afflicted. Lucy sat in a dayroom, one of a row of still, staring women sitting in armchairs six inches apart. Most of the other women were over seventy, and there by virtue of physical rather than mental infirmity. The curtains were bright, however, and the good sea air blew briskly in. The staff smiled. Sister was particularly nice, and did not make Praxis feel, as she felt so easily, that it was all her fault her mother was incarcerated.

"Praxis!" cried Lucy, getting to her feet, clutching her daughter's arm. "It's Praxis. This is my little girl Praxis," she said in pride to the others, but nobody stirred, or answered. Only Praxis, who cried; whereupon Lucy looked offended, displeased at the sight of the great blubbering lump she had mistaken for a pretty little girl, and withdrew back into inner blankness.

"She's getting better," said Sister. "We have so many new drugs. I wouldn't be surprised if you couldn't take her home, one of these days."

The sense of nightmare deepened. Praxis went to visit Mrs. Allbright, and discovered Baby Mary crying in her pram at the end of the garden, hungry and dirty, with all her covers kicked off, while Mr. and Mrs. Allbright cooed over their own new, warm, clean baby inside. They none of them had much to say to each other.

When Praxis went home Willie was playing Strip-Jack-Naked with Hilda. Whenever she or he turned up the same card she'd cry "rats" and take off an article of clothing. Her breasts were full against bony ribs, and brown-nippled. A dozen birds' nests hung by string from the clothes dryer on the kitchen ceiling.

"He's doing me a world of good," she assured Praxis. "It's so wonderful to be able to laugh."

And, indeed, her cheeks were pink and she ate heartily of the sausages and mash Praxis prepared for supper, stark naked as she was.

"Won't you get cold?" Praxis murmured, nervously.

"Oh, Pattie," groaned Hilda, "you are so insensitive. I am an art-form, don't you see?"

It was in the days before girls took their clothes off, easily, or anyone talked about living art-forms. Was she mad, or merely prophetic?

"Let her be," said Willie. "Let the poor girl be. It does her no harm. She'll get better soon, if we just all go along with it."

"But shouldn't she have treatment?"

"Your mother has treatment," observed Willie, "and look where she is. So long as things remain undefined, Hilda can yet escape." Praxis found his calm reason reassuring. She absolved him, rightly, of erotic intent towards Hilda. He relieved her of an enormous burden of guilt, anxiety and fear. She felt she loved him. Mannikin!

The next day Hilda was sallow, suspicious and more than adequately clothed. She watched Willie with narrow eyes all morning, and took to her room all afternoon.

"Perhaps we should go back to Exeter," said Praxis, hopefully.

"You can't run away," said Willie.

"I want to run away," said Praxis.

"What about Baby Mary?" enquired Willie. "Supposing your mother does get better? You need to be here, in Brighton.

"You have to face your obligations," said Willie.

"A branch of the Institute of Statistical Studies has opened in Brighton," said Willie. "They're prepared to take me on.

"I'll give up my further degree for your sake, Praxis," said Willie. "We can both live at 109 Holden Road. It's rent-free after all.

"You can get a job, Praxis," said Willie, "look after your mother, keep an eye on Baby Mary, if necessary, and on Hilda, as is certainly necessary.

"Praxis," said Willie, "where will a degree get you? To some kind of secretarial job?"

"Not necessarily," murmured Praxis. "I might do better than that. There are openings now for women graduates in the Civil Service and in Marks & Spencer."

"For girls with first-class degrees," said Willie. "Look at you!" She was washing the windows again.

If only, thought Praxis, we had gone to stay with his mother, instead of coming to Brighton. If only.

"Willie," said Praxis, lightly, "did you know before we came that they were opening this new branch of the Institute of Statistical Studies down here? Or afterwards?"

"Afterwards," he replied, vigorously. The sharpness of his response surprised her, but she had not the will, nor the interest, to ponder the matter further. He was clearly going to win. He had lapped her once, twice, thrice, and she had hardly noticed, thought they were both running neck and neck. But he still gave her a sporting chance: mannikin, white hairy legs twinkling before her on their way to the winning post.

"Unless, of course," Willie remarked, "I get a double first, when it would be worth my while staying on at Exeter. Then you might as well finish your degree."

Praxis spent the term organizing Willie's life so as to leave him as much time and energy as possible for study. To everyone's surprise, he got an average second, but luckily it would not affect his employment at the institute. Praxis didn't do too well in her end-of-term exams. There had not been much time for revision.

"You don't want to study too near an exam," Willie had said. "It addles the brain."

"You girls," said her tutor sadly. "You will put your personal lives before your academic future." He had seen her fall asleep many times in his lectures, and put it down simply to sexual excess. An element of malnutrition, mixed with anxiety, was in fact a contributory factor, but he was not to know that. Willie found he studied better when Praxis was sitting quietly in the room, and the hostel mealtimes had suited neither of them, so she more and more frequently had gone without.

"So," said Willie, when he had recovered from his chagrin at his foolish and ignorant professors, "it's off to Brighton, is it?"

"Yes," said Praxis.

"It's been a deliberate campaign," said Irma, "to get you where he wanted you. You realize that, don't you?"

Praxis realized nothing of the kind, and was right not to. Self-interest lay so deep, was so firmly rooted, in the very subsoil of Willie's nature that his behaviour could hardly be said to be calculating: it was simply what Willie was; he did not need to think: he simply did: and it turned out right for Willie. Praxis was to meet many, many others like him, and to grow more wary.

"At any rate," said Colleen, "you won't go short of sex." Irma had broken off with Peter: Peter had broken off with Colleen.

"He only went with me in the first place," wept Colleen, "in order to talk about Irma."

Irma had taken up with Phillip: she could see him as a world-famous film producer, and herself as a film star. She slept with him, too: delectable. Phillip ran his tongue round his soft, lovely lips. Praxis could not bear to see it. It was the final straw which broke the back of her resistance to Willie.

She was depressed.

In the hostel the smell of cabbage swirled round the corridors: at Holden Road the smell of dry rot, mingled with soapy water, surged out of rarely opened windows.

Mother, what kind of world did you bring me into? Father, why did you leave me here?

Hilda, have you no idea what it is to be me?

Willie, have mercy!

They moved to Holden Road and lived openly together, bold as brass.

"Like mother, like daughter," said Judith, cheerfully. She had a job on the buses, as a conductress. The uniform suited her: she seemed vigorous and healthy: her dark moustache was pronounced beneath her peaked cap. The children stayed with neighbours while she worked. Scarlet geraniums tumbled from her window boxes: the house was bright and cheerful. She had a bus-driver boyfriend. "But I don't suppose he'll walk out on you, like your Dad did on your Mum. He's onto too good a thing."

People kept telling her so but Praxis found it hard to believe. Lucy was getting better, but Praxis found that hard to believe too.

"If you have a suitable home," said the sister at Lucy's state nursing home, startling Praxis, "then I see no reason why your mother shouldn't be with you; the medication must be scrupulously maintained, of course."

Lucy weighed fourteen stone: little piggy eyes beamed out at the world, placidly enough. Was this getting better?

"You're a good girl," the sister added, gratifyingly enough.

Hilda took a good degree, and went to London, to sit her entrance exams for the administrative grade of the Civil Service. Part of the examination consisted of a weekend at a country house, where trained assessors could judge personality and manners.

"So long as she doesn't take off her clothes, or talk about rats, art or the stars," said Willie, "she'll be all right."

Hilda didn't and was. She went into the Ministry of Works—an odd thing, people thought, for a woman to choose, but it was the least-favourite ministry and there were vacancies available. She coped easily with the job, lived quietly in a little flat, and contented herself, when under stress, with writing lurid letters to Lucy's institution, and to Mrs. Allbright, telling on Praxis, and describing Willie's sexual activities in some lurid and accurate detail. Praxis put from herself any notion that Hilda might have actual personal knowledge of them. Willie never closed doors, let alone locked them: that was all.

"I threw the letter away," said the ward sister, kindly. "Has your sister ever received treatment?"

"No."

"Don't you think she should?"

"Not really," said Praxis, eyeing her moony mother.

"You probably have a lot to put up with," said her sister, surprisingly. "I really think we should keep her here a little longer."

Praxis was relieved. But why hadn't she said that before the end of term?

Mrs. Allbright held Hilda's letters in her hand.

"Of course I take them with a pinch of salt," said Mrs. Allbright. "Hilda's so wonderfully imaginative. All the same—

"If you are living in sin with a man," said Mrs. Allbright, "I can't accept you in my house. You understand that? I have to take a moral lead in the community."

Was Willie a man? Well, of course. It sounded odd, to Praxis, all the same, that sharing bed and board with Willie should be construed as living in sin with a man. He was a mannikin, forever twinkling in front of her, white hairy legs vanishing the other side of a winning post. Could this be sin?

"You could join my Friday nights for bad girls, I daresay," said Mrs. Allbright. "We've got a lovely sewing bee going. But I don't somehow think it would suit you." She held her plump young son to her plump young bosom. He smiled and gurgled.

Baby Mary cried and cried in the next room.

"Shall I pick her up?" asked Praxis.

"Crying exercises the lungs," said Mrs. Allbright. "She's such a difficult, dirty child. The longer I live the more I believe that the sins of one generation are visited upon the next. And now look at you, Pattie! Thrown everything away. It's very bitter. My husband and I used to pray for you, before we went to bed at night. Please, for our sakes, ask this man to go. I'm sure God will forgive you."

"It's not as simple as that," said Praxis.

"Doing God's will is always simple," said Mrs. Allbright, firmly.

Mr. Allbright no longer sucked her of sweetness, as a bee sucks nectar from the honeysuckle: he respected her too much, alas. She was the mother of his child: his holy Madonna. Only sometimes, at night, in the dark, she would hear him groaning with torment in the other twin bed; and then he would succumb and fall upon her, and there was very little pleasure in it for either of them. She was confused: she caught the infection, or perhaps came to the realization, of sexual guilt. The memory of the early days of their marriage horrified her, as it did him. Pattie was linked with them, and Baby Mary, too, conceived in sin, born in violence.

Baby Mary lay neglected in her cot: thin and snivelly.

"I could take her off your hands during the day," offered Pattie, cautiously. "You must be so busy.

"Unless," Praxis added, "you think I might corrupt her."

"She was born in corruption," said Mrs. Allbright, clearly and unmistakably. Praxis had been joking, but Mrs. Allbright was not.

Pattie wheeled Baby Mary home. Baby Mary smiled and laughed, as if recognizing her good fortune. Pattie did not take her back to the Allbrights, and the Allbrights did not ask for her.

Her birth certificate, identity card and ration book arrived eventually, by post, without a covering note.

"I'd like to buy a book on baby care," said Praxis tentatively.

"What for?" asked Willie. "You have your instincts, surely."

"They might be wrong."

"The point about instincts," said Willie, "is that they're never wrong. Wrong simply doesn't apply. However, if you're worried, I'll see if I can pick one up somewhere."

"I want a *new* one, Willie. Up-to-date."

"What for? Babies have been the same since the beginning of time, surely."

"Yes, but—" Praxis gave up more and more easily. It was Willie's money, after all. He was earning eleven pounds a week at the institute, working by day, and in the evenings and at weekends, using their facilities to study for further examinations. Light, heat and so on being free.

He posted a timetable on the kitchen wall, and they kept to it, rigorously.

Willie had his breakfast at eight, and left the house for the institute at eight-thirty. He cycled, and in wet weather wore a rain-cape. The bicycle was Policeman's Issue, 1928, and massive. She did not know how he managed it, but his calf muscles, as she well knew, were very strong. He returned for dinner at twelve-thirty, went back to the institute at one-fifteen. At five forty-five he came home, played with Mary and had supper at seven. At eight he would cycle back to the institute for three hours' study. By eleven-thirty they were in bed. It was a quiet life but a busy one for Praxis. Willie liked to have his meals set promptly upon the table. Sausages, baked beans, mashed potatoes and oranges remained his staple diet.

"Couldn't we try something from a recipe?" asked Praxis.

"Why?" asked Willie. "We have a perfectly balanced diet." He developed ulcers on his shins, however, and thereafter, on the doctor's advice, supplemented the diet with kippers.

"You see!" he said, triumphantly, to Praxis. Praxis saw.

They shopped on Saturdays: or rather Willie did. Praxis seldom held actual cash in her hand. The little illicit family, all the same, were well fed and well clothed, for remarkably little money.

Praxis imagined, rightly, that Willie's savings would soon be into the thousands. He was keeping them for a rainy day. Praxis might be drenched in cloudbursts, but Willie kept warm and dry, feeling not a spot.

Baby Mary proved in time to have a highly moral nature. She would do nothing, put on a sock or take off a shoe, without first discussing the significance and rightness of the act. Sometimes it would take an hour to dress her. Sometimes Praxis wondered what she had done, and why, but not often.

She felt sure it all couldn't go on like this. But it did.

There were few visitors. It seemed a house doomed to have few visitors. Elaine came, once, but did not return. She talked about the price and quality of ham, and clearly found the house eccentric and not to her taste and pitied Praxis. Nor was she accustomed to such as Willie, who had grown a beard and wore his shirt unbuttoned to the waist, so that his hairy ribs showed. Elaine, Praxis felt, had never seen an unbuttoned shirt, except possibly on the beach on a hot day, in her life. And who of the inhabitants of Brighton went down to the pebbly beach on a sunny day? That was visitors, who had nothing better to do.

"At least," said Elaine, as she left, "you've got a man." And it seemed to Praxis that whole wide leafy avenue of communication opened up, but she had left it too late. Elaine's broad energetic back was already disappearing into the mist that blew in from the sea that day.

Praxis comforted herself with the thought that she did not like being pitied by a grocer's daughter. She wrapped eccentricity around herself like a protective cocoon.

Every time she visited Lucy, Lucy was fatter.

"It's the drugs," said Sister. "But it saves locks and bars and keys, and you can see she's happy, the dear!"

Hilda was having a good time in London. She seemed to be in a good frame of mind: or perhaps no one bothered, any longer, to let Praxis know she was writing letters.

Mary grew talkative and pondered, in infant prattle, about the nature of the universe and the existence of God. She demanded concentrated attention.

"Oo hear wat I say?" she would demand, in the manner of a child in a Victorian novelette, if Praxis' attention wandered.

What have I done with my life? Praxis wondered. It can't go on like this. Willie thought it could.

"Nothing happens," complained Praxis.

"Thank God for that," said Willie.

"But are we going to go on like this forever?"

"I don't see why not. You've got what you wanted. It's what you wanted. Have you changed your mind?"

"No. Perhaps we could go on holiday?"

"Your life is one long holiday," commented Willie, and Praxis had to concede that it was more or less true. Was housework work? Child care? No. That was simply what one did, all day.

"You could always do good works," he added, laughing, impaling her up against the old gas cooker. It was no longer greasy, but somewhat corroded, and afterwards she seemed for days to be brushing flakes of rusted metal from her buttocks. Willie, these days, reserved more of his energies for his work, now that he had found a mental discipline which absorbed him, and rather less for sexual activity. She thought she would have been glad, but found she was sorry. She had become all but addicted to their sudden, if temporary, escapes from reality. They broke up the day. He was warmer, too, than he had been. She no longer found his body cold—or had she merely become as used to it as she was to her own? Or worse, had she grown cold herself?

"Good works?" she laughed. "You don't understand, Willie, I *am* the good work."

He didn't like her to become too discontented. They started going to the pictures, for the first showing, every Sunday evening. Mary would sit between them. They went in the first six rows, where the cost was nine pence a seat, and the town's children banged their seats up and down, and you had to crane your neck to see the screen. Praxis rather liked sitting here—watching the great distorted black and white shapes of someone else's truth— and in later life never quite became accustomed to sitting far back from a wide curved screen. But the pictures had lost their magic by then, in any case.

"Willie," said Praxis, "make something *happen*."

"In another couple of years," said Willie, "Mary will be at school and you could get a job."

"What doing?"

"There must be lots of things."

"Being a bus conductor, I suppose, like Judith?"

"Why not? It's useful work.

"A pity you didn't stay on and get your degree," said Willie to

Praxis. "You could have got something more interesting, and better paid, like Hilda."

He had misjudged his investment. Gone for short-term profit rather than long-term gain.

Hilda was earning a thousand pounds a year. It was an unheard-of sum for a woman to make. Few at the ministry cared to stand in her way. She dealt fearlessly and efficiently with problems as they arose, provided they were conveyed to her on paper, and not verbally, when she would tend to dismiss them too quickly as insignificant. She made decisions without anxiety or effort. On the rare occasions she was proved wrong, and her judgment in error, she merely sighed, and shrugged, and accepted blame. Others found her attitude reassuring. As if all one was supposed to do in life was one's best.

Praxis bit her nails with impatience. Willie disapproved of that.

"It's the evenings, Willie," she said. "If you'd only work at home instead of the institute!"

"When I've passed my next lot of exams," said Willie, "I'll be earning more money."

"But you know you won't spend it."

"Why should I spend it when we have everything we want? What else do you want from life, Praxis, apart from what you've got?"

What, indeed. A man, a house, a child. It was what most women wanted.

She developed bronchitis. The doctor said the house could do with heating. Willie bought an oil-stove.

"Willie," screamed Praxis, "I want some *new* clothes. I want to go shopping for myself."

He eyed her, thoughtfully.

"Perhaps you really want me to marry you," said Willie. "I will if you like."

"I'll think about it," said Praxis, thus rather hurting and certainly surprising Willie.

"Don't you marry him," said Judith. "All he's after is a legal right to that great house. It must be worth a fortune."

Praxis knew that it was not: that 109 Holden Road was a millstone rather than an asset. Willie would spend nothing on repairs: the neighbours complained about the dilapidation and the weeds in the garden: rain leaked through loose tiles into the attic rooms:

Hilda never came down to see what was happening. No one, not even Willie, could plot to gain possession of such a property. The look of surprise and horror on Elaine's face as she had looked round Praxis' home remained with Praxis; the mere memory of it shamed and embarrassed her.

"If you marry Willie," wrote Irma from London, "don't think I'll come to the wedding because I won't. He'd water the sherry. You must be mad to even think of it." She was officially engaged to Phillip, she wrote. There had been a big party, out of funds provided by her guardian, in South Kensington. Young people in sports cars turned up, and there was a good deal of hooting, calling, slamming of doors and angry neighbours in the night. She had a diamond as big as the Ritz.

"Don't marry Willie," wrote Colleen from Manchester. "It's a mistake to marry too young, before your character's settled down. I find mine changes all the time. I used to think I was the athletic type, but my boyfriend Harry, who's doing abnormal psychology up here, explains it's just a retreat from sex, and in the meantime I've developed the most dreadful leg muscles."

"I don't think I'll marry you," said Praxis.

"Praxis," said Willie, "just on practical grounds, I think you ought to marry me."

"But what about the cost of the licence?"

"I am perfectly happy to pay it. I will pay for anything necessary, and gladly. You know that. Don't try and be unpleasant. It's just that someday, sometime, Baby Mary's papers are going to rise to the top of a file somewhere, and if we're not married, they may say she's in moral danger and take her away."

"I'll take the risk," said Praxis.

Willie waited until Praxis was home from visiting her mother, on Sunday, and they were setting off for the pictures.

"I begin to think," said Willie, "that you don't really want your mother home at all. You know why they don't let her out? It's because you're living with me."

"It's no use, Willie," said Praxis, sadly. She could almost feel his body temperature dropping: the flesh stripping away again from his by now quite plump limbs: the anxious, desperate trembling of the muscles returning. She thought his mother had a lot to answer for.

But she was sustained by a vision, and there is no one so strong as she who is so sustained. She would not marry Willie for a reason she could hardly communicate to anyone—except, oddly, this time, Hilda might understand. How could she say that the red dwarf Betelgeuse had bent down out of the night sky over Brighton Beach and told her not to marry Willie. But it had happened.

She had walked out late one night on the pebbly beach. She seldom did so, for gangs of youths now roamed the water's edge, mostly with the intention of fighting each other, but occasionally they were reputed to attack, or rape, or knife some harmless passer-by. Willie said the rumours were exaggerated: people loved to be frightened and feel they could not sleep safe in their beds any more—or at any rate go down to Brighton Beach anymore.

Praxis went walking; the night was moonlit and bright; she felt she would at least see danger approaching, if approach it did.

The pebbles gleamed beneath her feet; the sea lapped and glittered; in the distance Brighton Pier flung its dark man-made shape out into deep waters. The arch of the sky was vast and deep. Praxis felt elation rising: and with it the desire to worship, to bow down before the Maker, along with the seas, the skies, the valley and the mountains. She felt a sense of destiny, as if someone had turned and touched her on the shoulder.

"What shall I do?" she asked the universe. Betelgeuse replied, leaning down out of the sky, all spears and pale fire.

"Wait. Be patient. Do nothing. Your time will come."

She did not doubt that there was some force guiding the affairs of the universe, working its way peacefully through the chaos of human societies towards an end of its own devising: and that she had some part to play in it, however humble.

I must be mad, she thought, as the star retreated, and the heavens grew less brilliant and more ordinary, and the sea turned back into sea, and the pebbles did not exist to reflect the glory of the Creator, but merely crunched beneath her feet, and made it difficult to walk.

But she knew she wasn't, and that she wouldn't marry Willie.

Praxis settled down.

She bought some washed-out prewar woollies for herself, from Mrs. Allbright's summer sale. She gave up looking in a mirror altogether. She cut and stitched her old clothes into passable garments for Mary, who was happy with what she was given.

Praxis was becoming quite good at sewing.

She did not read much, although, as Willie pointed out, the free library was only round the corner, and it was a pity not to make use of it. Words blurred on the page: notions failed to penetrate her mind. She seemed to have thrown away her brain.

Hilda said as much. Hilda eventually came to visit, looking serene and well-dressed. She had a little car. There was no talk of rats, art or stars; nor did she take off her clothes. Mary was frightened of Hilda, however, for no apparent reason, and Praxis found herself glad to observe it.

"She's a G.I. child, isn't she?" said Hilda.

"What makes you think that?" asked Praxis, surprised. Hilda shrugged, and did not pursue it.

In truth, Mary had a serene and hopeful turn of mind, which seemed to belong to another continent; to the future, not the past. She had a long face, a pale skin, thick pale hair, long legs and slightly buck teeth, kept back by a bar, which she tried to avoid wearing. Praxis liked to think she was very clever. She could read when she was three.

"So could I," said Willie, jealous.

Hilda left.

It can't go on, thought Praxis. It could. It did. On Sundays she would visit her mother and stare companionably, if wretchedly, into space. At Christmas they would visit Willie's mother and eat the ritual chicken and Mary would catch cold. Willie passed one set of exams and started on another. His savings were immense. He spent forty-three pounds on new tiles for the roof. He would at least eat fish fingers now, but had gone off sausages, complaining they were mostly bread and bad value. She served them at her peril. Sometimes they would have herrings as a change from kippers. Mary swung on the gate as once had Praxis, and watched the children from the council school, and longed to go. Willie became more sexually experimental. Judith fell off the platform of her bus and broke her ankle: it was badly set and afterwards she limped and lost her job. There was a whispered scandal relating to Mr. Allbright: he had exposed himself to a young lady member of the choir, but the case never came to court. Mrs. Allbright had twin girls. Sometimes she left them with Praxis to look after. She did not care for them much, Praxis thought. She loved her son. She asked after Mary, but never closely.

Irma married Phillip, who had a job with J. Arthur Rank, King of Starlets. So much for film as a force for social change, said Willie. Willie and Praxis went to the wedding. Irma was dressed in white sharkskin; Praxis actually wore a new dress. Praxis found she loved Phillip as much as ever, but he, of course, was marrying Irma.

Colleen was in London studying archaeology. Her chin was hairy, but her eyes were bright. She had no boyfriend. She played tennis and hockey in the evening: her calves were certainly large and her hands were blistered, but she seemed happy. Praxis refrained from asking her why she didn't just take a pair of tweezers and pluck out the offending hairs. Some people, she had gathered, waved such hairs as an act of defiance to the expectations of the world.

"Why do you put up with it?" asked Colleen.

"Put up with what?"

"Willie. Living down there."

"Because of Mary. What else can I do? How else can I live?"

Colleen had no reply to that. Who had?

"There's only one way to get out of the fix you're in," said Irma. "And that's to sleep your way out of it. Sorry, and all that."

Betelgeuse glimmered low in the sky as Willie and Praxis went home by coach. To go by coach cost half what it did to go by train. It took twice as long and was twice as uncomfortable, but Willie could work anywhere, so long as Praxis was beside him. He had his papers on his knee and could apparently make sense of them, even in the dusk light, and on the jogging vehicle. To Praxis the figures seemed a blur. Perhaps he just stared at them, to save himself the energy of talking? Perhaps he feared his voice would wear out if he used it, as he feared that records would wear out if played too much.

"It can't go on," said Praxis, aloud. Willie did not hear, or pretended not to hear.

And still it went on.

Praxis wrote to Hilda suggesting that the house could be sold and the proceeds divided between Lucy, Hilda and herself. Hilda wrote back to Willie saying it was out of the question: what was he thinking of? Praxis, fearful, told Willie it was just another of Hilda's mad letters: Willie seemed to believe the lie. Praxis' panic, or determination, call it what you will, subsided.

Elaine's father died. He had a heart attack at the wheel of the delivery van and drove it into a wall. Praxis plucked up her courage, called on Elaine, to extend condolences, and found her behind the counter, slicing ham.

"No matter where you go," said that young woman, pink with distress and determination, "or however hard you try, you end up where you began."

"It isn't over yet," said Praxis. "It's only just beginning." She spoke bravely, but found it hard to believe.

"I suppose sooner or later I'll get married and have children and apart from the marriage ceremony, that will be me more over than ever. Come to think of it, we only have until we're twenty. After that it's all downhill."

She had given up her job in the Social Security Office and come home permanently to be near her mother and help run the shop.

"Why does it have to be me?" she complained. "Why couldn't it be my brother who came home?"

"Because he gets paid twice what you do," said Praxis.

"It's good of you to talk to me at all," said Elaine. "My dad always used to have hysterics about you. First because your mother was in the loony bin and then because you were a scarlet woman. I wonder what he wanted for me? To stand here and slice ham, I suppose. Anyway he's dead now, and I'm free to do what I like. My mum's nearly blind, not to mention stone deaf. I'm sure it's hereditary."

She had grown into a sturdy young woman with the same mixture of placidity and vigour which had characterized Judith in the old days: but blessed—or cursed, considering her circumstances—with intelligence.

"The only way out," Irma had said, "is to sleep your way out."

So they did.

15

LISTEN! I am not anxious. I am angry, resentful, spiteful, plagued with self-pity, frightened by death, but I am not anxious; not plagued by the Worm Anxiety, which gnaws away at the foundations of female experience, so that the patterns of magnificence fail, time and time again, to emerge.

Don't pity me, down here in my basement. Don't blame yourselves for your neglect of me. Old woman and a nuisance. I am all right, I tell you. The worm is gone. I am everything disagreeable, but I am not anxious.

I feel no anxiety because I have no one to love. Parents, spouse or children; above all, I have no children anymore. They have grown up now. I have disowned them and they have disowned me. We are free of each other: I should be, and am, proud of that. We do not need each other anymore.

There comes a time when the Alaskan brown bear gets fed up with her young. She leads her brood to the top of a tall pinetree: and leaves them there. She knows how to get down, but they don't. By the time they've found out, she's off and away, the other side of the mountain; and they do without her, well enough. They have to.

And she can live without the thought—are they all right? Where are they now? Altogether free from the instinctive anxiety that plagues the maternal life, animal or human. It starts before the child is born—will it have arms, legs, a brain? Will it be birth-marked, deformed, monstrous? Where are their teeth? Why don't they talk? Why do they steal/lie? Why can't they read? Why do they fight, why don't they fight? Are they happy? Why can't I make them happy?

There is no end to it.

Do you think I could be happy, with my mother in the loony bin? Waking every morning knowing she was there? Myself part of her, never grown out of her, away from her, as I left my children free to grow away from me?

My children are ungrateful: they don't care. That is my great reward. They are free.

Anxiety, I think, is part of women's lives more than it is men's. Men shake it off more easily: whether it is in their natures or the mere product of their lives today, how can I tell? I do know that the Worm Anxiety snips some nerve in the minds of women, and keeps their heads bowed.

16

RAFFLES ESPLANADE DIVE was a lunchtime drinking club down on the seafront. Ordinary pubs shut by law at two P.M., but the Raffles had a licence which enabled it to go on serving drinks until three o'clock, provided that food was served at the same time. A few curled ham sandwiches were therefore passed, as tokens of respectability, from table to table while drinks were served between two and three. The club's name and its decor—red plush, with candles in Chianti bottles, not to mention its prices—served by and large to keep the lower-born drunkards out; those who might stumble out of the pubs and instinctively down the steps, out of the bracing sea air and spray back into the warm, familiar embrace of alcoholic fumes.

The seedier gentry of Brighton drank here: estate agents clinching deals, businessmen in financial difficulties, farmers in search of a good time, a sprinkling of unemployed gentlemen of nebulous means; the well-spoken, gin- and whiskey-drinking, cigar-smoking riff-raff. The clientele was almost exclusively male—although occasionally an illicit girlfriend would sit dangling long legs at the bar; or a secretary searching for a missing boss would come in, or an angry and desperate wife, trying to trace a drinking husband.

Here Praxis and Elaine would sit, most weekday lunchtimes when Willie was at work, Mary eating her school dinner of stew and mash, cake and custard, and Elaine had someone to help in the shop—swinging their legs, raising slow glasses to provocative lips. Douglas, the Raffles' owner, was happy to have them there: a pair of well-spoken, educated girls, not obviously tarts—which might endanger his licence—but nevertheless providing a useful service, and good for business.

Sometimes the girls were content merely to increase the flow of drink across the bar, and the money over it: drinking yellow water while their admirers paid for whiskey, and sharing the profit with Douglas. Sometimes one or other of them would leave with a customer, and what happened then Douglas neither knew nor cared. In fact, the client would be led, or supported, if he had had a lot to drink, to the summerhouse at the bottom of Elaine's long garden. Here a gift of money would change hands, in return for the promise, the prospect and, indeed, if still required, the actuality, of sexual congress. A gift was tendered: not a charge made— Elaine and Praxis were definite about that. They were not prostitutes; just a couple of girls living life to the full, working their way out of difficulties, in a world which made any other solution impossible.

Why not?

Why was it better, Elaine asked, to give sexual services free, as she was so often required to do? Didn't the exchange of money, as in psychoanalysis, raise rather than lower the value of the therapy offered? The more was charged, the more the client enjoyed himself. He had to.

"It's like when you want to increase the sale of a lipstick," said Elaine, "you don't lower its price, you double it. What you're selling is magic."

Elaine had worked for a time in marketing, before her father's death had brought her back to her beginnings.

"It's not," said Elaine, "as if most women enjoyed carnal knowledge, or got anything out of it."

"Some do," said Praxis.

"Do you?"

"Not much," Praxis was obliged to admit, at that stage of her life. She had, after all, until the days of the Raffles Esplanade

Dive, carnally known, as Elaine put it, only two men. One being Phillip, and he and she had been drunk at the time; and the other being Willie, who drove into her incessantly if briefly, and usually when she was standing up.

"There you are!" said Elaine, her point proved from her sample of two. "I think it's disgusting; but I admit I quite like doing it. I like to see men out of control, I really do. It's the peripheral bits of sex, not the sex itself, that women go for."

They felt the need to justify themselves to each other, all the same.

Sometimes fear, disgust, boredom or an acute sense of waste would intervene, and Praxis would elude her escort, or her trailer, or the drunken bumbler at her side—however he was best described—and slip off home, and bath, and wait for Mary to get back from school. But just as often and increasingly, she would complete the journey to the summerhouse, undress, display herself, watch her partner's mounting excitement, or if it did not mount, assist him as best she could, and do whatever was required of her: things she had never thought of, which Brighton wives were not required to do. To masturbate openly, suck and be sucked, spank and be spanked, be tied, tie up, bugger with dildo, be buggered herself; but mostly just to lie there, in a fume of alcohol, her face wet with a stranger's tears, while he inexpertly plunged, lunged, failed, gave up, tried again, spoke his griefs and unburdened himself, via his ejaculation, of his troubles.

Magic, as Elaine had said.

She asked, in payment, beforehand, what the man thought the experience would be worth. If he seemed reluctant to hand over the money, she did not press the matter. Booksellers, dentists and whores, she had read, have the most trouble in exacting money from clients. It seemed a modest expectation of life to have free books, painless teeth and love freely offered, and she sympathized.

The more bizarre requests puzzled her: yet it was the fulfilling of these which seemed to give the greatest relief. Afterwards, she liked to think, there would be little remembrance of the event, let alone of Praxis. She seldom took sober men home: and if she was lucky not to catch a venereal disease, or end up murdered, a true victim of the sadism her masochism provoked, then she did not

know it. The world in those days was, after all, a gentler place—
sex crimes were a rarity: girls went hitch-hiking with impunity:
front doors were seldom locked, at any rate, by day.

All the same, in retrospect, Praxis marvelled at herself and her
foolhardiness.

If, as sometimes happened, both Elaine and she were partnered,
they would move a screen to divide the two summerhouse beds,
and let the sounds from one incite further sounds from the other.
Then indeed Praxis could, would, become orgasmic herself, but
she did not like that. She told Elaine that it interfered with business, but what she meant was that it drew more from herself than
she was prepared to give. She could offer her body as an instrument of relief, her sympathy as salvation; she could stretch out her
hand and receive money in anticipation of these blessings, but she
could not give her own abandonment.

Praxis acquired two regulars, married men whose discretion
could be relied upon. Jack, whose pleasure it was to whisper in her
ear in detail all the things he was going to do to her, and then do
nothing. And Arthur, who had just had mumps and had been told
he could not have children: but could not, would not believe there
was a difference between impotence and infertility, and lay there,
limp of penis, bemoaning his fate, while Praxis read the definitions
from the dictionary, over and over, until at last it would spring to
life—only to fall once more.

Growing bolder, she would occasionally take these two home to
Holden Road instead of to the summerhouse. They were so clearly
both good works: and no possible pleasure to herself.

"Do you think it's making us hard and crude?" asked Elaine,
standing naked in front of the summerhouse mirror, after one of
their double sessions. She looked better undressed than dressed,
Praxis thought. Her skin was very white, and her breasts, which
seemed top-heavy clothed, were firm and strong, seen naked.

"Do you think we should stop? Are we being brutalized? Are we
on some slippery downward path? Are we doing things we wouldn't
have done before?"

"Yes," said Praxis.

"I like doing them more, not less," said Elaine. "The dangerous
thing, I'm sure, is when you stop liking things, not when you start.
Because if you stop it might just spoil you for your loving husband,

later on. I suppose it's different for you; you have a kind of husband already. Do you still fancy him?"

"I never did," said Praxis.

That much she had learned.

Praxis had one hundred and thirty pounds saved. A fortune! Elaine, with rather fewer sexual encounters to her credit, but a rather more forceful approach to money, had one hundred and ninety. Both now could afford to run away, start life again somewhere else: get to London, job, men and future. But still the people, the obligations, did not go away. Willie, Lucy, Elaine's blind old mother. Perhaps the lack of money had been the excuse for, not the cause of, their apathy and their indecision.

To all intents and purposes, Praxis now realized, Willie was Mary's father. If Praxis took Mary to London, away from Willie, Mary might suffer all her life, as Praxis had so far, and presumably forever would, from the loss of her father.

It made her pause. Something made her pause.

She dangled clues to her lunchtime life in front of Willie's nose. He took no notice: he changed his thick glasses for even thicker ones; he spoke even less: studied even more: read throughout meals: kept his eyes closed as he impaled her: she felt more and more like a butterfly run through with a pin. She bought new dresses and he made no comment: she yawned with much languorous stretching: she even made sexual advances to him, of an adventurous kind, which he ignored.

Perhaps he knew? No, that was impossible. He would kill her. Surely he would kill her. The prospect, while it frightened her and made her wake breathless in the night, at the same time made her feel safe. She could only leap and cavort at the end of her leash, because Willie held the other end, in his quivering, unseeing, murderous hand.

Could it really go on?

It did. It seemed to.

Until the event occurred: the extraordinary happening, which divided her life in two: into before and after.

He bought her a double whiskey, and for once that's what she had, instead of the sweet yellow liquid from the bottle Douglas kept especially for her and Elaine. By so doing she lost some two shillings and fourpence, but she needed the whiskey, for although he was suave and charming, he made her nervous and self-conscious. He was, she supposed, rare in the Raffles, a man difficult to despise. He was not young; perhaps even about sixty, but his hair was still thick, though grey, and what was more, it was his own. Too often her hand had encountered hair which moved not strand by strand, but in whole slices, tipping here and there across the scalp, and would turn out to be a toupee, or a wig. He drank double whiskey after double whiskey but seemed unaffected by the alcohol. His voice was low, smooth and gentlemanly: he smiled at her, and seemed to appreciate what he saw.

Elaine and Praxis had tossed up for the privilege of sitting beside him; and that they had never done before. He was wealthy: you could tell from his shirt and his shoes, and not just the thickness of his wallet. Estate agents and farmers could be rich, and often were, flashed gold signet rings and watch chains to show it, but that was no guarantee that the money would easily come the girls' way. This man was what Elaine and Praxis described as Bond Street rich: he had an easy affluence.

"The sort of man," as Elaine said, romantically, "who steps on a bus and finds he doesn't have the money to pay the fare, because he has better things to do than think about it."

However, Praxis won the toss, and then wished she hadn't. He asked her name.

"Pattie," she said.

"An ordinary name," he said, "for a not very ordinary young person." His blue eyes travelled, with not so much speculation as was usual, but, rather, with a contemplative admiration, over her breasts and down to her legs, and up again to meet her eyes, quite frankly.

"What blue eyes you have," he said.

"I like blue eyes, better than brown," she replied. "Brown eyes hide feelings: blue eyes show them." Hilda had brown eyes.

"I agree," he said, "but perhaps that's just because we both have blue eyes."

"We both," he had said, and the feeling of inclusion warmed and satisfied her. Nor did he ask, as so many did, what's a nice girl like you doing in a place like this, before going on to make sure that the notion of niceness did not apply. He accepted her right to be there, as much as his own: her right to be penetrated by him, as much as his to penetrate. Nor, on the way to the summerhouse, did he go behind, or before, as one ashamed, but took her arm in his and walked beside her, talking about himself and her.

Was she married? More or less.

Children? More or less.

"You don't say much about yourself," he complained.

"There is so little to say," she complained, in return.

"Only because you have not investigated yourself," he maintained, "or no one has yet investigated you. If you had, or they had, you would be of infinite interest to yourself.

"I am," he assured her. "I may bore other people, but I never bore myself, and that's the main thing." Did she like Brighton?

"No," she replied.

"Neither do I," he said. "It makes me feel desperate. Perched on the end of the world, in danger of falling off. That's why I'm behaving like a man half my age. I am rather old," he apologized.

"Not nearly so old as some," she remarked.

"If I lived in Brighton," he said, presently, as they reached the summerhouse, "more or less married, more or less with children—" He stopped.

"What?"

"I'd get out," he replied.

Her hands shook as she tried to disengage her brassiere strap.

"Why are you trembling?" he asked, doing it for her.

"I don't know," she replied, truthfully.

"You're not new to this?"

She shook her head.

"It's the terrible effect I have on people. My wife trembles all the time, but mostly with indignation."

So, he was married.

She stood naked. He knelt, with his head pressed against her belly, in his grey expensive suit, well-manicured hands clasped behind her back.

"I love young women," he said. "All young women, any young women. I love to hear them talk, and feel them breathe. They are the centre of the universe. And their centre is the nearest a man can ever get to it. When their centre moves, when I make it move, the world shifts."

She hardly liked to ask for money.

"We all try to do it," he said, lying white and pale beside her, his skin not young but smooth from health and care. "We all try to do it, to move the universe to our way of thinking."

She wished the sheets were cleaner, less familiar, the bed more unsullied by the fumes, the tears, the odours and the struggles of the many who had lain upon it. He did not seem to mind. What was she to call him? He had not given her a name, and it was not her place to ask for one. What was she, after all? A whore. But titles were absurd, definitions were absurd; she'd always known that: words used to simplify relationships between one person and another: granting one privilege, the other disadvantage. Bastard, Jew, student, wife, mother, prostitute, murderer: all made assumptions that reduced the individuals, rather than defined them.

His hands moved over her body, her breast, between her legs.

"Pattie," he said, "smile, smile."

It seemed more indecent than anything she had ever been asked to do.

"Keep your eyes open: look at me."

Willie always kept his eyes closed: so did she. Her clients would watch what she did, to herself, or to them: they would look for pain or pleasure on her face, but it was the reaction they needed and one brought about by themselves; it made no difference whose it was. This man acknowledged her: it was not comfortable or what she wanted.

"Pattie," he repeated. "Pattie," when she tried to retreat into solitary isolation, bringing her back into contact with him.

His methods were straightforward: himself on top of her: admiring, leisurely, talking at first, later busy and exciting. She cried out, in genuine orgasm: she had all but forgotten how not to feign them.

"Pattie," he said again, "Pattie," almost as if her climax had been all he wanted, but then he came to his own, and lay there for a time, half asleep.

"You're very restful," he said, although her mind kept racing ahead to Mary's return home from school, and the necessity, usually fulfilled, of being there first. But she felt, for once, happy where she was.

"And more beautiful supine than upright," he added. "All the best women are.

"A pity we can't have children," he said. "I always want to have children. But I suppose it's impractical."

"Yes," said Pattie.

He made no suggestion that he might see her again, and for once, she was disappointed. But what else could she expect? His hand continued to run over hers, however, as if, although the prime purpose of their encounter had been met, his interest and concern for her remained.

"I used to live in Brighton once," he said. "It was a terrible time. Before the war. I was more or less married and more or less had children. Lucy, she was called. Loony Lucy. I think she was even more impossible than me, but it was a long time ago. How could one tell? Who was right and who was wrong?"

"What became of her?" asked Pattie, eventually. Her mind moved quickly to the defence, while her feelings remained stunned. Incest, she told herself, rapidly, was merely another label: so, come to that, was father. A father was someone who brought up a child: not someone who abandoned it. Incest was something disturbing which happened, inside families.

"She was provided for," he said. "I'm sure she was better off without me. People usually are."

"And the children?"

"Better to keep out of their way," he said. "They were her idea, not mine. It would only be an embarrassment now, to seek them out. It was a long time ago."

Pattie lay quiet. His hand moved up from her hand, to her arm, to her breast.

"You're lovely," he said, as if surprised. "I want you again. You make me feel young again."

To commit incest knowingly, Pattie supposed, was a great deal worse than to do so unknowingly and that was bad enough. Oedipus had put out his eyes, and been pursued by furies, forever after, for such a sin. But she was committing nothing: she was lying there, while her progenitor plunged and frayed in the body of his own creating. She was glad he liked it. She would say nothing. She would take his guilt upon herself.

He was a charming, impossible man; a hopeless, dangerous romantic. No wonder he had driven Lucy mad. Had he lain his head upon her belly and tried to listen to the breathing of the universe?

No doubt, and then gone straight down to the golf club, listening in to the waitress's hot line to infinity, as well.

Pattie laughed aloud, with bitterness and exultation mixed, at which orgasm shook her body, so that the laughter turned almost to a cry of distress.

"Christ," he said, with reverence. But she had altogether demystified him: turned him from saint to client, from father to man, from someone who must be pleased to someone who could pleasure her. He was a natty, grey-haired old gentleman, spending the afternoon with a provincial whore, and that was all there was to it. As to being her father: he had renounced his rights to that a long time ago.

As if sensing the change in her, his erection wilted and all but died, and she obliged it up again, and used it for her own purposes, and found she could. She had become, at his expense, autonomous, wresting from him what he had failed to offer.

What am I doing here? wondered Praxis. What am I trying to prove, and to whom? Who is there in the world to care how low I've sunk; to take the blame for it? It has all been my own doing.

He dressed: Praxis lay naked on the bed and watched. He left her twenty pounds, white five-pound notes. It occurred to her that perhaps the same knowledge had come to him as had to her, mid-intercourse, causing the momentary lapse in psychic energy, the temporary failure of desire.

He paused before he left.

"So long as this is only part of your life, not all of it," he said, and she was conscious once again of affection between him and her: of something he was trying to offer her, within the very narrow limits of what he saw as his responsibility.

"All right," she said, and he gave her the most paternal of pecks upon the forehead, and a rather less paternal one on each of her breasts, and left.

Pattie got up, washed, dressed, went home, packed, met Mary out of school, took a taxi to the station, the train to Waterloo, and within hours was knocking on Colleen's front door.

17

ARGUMENTS FROM NATURE.

It is natural, they told me in prison, waving their keys, to want to be free. The prison I was in, actually, had a secure perimeter, but once inside the high brick walls, the ring of alarms, dogs, and surveillance, there was a fair degree of free movement. The difficulty lay in wanting to move, freely or otherwise. Prison was as much inside the head as outside it.

It is natural, they told me, to miss the opposite sex. Sexual deprivation, of course, though it is seldom mentioned, is what prison is all about. Thirty years without fucking, to this robber or that. A year without fucking, to this or that rowdy young man. It used to be more awe-inspiring a penalty, in the days when the general degree of sexual disgust was higher. Now the men masturbate in cheerful unison over girlie magazines, and the girls fall in love with each other.

That's natural.

It is nature, they say, that makes us get married. Nature, they say, that makes us crave to have babies. You must breast-feed, they say. It's natural. Best for baby. Eat raw carrots, yeast tablets, sea salt, honey, and so on. Natural. Eschew white sugar, chemical salt, artificial sweetness, preservatives. Unnatural.

It's nature that makes us love our children, clean our houses, gives us a thrill of pleasure when we please the home-coming male.

Who is this Nature?

God?

Or our disposition, as laid down by evolutionary forces, in order to best procreate the species?

I suppose, myself, that it is the latter.

Nature does not know best, or if it does, it is on the man's side. Nature gives us painful periods, leukorrhoea, polyps, thrush, placenta praevia, headaches, cancer and in the end death.

It seems to me that we must fight nature tooth and claw. Once we are past child-bearing age, this Nature, this friend, we hear so much about, disposes of us. In drying up our estrogen, it bends our backs, brittles our bones, rheums our eyes and clouds our tempers: throws us on its scrap-heap of useless though still moving, stirring, moaning flesh. It is not *natural* to be a grandmother: it may be nice, but it is a social role, a consolatory one: no, it is natural to be dead.

What I am saying is, I am useless. I do not mind dying. I have given up. I, little Praxis Duveen, bastard, adulteress, whore, committer of incest, murderess, what else? Hand me your labels. I'll wear them for you.

But as for the rest of you, sisters, when anyone says to you, this, that or the other is natural, then fight. Nature does not know best; for the birds, for the bees, for the cows; for men, perhaps. But your interests and Nature's do not coincide.

Nature our Friend is an argument used, quite understandably, by men.

18

"YOU SHOULD GO BACK," said Colleen to Praxis. Colleen was eight months pregnant. She was married to Michael, a thin, dark, kind, silent man, who suffered from asthma and depression. He had been a business executive for a farm machinery firm when she married him, but his illness had forced him to take a less responsible job, and now he sold Rolls-Royces in Berkeley Square. His asthma and his depression, alas, had merely been accentuated by the move, by contact with motor fumes and the very rich. He longed for the rural life. He did not see how he could support a child, let alone Colleen, on the money he earned. He had been to university, but despair and wheezing combined had induced him to leave just before his finals. He suffered from nostalgia, from the belief that once things had been better than they were now: sometimes he would lie in bed for days trying to summon the courage and strength to get up: or else wheeze and choke, so that Colleen would call the doctor. By the time the doctor came, he could breathe quite easily. Yet on good days he was charming, and interested, polite and clever, and kind.

"I thought I could cheer him up," said Colleen. "I'm quite a vigorous person, really. I thought I might infect him, somehow,

134

with energy. Make him look forward instead of back." She spoke doubtfully, as if she now knew it would never be. The flat was small and poky. Praxis slept on the couch: Mary on pillows on the floor. In the bedroom Michael wheezed and Colleen murmured consolation through the night. She had given up tennis and hockey. She could not share them with Michael.

There were wedding photographs on the mantelpiece. Michael looked handsome, sombre and well-bred; Colleen lively and pretty. Colleen's mother wore a hearty felt hat pulled down over her eyes, and Colleen's father had insisted that his elderly flower-arranging mistress be in the picture. "Such a good friend of the family."

"You should go back," said Colleen. "Marriage is sacred."

"But I'm not married. I never married him."

"You're as good as," said Colleen, with truth. "He's been keeping you all these years."

Colleen sat with her legs apart, arms clasped over her eight-month lump, occasionally gasping and groaning. "And it's not as if Mary was his own. Besides, you can't just wander round London homeless with Mary; someone will catch up with her and take her away."

"She's mine," said Praxis. "They can't."

"Not unless you officially adopt her," said Colleen primly. "And that means being married. Go back home and marry Willie."

"Never," cried Praxis.

"I don't think you've given it a fair chance," said Colleen. "Living in sin is very different from being married. What you need in your life is more commitment, not less."

At which point Michael loomed through the door, home early from work. His face was white and his eyes glazed: he took to his bed. He had triumphed that day, sold a Silver Ghost to the nineteen-year-old son of an earl, but at once had started wheezing.

"Asthma's a terrible thing," said Colleen when she had settled her husband, and he was breathing more easily.

"So's envy," said Praxis, tartly. "He should get a job where he mixes with people less fortunate than himself."

"That's nothing to do with it. Michael despises worldly privilege and wealth."

There seemed to be little left of the original Colleen. She had become her husband's spokeswoman.

"What's happened to the archaeology?" asked Praxis.

"It's not really practical, is it?" said Colleen. "Though I must say," she added, more brightly, "I did get interested in tracing trade routes via artifacts. I might go back to it later. But one has to settle down, doesn't one? All that sleeping around—you can't think how wonderful it is just to have Michael, and be married and secure. And now the baby. After the baby's born I'll make Michael join a tennis club. I expect all he needs is exercise."

But she spoke without conviction. She looked at Praxis mutely, appealing for help, but Praxis had none to offer. She did not doubt that Colleen still filled the night with the sound of her tears, carefully controlled so that her husband did not hear.

As you start, so Praxis decided, you have a terrible tendency to go on.

Not me, thought Praxis, not me.

Colleen lumbered about the tiny kitchen, washing chipped cups in cold water, wedging herself perpetually between table and cupboard. She did not seem like an object of love, but Praxis supposed she was. This at any rate was where love led. Mary watched, open-mouthed.

"How's it going to get *out?*" she whispered later to Praxis. "Won't she burst?"

"Of course not," said Praxis, briskly, but she shared Mary's fears.

They stayed with Colleen for two nights. A sense of nightmare assailed Praxis.

The welcome inside the house was dutiful but strained: Colleen's loyalty was to Michael: her desire to protect him from her former girlfriends in distress quite understandable. The welcome outside the house was nonexistent. Nothing familiar met the eye. The London streets seemed strange and the people who thronged through them were indifferent to her plight. How could she ever get the better of this place: get the crowds to part and to acknowledge her?

Willie had made no attempt to get in touch with her, and Praxis was confused. She had expected him to come after her with axe, or writs or reproaches. Instead, there had been silence. Even the sense of having someone to have run from would have been welcome: would have given her some sense of scale.

"When are we going home?" asked Mary.

"I thought we might live in London," said Praxis.

"I don't like London," said Mary.

"Why not?"

"You have to sleep on the floor."

"Not for long. I'm going to find somewhere lovely."

"And what about Willie?" Mary looked at Praxis with clear, accusing eyes. "And what about my friends?"

She sulked: shuffled and whined.

"You took her on," said Colleen. "You're behaving very selfishly. Just because you're bored . . ." Her own eyes were glazed with boredom of late pregnancy.

"I'll feel better when it's born," she kept saying, "and I can get on with things. It's just not being able to *bend*."

But she offered to look after Mary for a day or two while Praxis tried to find somewhere to live.

"If it's not too much of a burden," said Praxis, falsely. "It seems bad to burden you at such a time—"

"She can do things for me," said Colleen, practically. "I can sweep and she can use the dustpan and brush."

Colleen, thought Praxis, where are your dreams now? Your hockey cups and netball trophies: your nights on the downs with the boys?

Praxis, not without reluctance, went to visit Irma and Phillip. Irma would feel sorry for her, she knew; as sorry as she herself felt for poor Colleen. Phillip would patronize her, and the memory of their first encounter would remain between them like some extravagant vase of flowers on a dinner table, preventing the easy flow of conversation and ideas.

He would, besides, presumably be on Willie's side. Whatever Willie's side was.

"Phillip's given Willie up," said Irma, loftily. "Don't worry about that. Willie's of no value to him. Phillip only associates with people who can get him on in his business of improving the world."

"Where is he now?" asked Praxis. Phillip was at work, said Irma, in tones of amazement, as if the activity was bizarre. He sat in a room composing television commercials in preparation for the opening of ITV, the commercial television network set up to rival the BBC.

"Doesn't that rather go against the grain?" enquired Praxis. Willie regarded the arrival of ITV as the death of socialist aspirations.

"TV commercials," said Irma, smirking, "by increasing demand, reduce capital costs, and thus the consumer benefits and the revolution approaches. Phillip hasn't joined the system, of course, he's only infiltrating it. Phillip always has a good argument for doing what he wants to do. They sit in this room," said Irma, "composing TV commercials, and none of them has ever even read the script of one, let alone seen one. And they call it work and come home tired."

It was, Phillip had told her, a prime example of the eccentric amateur charm of the English, a proud lack of professionalism, which was presently going to bring the nation to its knees and the revolution nearer.

Praxis had never heard of the revolution.

"Phillip's nothing if not clever," said Irma, with a curl of her scarlet lips. "And always in the forefront."

Phillip and Irma lived in a high, narrow, clean house in a crescent of high narrow dirty ones. There were pot plants on the window sills of Irma's house. Up and down the street common children played, vulgar women sat on steps, and bored young men mended cars.

"The area's bound to come up," said Irma. "The estate agent thought we were mad, but Phillip knew better."

The last three words came out spitefully. Was it hate, or habit? Praxis couldn't make out.

"Of course we only have the middle floors," said Irma. An eighty-five-year-old woman lived in the basement: twin brothers of seventy-three had the attic floor. Both had the protection of the law and could not legally be driven or bribed out.

"When they die," said Irma calmly, "at least I'll have the whole house. I look forward to it. Playing houses is all I do have to look forward to. I play Phillip's LP's very loudly in order to hasten the old folks' end. In the meantime, the twins piss through the ceiling and the old lady craps by the dustbin. Yellow liquid dripped through the ceiling rose the other day, onto the table. We were giving a dinner party for one of Phillip's clients. I laughed."

Irma trilled her pretty laugh. She had a baby and a girl to look after it, but there was no sign of either.

"Can I see the baby?" asked Praxis.

"What for?" demanded Irma. "It doesn't say or do anything interesting. It just crawls about, making a nuisance of itself." She was expecting another one.

"I put a knitting needle up me, darling, but nothing happened. I expect the baby will have a hole in the head; like mother, like baby. Of course Phillip's over the moon. Anything that reduces me enhances him. I've had two abortions. I couldn't stand another. They come and stand at the bedside in their Harley Street suits and stretch out their hands for the money. In cash. They won't take cheques, which means somehow I have to get the cash out of Phillip, without letting him know what it's for. According to Phillip, the more children we have the better. He wants to use them in commercials. Soft as a baby's bottom, that kind of thing. He says there's a fortune to be made."

Irma was, by and large, indifferent to the details of Praxis' fate, though she sympathized in principle.

"Of course you can't go back," she said, "to that dreadful smelly little man."

"But where can I live? And how? I can't stay on Colleen's sofa forever."

"I should think not. I'm sure it's damp and lumpy, like its owner."

"And there's Mary."

"There doesn't have to be Mary, Praxis. You only choose Mary. We all think you're slightly dotty. Leave Mary behind with Wee-Willie-Winkie, or send her back to the clergyman's wife."

"She's like my own child. And she hardly knows the Allbrights anymore."

"Well," said Irma, buffing her red nails, straightening a picture here, blowing a speck of dust there, "I suppose we must all have something to love. Except me, of course. I can do without."

"Surely you love your baby."

"I leave all that kind of thing to Phillip."

Irma tripped about her glossy home, on high stiletto heels, which marked the parquet floor at every step, head high, middle lightly corseted so that her new pregnancy didn't show, scarlet-lipped, doe-eyed, heavily scented, infinitely angry, infinitely bored.

She turned to Praxis suddenly, tears in her eyes, smudging the mascara on her lower lashes.

"It can't go on," she said to Praxis.

"You'd be surprised," said Praxis, "how it can. Or what it takes to make it stop."

Irma did not offer Praxis, even temporarily, the shelter of her spare room. Praxis, it was mutely understood by both of them, was neither grand enough, interesting enough nor beautiful enough to occupy it. She had, besides, a bad cold in the nose, and Irma feared lest she catch it.

Praxis was receiving the world through slightly watery eyes and dimmed ears. The rims of her nostrils smarted.

"You should be in bed," said Irma.

"I haven't got a bed to be in," said Praxis.

"Well, tucked up on Colleen's sofa then," said Irma. "I'm sure she's glad of company; and the snufflier the better. It's clearly what she likes. Her car salesman wheezed all through the wedding ceremony. Or do you think she's just desperate?"

"I think she loves him," said Praxis, and Irma eyed her pityingly, and then took a broom and banged the kitchen floor to startle the old lady in the basement and then ran up the stairs—the price tags, Praxis could see, were still on the soles of her shoes—to the bedroom, to bang the ceiling there and annoy the twins.

"I don't think you've got enough to do," remarked Praxis. "Why don't you go to work?"

"Because of the mother-baby bond," said Irma, calmly enough. "Phillip says it is detrimental to the child's emotional and mental development if the mother goes out to work: and I want no comments from you, please."

Praxis closed her mouth.

"Phillip will be back soon," said Irma, dismissing her friend, and closing the conversation at the same time.

"I'm afraid you caught me on a bad day," Irma said on the doorstep. "It's been lovely seeing you again and as soon as you're settled do come round again. It's no use me trying to help you. I'm hopeless at that kind of thing. I'm only good for entertainment value. Now what you must do, Praxis, is get married to some exciting man with a future, and bring him round to dinner. You'll have to do something about your clothes, mind you. So long as I've known you, you seem to have been wearing the same dusty black sweater. Why?"

Because there's a never-ending supply of them at church sales, Praxis could have said, and because if I wore the tight black satin blouse and flounced red Spanish skirt that was my Raffles outfit, you'd know altogether too much about me.

You might even tell Phillip. Praxis reserved Phillip in her mind, as it were, for another occasion.

Praxis met Hilda out of her office. Her sister came down the steps at a quarter to six, brisk and efficient, in earnest conversation with a grey-faced colleague. She motioned to Praxis to wait quietly, finished the conversation and then came over. She was wearing a fur coat, in spite of the warmth of the day; but she seemed palely cool, and her brown eyes cold.

"You should have rung to make an appointment," said Hilda. "I am going to the opera tonight, and I haven't much time." But she consented to have a cup of coffee with Praxis, in a sandwich bar.

"I had a phone call from Willie about you," said Hilda. "I think you're being very irresponsible. Who's going to look after the house and who's going to visit mother if you just walk out like that?"

"There's no reason," said Praxis, bravely, "why it should be me and not you."

"I'm the eldest and I'm earning," said Hilda. "You have nothing better to do. How can I possibly get down to Brighton? He told me to tell you he wants Mary back. He'll go to the Children's Department if she's not back by the end of the week."

"How can he look after her?" protested Praxis. "He's out at work all day."

"I expect he'll move Carla in," said Hilda.

"Who's Carla?"

"Willie's girlfriend," said Hilda, blandly.

Praxis found her coffee cup trembling in her hand.

"Willie wants to marry Carla. She's only a shop girl but Willie doesn't mind. He doesn't come from a particularly good background himself, I suppose. Not like us."

Praxis studied her sister's cool, unimpassioned face. Her expression was not malevolent: that she could have understood. Rather it was cautious, interested, without empathy. She wanted to embrace her and say this is me, me, Pattie, your sister, help me, but Hilda would merely have been puzzled and embarrassed.

"Don't you know about Carla?" enquired Hilda. "He told me about Carla; why didn't he tell you? She works in the canteen at his office. She's very practical and very clean, I believe. She'd look after the house well. I daresay we could ask her to visit mother: we could even club together, Pattie, and pay her to go. Then she'd be sure to. Though when I think of how little mother did for us, I'm sure I don't know why we should bother."

"She did what she could," mumbled Pattie, through shock and tears. It was one thing to leave Willie: another for him to be gratified by her leaving. One thing for her to leave her home: quite another to see herself so instantly supplanted.

"She should never have deprived us of a father," said Hilda, looking at her little diamond watch.

"It's our house," said Praxis. "Willie can't just move someone else in."

"Someone has to look after it," said Hilda. "And as I said, he wants Mary back."

"He can't have her."

"Do be practical," said Hilda. "After all, you're a known prostitute. All Willie has to do is lift his little finger and say she's in moral danger, and you'll never see her again."

"Is that what Willie said about me? A known prostitute?"

"It's not surprising that's what you turned out to be," said Hilda calmly. "You caught it from Miss Leonard, and of course Mary has made things worse for you. She is the Antichrist. I warned Willie but he laughed. Well, he'll find out."

She rose to go.

"Do you like my coat? It's anti-static. If you had one, you might find it some protection."

She looked almost sad, for a moment, as if some inkling of her sister's plight had pierced her carapace; but then she shook her head briskly, as if to shake off doubt and gloomy thoughts, and walked away. Praxis paid the bill and took the train back to Brighton. Mary was safe with Colleen.

Praxis reached 109 Holden Road just before six o'clock in the evening. It was Willie's habit, these days, to be home by six-thirty.

But it isn't his home, Praxis told herself, it's my home; Willie is some small painful parasite who has wormed his way into the flesh of my being. I must dig him out.

The sense of nightmare which had descended upon her in London did not disperse as she neared Brighton. Rather it intensified. She dreaded the place; the past it contained; the present it had; and the future it might still have waiting for her.

Praxis stopped outside her gate. It was a gloomy evening. The sea sky was heavy and tumultuous. Black clouds formed themselves into monstrous bat wings, which hovered, it seemed, just over her house. The sound of the sea, so familiar to her as to go mostly unheard, was tonight loud in her ears: a restless spiteful background to her life.

She opened the front door and heard the sound of singing. For a moment she thought it must be Lucy, back home again, and young again, singing in the absent kind of way she had, as if to cover up the blackness of her thoughts: the better to raise a smokescreen between the world and herself. Praxis had hated to hear her mother sing. Others had thought: There! Lucy's happy. She sings. The child knew better.

Praxis went through to the kitchen. The light was on. There was a young girl on her knees on the floor, scrubbing; she was wearing rubber gloves; she sang as she worked. The kitchen was tidy, bright and cheerful. Flowers had been put in a vase, the mantelpiece cleared of bits and pieces, the Aga stove blacked. Once long ago, Praxis remembered, the kitchen had looked like this. That was in the days when the grey-haired gentleman with the philosophical turn of mind and the admiring nature, and the wooing, caressing, dreadful penis had been young, and had even—had he?—sat by the Aga and bounced Praxis on his knee, and chucked her under the chin with his smooth well-manicured finger.

Oh, I am old, thought Praxis. I am so old. I am too old to go on living.

The girl straightened up. She seemed embarrassed. She had what Hilda would have described as a common little figure, and a common little face. Her hair was fair and permed, and her eyes blue and watery. Her voice was nasal.

"I suppose you're Praxis," she said. "I told Willie you'd come back, but he wouldn't believe me. He said you wouldn't dare. I'm Carla."

She took off her apron and her gloves and offered her red and wrinkled hand to Praxis. Praxis did not shake it: not from any sense of animosity, but from a sudden vision of the hand in intimate contact with Willie's flesh.

She ought not to mind: she could not mind: but mind she did.

"I used to feel bad about it at first," said Carla, "but when he told me what you were doing, I didn't see how it made any difference.

He was ever so upset. He only came to me because he was upset. Well, I knew that. It was just afterwards things became different. You can get very fond of Willie, can't you?"

"What I was doing?"

"Well," said Carla, blushing. "Down at the Raffles with that girl from the grocer's shop. My dad has a garage. He had to tow away her dad's car after the accident. Blood everywhere. It was terrible."

Men, reflected Praxis, are commonly expected to marry someone poorer, less educated and of lower status than themselves. Women, likewise, are expected to marry above themselves. Thus every wife in the world will automatically feel, in her domestic life and status, inferior to her husband. Because in fact she will be: and perhaps this way happiness and acceptance lie. The husband looking down. The wife looking up. If only I could have looked up to Willie.

Perhaps, thought Praxis, that was the whole trouble. I was too nearly Willie's equal. He did his best: stopping my education, forbidding me to earn, reducing me to whoredom: yes, he certainly did his best. Except, alas, that to blame Willie for these things is ridiculous. He didn't do them. He pointed a finger, and I ran, willingly, in the direction he pointed.

She was silent. She sat down, without asking permission. It was, as she had reminded herself, her kitchen, her chair. Carla was wearing a pale pink fluffy angora jumper.

"I like your jumper," said Praxis.

"Willie bought it for me," said Carla. "Well, we thought we'd get married. I could hardly marry him in white, could I—not after all that. Well, you know what he's like. Always at it. And you wouldn't marry him. He did ask. I said he should. You turned your back on him. What did you expect? He was bound to find someone else. He wants a wife. A man has a right to a wife."

Her nasal voice rose high in indignation, in defence of Willie.

"The last time I saw Willie," Praxis could have said, but didn't, "only a couple days ago"—can it have been so little?—"he had me on the stairs in the two minutes between Mary leaving for school and his own leaving for work. I waved goodbye to him, still sitting on the landing. He has been telling you lies, shop girl, of a kind only a shop girl would believe."

A canary sang in a cage which hung from the window.

"I brought my bird along," said Carla. "I'm ever so fond of my bird. It sings its little heart out. Willie said bring it. I said you'd be back, he said you wouldn't dare."

I have been telling you lies, Willie, of the kind a whoring mistress tells. No, perhaps I don't dare. Perhaps I'm going to leave.

"You can't get married in a jersey you've been scrubbing floors in," observed Praxis.

"I wore my apron," said Carla, anxiously. "It's just the angora's so soft and lovely. I couldn't resist it. I meant to take it off before Willie got back."

Praxis, recognizing something of herself in Carla, felt more kindly towards her.

"I feel bad about all this," said Carla, "but the thing is, we haven't anywhere but here to live, Willie and I, and your sister Hilda—I do admire her, she's so clever and smart, I'd no idea about anti-static and how it eats into the brain, do you think it's true?—says it's all right if we stay here till we find somewhere, and I can keep the house nice and look after Mary—you can't take her away from her school and everything she knows, I mean, if you really love her, you can't—and I've heard so much about her from Willie I feel I know her already: and Hilda asked if I could pop in sometimes and see how your mother was getting on—" She broke off. There were tears of entreaty in her blue eyes.

"You know what Willie is—" she said. "It's so difficult sometimes. He has his savings. We could put them down on a little house, near the seafront. I could take in boarders—but you know what Willie is."

"Yes," said Praxis. "I know what Willie is." But if you got a pink angora jumper from him, you might get a house of your own yet. In the meantime, she said, "By all means, stay. And do visit Mother. I'd be grateful. She might even think you were me, if you told her so. These days she believes what she's told. It's the new drugs she's on."

"What about Mary?"

"I don't know about Mary," said Praxis. "I'll have to think about Mary. Could I just ask, is it a new pink angora jumper or is it second-hand?"

"New," said Carla, not without indignation. "Of course."

The wind had risen; it buffeted Praxis about the ears as she went back to the station. The black-bat shape of the high clouds held its form, however, and seemed to follow her as she went, as if Praxis was the object of its particular attention. She walked close to hedges and fences; she was frightened. Her mind held oddly little; she was conscious of some relief as the train pulled out, and Brighton was left behind, and the clouds changed into something more normal and less personal. The shock of having encountered her father, in the manner she had, loomed over all the other minor assaults her dignity and feelings had lately suffered; it incorporated them all, as a major devil might sweep a whole host of lesser demons beneath its bat wings and take them into itself, biding its time before disgorging them again.

Truth and the devil, thought Praxis, being the same.

19

I CAN SCARCELY REMEMBER, on a hot summer's day, what it is like to be cold. When I am replete, I cannot remember hunger. I can, mind you, when rich, remember what it is like to be poor. Though I may tend to look scornfully at the poor and wonder why they stay that way, I try to remember, and not to despise.

I remember wandering through London streets, crying for grief because I had lost Willie and was about to lose Mary; not seeing that my own actions and my own obtuseness had brought these losses about. Or that, in any case, neither Mary nor Willie was mine to lose.

Had Mary been my own child, had Willie been my legal spouse, I still would not have had the right to call them mine. We shelter children for a time; we live side by side with men; and that is all. We owe them nothing, and are owed nothing. I think we owe our friends more, especially our female friends. I might have been justified in feeling angry with Irma, for not helping me when I needed help, and with Colleen because the help she offered was limited by her desire not to inconvenience her husband. But I was not angry: I assumed, along with everyone else, that a man's convenience rated more in the great scheme of things than a woman's pain.

In retrospect, I see as quite ridiculous my agitation because Willie chose to buy another woman a new pink sweater, when I had had to make do for so long with second-hand dusty black. Why didn't I buy my own sweater? Why did I expect to be provided for, and resent it when I was not?

And why, when being a part-time whore at the Raffles seemed neither particularly disreputable nor disgraceful at the time I was doing it, did I allow it to turn into a disgraceful and shameful secret? I was earning, after all, offering one of the few services the world allowed me to offer—apart, I suppose, from my dubious skills as a cleaner or washerwoman, and I was doing that at home, anyway, unpaid. I was gaining some agreeable physical sensations, and stretching my vision of humanity; I was free to pick and choose my clients, and had time left over to look after home and child. Why was I so easily made to feel it was distasteful, when my own experience indicated that it was not?

Certainly it is true that many, even most, whores are debased and wretched-looking creatures, but I suspect the debasement and wretchedness came before the streets (or the bar stool) and that whoring, for male or female, is a way out, not a path down. It certainly was for me.

And is it really any better at the other end of the spectrum? Is the ordinary domestic woman, lumbering about in a hospital maternity ward, less debased, less wretched? She seems to me to be neither spiritually exalted nor greatly loved; fulfilling no higher purpose than a mindless biological destiny.

And as to Hilda's madness, it at least enabled her, in whatever form it happened to take—rats or stars or anti-static—to function as a man might do, to earn the respect of her peers and get to the opera of an evening. And I do not believe, had she been a man, that her lack of rationality would have been so easily interpreted as madness, paranoia. If it was madness, it served her very well, as obsessional interests—company, religion, country, politics—serve men well, to relieve them of the more exacting chores of family and domestic relationships.

Do you know, I am beginning to feel better.

20

LETTERS FROM WILLIE pursued Praxis for a time, accusing, pleading, threatening, reasoning; but the truth was, alas, evident—he did not really want her back so much as he was reluctant to commit himself to marrying Carla. Praxis feared that his determination to have Mary rose from his belief that so long as he had her his tenure of the house was secure.

But Mary wanted to go back.

"Even if I don't?" asked Praxis, hurt.

"You could always come and visit me," offered Mary, kindly, and Colleen remarked on what a well-balanced and secure child Mary was. Michael, as sometimes happened, had been taken into hospital with a particularly severe attack of asthma, and Colleen now welcomed Praxis' presence: apart from anything else she was so pregnant as not to wish to be left alone. There was no telephone in the house, and the neighbours were out at work all day, and unhelpful by night. Michael's job was in jeopardy, too, and Colleen tended to "brood," as she put it, if left alone.

"I have my seven-plus reading text next week," said Mary. "I can't miss that."

"You know how well you can read," said Praxis. "Does it matter what other people think of you?"

"Yes," replied Mary. She was an orderly child with an untroubled gaze and a sternly practical nature. Sometimes Mary would confound her by hugging her and assuring her that she loved her, with a straightforwardness of which Praxis herself was scarcely capable. Mary meant to be a doctor: she had been determined on it since she was five years old. When Mary was six she asked Willie if she could have a microscope for Christmas. Willie had provided one, albeit second-hand. Mary took more of an interest in his work than did Praxis, and he appreciated it and was happy to show his appreciation. To all practical purposes, Willie and Mary were father and daughter: he a rather clinical and remote father, if concerned and interested; she a dutiful child, and likewise. They seldom touched each other: for some reason Praxis felt nervous when they did. Mary knew something of the circumstances of her birth, and would proudly point to the rubbled bombsite on the esplanade—later to house a ten-storey office block, but in her childhood still uncleared—and say to her friends, "That's where I was born." Her father, Praxis let it be vaguely known, had been an American serviceman briefly married to her mother before being killed in action, and Mary was shrewd enough—as perceptive children can be—not to pursue this particular story in detail. She had a sense of destiny.

"I wonder what I was saved *for!*" she'd ask.

Mary went back to live with Willie, and took her seven-plus reading test, in which of course she excelled. Willie married Carla. Carla looked after Mary, 109 Holden Road, Willie, her job in the canteen, and visited Lucy on Sundays. When Praxis stopped crying, she felt quite sorry for Carla.

In the meantime, Colleen had her baby. It happened, as is the manner of these things, on the same day that Michael, still in hospital, lost his job. He had been too often absent, and too long-faced when present, for comfort. A letter came through the post as Colleen set off for hospital. She had a daughter, with a good deal of reddish curly hair and a stoical face, who reminded Praxis of Colleen when young, a player of hockey, and a weeper merely by night, and not by day and night, as she now was. Colleen's mother came to visit her in hospital and lamented the past, and never once made a helpful contribution to the present, let alone the future. Colleen's father brought an arrangement of flowers by his mistress: wired winter bulbs stuck in green foam moss. Praxis got a job filing in an office, and stayed on in Michael and Colleen's flat, to look after Michael while Colleen was in hospital, for Michael was discharged in the afternoon of the same day on which Colleen was admitted.

Michael and Praxis behaved towards each other with careful, self-conscious and distant civility—those being the days when members of the opposite sex, if left alone together, were expected instantly to fornicate. Both lay awake at night, on different sides of the wall, envisaging the comfort and possibilities of sexual congress with the other, but both, happily, were loyal to Colleen.

Michael went to Australia House and investigated the possibilities of emigrating, and within the month, he, Colleen and the baby were gone, leaving Praxis with a five-year lease on the flat, some furniture it would cost more to move than to replace, a single cold-water tap and her future before her.

On the first Sunday in every month Praxis went to Brighton, to visit Mary, and was made barely welcome by Willie, and rather more welcome by Carla. Praxis would help Carla with the Sunday lunch and chat to Mary. At twelve Willie would emerge from his study—for so he and Carla now referred to it—look at his watch and say: "Well, you'll be down to the Raffles now, I suppose," and Praxis would grit her teeth and smile and say nothing. "Don't you miss it?" he'd ask presently, and Praxis still would say nothing; but there was a look of wounded desperation in his eyes which made her all but forgive him for his disgraceful behaviour. She had, after all, betrayed him sexually, and most dreadfully, and as it turned out, indiscreetly, one of her more distasteful occasional clients being, it transpired, a junior of Willie's at work.

Once, when Carla was out getting coal for the Aga, Willie tried to force her back against the wall, in the corridor, against the door of the old darkroom under the stairs, and though part of her did, insanely enough, miss the rapid coupling which had been part of her life for so long, she pushed him away, for Carla's sake.

"I still love you," he said, insistently. "I still want you."

"You should bring the coal in, not leave it to Carla."

"It's all she's fit for," he said, bitterly. "You should never have left."

"Then make me more welcome when I come here."

"Why should I? You're a tart and a whore. You're mad, like your mother and sister."

But he could not hurt her anymore. When she cried it was because the past had changed and the present had failed her; and she had no hope of the future, not for the loss or love of Willie. Rather, she enjoyed the power she had over him. He had become the one person towards whom she could be liberally unpleasant, without risking the loss of his love.

She had been wrong about Phillip and Willie. It was Phillip who loved what he had, however disagreeable it tasted: it was Willie who loved what was out of reach. Carla, she was gratified to see, was these days dressed in matted brown.

In the afternoon of those once-a-month Sundays she would visit her mother.

"Are you the same one as comes the other days?" asked her mother, slightly puzzled. "She looks smaller than you, or perhaps you've grown." When Praxis murmured an unintelligible answer she seemed satisfied enough.

"See," the sister said, proudly, "how much better she is. I really think one of these days you'll be able to take her home."

Sister had short, straight, dark hair, an almost mannish face, and a scar running round her chin. Flying glass, from the look of it.

On one of her visits Praxis raised the question with her mother of selling Holden Road, more in speculation than anything else, but Lucy's vague eyes instantly focused, with a distressing intensity, and she shook her head violently from side to side and trembled all over her body, so that Praxis had to call Sister, who sedated and soothed her patient kindly.

"What did you say to her?" Sister asked, crossly, when it was done. She had been called from tea to deal with the situation.

"But that's her home," said Sister. "You can't sell her home, over her head. It's all she has.

"After all the struggle she had," said Sister. "Two little girls and no support, and those dreadful solicitors!" Sister seemed to know as much about it as anyone.

"We have little chats, you know," said Sister. "Before bedtime medication, when the morning doses have all but worn off, your mother can be quite talkative."

"We have so many deserted wives in here," said Sister, "it's surprising. Or wives committed by their husbands. It quite puts you off marriage." She laughed gaily.

The world pities you, thought Praxis, for a spinster, and so you pity yourself. All you're fit for, they think, and you think, is to look after others. Since you have no helpless children of your own, you must look after helpless adults. A good woman, they say, pityingly: what a tragedy about the scar. I am a good woman, you persuade yourself, through your grave, lonely nights, preferring to be safe than sorry.

I would rather be sorry a hundred times, thought Praxis, than safe.

Well, I am, aren't I? Very sorry and not at all safe.

"It's better for your mother not to have visitors at all," said Sister sharply, "than visitors that upset her. I never have this trouble with the other girl who comes. Is she a relative too?"

"Carla? She's a relative, of a kind."

"That's the trouble, these days," said Sister. "There's a great deal of vagueness in family relationships, and far too much loose living."

She spoke in general terms, but with too knowing and rebuking a look for Praxis' comfort. Perhaps she had a brother who frequented the Raffles? Praxis left before visiting hour was over: her mother kissed her on both her cheeks, which was unusual, and brought sudden tears to Praxis' eyes.

"Don't fret," said her mother, astonishingly. "You'll be all right."

As she left the hospital grounds, Praxis felt her face set into an expression which was recognizably Hilda's, and had to carefully rearrange its lineaments. To suspect her mother of being perfectly sane, if very cunning, was in itself madness. Sane people did not prefer mental asylums and sedation to the real world.

Praxis went to visit Elaine; she was behind the counter arranging jars of barley sugar and mint humbugs.

"Why did you go off like that, so suddenly?" enquired Elaine. "All the fun went out of it. I hardly ever go down to the Raffles anymore. Douglas got in another girl, but she wasn't a nice type at all. And I got beaten up by some madman and ended up in Brighton General with my ear half bitten off. But it's an ill wind. I'm going steady with one of the young doctors there. I must say," she added, speculatively, "it did all teach you a thing or two. Of the kind you wouldn't read in books."

Praxis supposed that it had. She had not learned the arts of seduction: that required the projection of an erotic fantasy, the suggested offering of something beyond the power of any human being to offer to another; but she had learned the techniques of arousal, and culmination, and rearousal. For what it was worth.

"Well," she said vaguely, "you live and learn." She remembered Elaine as a little girl, her braid of embossed bars almost as long as Hilda's, and here she was, arranging sweets, back where she started.

"I hope it works out with the doctor," she said.

"That elderly man with the soft voice was back looking for you," said Elaine. "I told him you'd gone up to London suddenly and he seemed quite put out."

"Did he go back with you?"

"No. I offered but he didn't seem to want to. I was sorry. He was rather nice. A real gentleman, for a change. Was he a Jew? He had that kind of nose."

"A descendant of King David," said Praxis, "I seem to remember."

"They all have to be something. I wouldn't mind being Jewish. You could go to Israel and fight Arabs and really start something. Build a new country."

"New countries are in your mind," said Praxis.

"They have to be, if you're a woman," said Elaine. "Personally, I'd rather carry a gun," and she went on arranging a tray of penny sweets for the children—bubble gum, raspberry chews, all-day suckers—an ordinary-looking young woman with a plaster on her ear, and a shop to run.

"Now you have really left Willie and done the sensible thing about Mary," said Irma, who was quite helpful now her spare room was not in danger and Praxis had stopped showing signs of tears, "we must start doing something with you."

She took Praxis to the hairdresser and had her hair cut short and dyed blonde, at considerable expense to Praxis, and sold her, at half-price, which Praxis suspected was a great deal more than they were worth, a collection of clothes Irma no longer needed, mostly in bright reds, yellows and greens. Praxis stared at herself in Irma's mirror. She looked rather like a doll: blank and characterless, if pretty. She had a memory of herself, on a beach, as a small child, and of a photograph; but the memory closed in—it was painful. She did not pursue it.

"It's all a matter of presentation," said Irma.

Phillip came home from work and framed Praxis between the square of his two hands.

"Portrait of a transformation," he said.

"I'm not sure about it," said Praxis.

"Neither am I," said Phillip, "but if that's what Irma wants, that's what Irma has."

Irma sighed loudly and left the room. It seemed to Praxis that whenever Phillip walked into a room Irma walked out of it. Phillip had lost his boyish look. Praxis found him slightly formidable. He still smiled sweetly but his smile now hid something, and she did not know what it was. Irma seemed perpetually angry with him, that much she knew: but Phillip seemed not to notice it. Praxis could see that this in itself was singular unkindness. She began to feel easier in his presence, perceiving that Irma was more his victim than he hers.

Praxis applied for a job in a research department of the BBC, and failed to get it, inasmuch as she had no qualifications. She was however offered a job on the reception desk, because she was blonde, pretty, sensible and had an easy manner—a combination of qualities rarely found, or so the Appointments Board said, in the same woman.

She quite enjoyed it. She sat on a stool at a high desk which somebody else dusted and polished. Cups of coffee appeared at regular intervals, and she did not even have to wash the cup. She had nothing to do but make, all day, a series of minor decisions, which gave her no difficulty, but seemed to exhaust and agitate the two other girls who sat alongside her. Ring this person, ring that one, keep this one waiting, let another one through: ignore the bombastic, who were usually unimportant: succour the modest and retiring, who frequently were not: apologize, emphathize, organize. Compared to dealing with 109 Holden Road, Willie, Mary and the Raffles Esplanade Dive, it was nothing. Her fingernails grew long: she painted them: had her dark hair roots seen to frequently, and was made reception desk supervisor.

Well, thought Praxis, it isn't what I meant, but it isn't bad. She went to parties, unescorted, and slept with the occasional guest, or even host, but it came to nothing.

"Of course it comes to nothing," said Irma, irritably. "You shouldn't lead them on."

"I can't be bothered," said Praxis. "I am way, way beyond cuddling on doorsteps."

"I don't know where it will all end," said Irma, "I'm sure. Do be careful of V.D."

Phillip was promoted. One of the elderly twins died of bronchitis and pneumonia—the roof was leaking; Irma either refused to have it mended, or Phillip forgot, Praxis could not be sure which, and Irma certainly claimed the former, and the other twin, Irma hoped, could not long survive. Already he was pining. Then she would be able to have the attic floor converted to a proper nursery wing, and see even less of the two children, by name Victoria and Jason. Or so she said.

Now that Praxis had tales to tell of the great and famous, and ate her sandwiches and drank her shandy in the BBC bar, Irma occasionally asked her to dinner, to sit opposite a spare man.

"You have to be especially nice to this one," said Irma, on the telephone to the reception desk. "He's the product manager on a new soup mix and it's going to be a big account for Phillip. Wear a low dress, for heaven's sake."

"What do you mean by especially nice?"

"You *know*," said Irma. "He's down here in London all by himself, and not even married. I wish I didn't have to live like this; it's all so sordid. I wish Phillip was Nobel Prize material, and not commercial. As it is, I have to do the best I can."

"You don't, you know," said Praxis. "He's only in advertising to keep you in nannies. And it can't help to have you despising him every step of the way."

"You wait till you're married," said Irma, and rang off. She dialled through again, almost immediately, to Praxis' great inconvenience.

"Except I don't think anyone ever is going to marry you. You're much too sharp."

"Irma, I have to go. The director general is in reception and his taxi hasn't turned up."

"Now I'm married," said Irma, "I can be as sharp as I like. It's lovely. I speak the truth; you can't think what a treat it is. But you can't afford to."

"Irma, I'm working."

"What a treat!" said Irma. "I wish I was." And rang off.

Within three months Praxis was married and within four she was pregnant. Married to and pregnant by (there's posh for you, cried Irma, one and the same man and all!) the product manager of the soup mix firm, for whom she had worn, on Irma's instructions, a low-cut dress. His name was Ivor, he was the only son of a county surveyor in the Midlands, had been to grammar school and business school, and was at the age of thirty on the middle rungs of a company ladder, doing well and pleased with himself. He was handsome; his hair short and dark, his brown eyes wide and bright, his mouth shrewd, wide and narrow, and his teeth very regular and very white. He was broad-shouldered, narrow-hipped and well-suited. His shirt was very white, his tie conventionally and carefully knotted, his shoes polished, and his voice quiet and confident. One day, he knew, he would be chairman of the board. He found Phillip and Irma, as he confided to Praxis, bohemian and exciting. He had been pleased by their invitation to dinner. He wore his boldest tie for the occasion. He was nervous of Praxis' cleavage, and kept his eyes firmly on her face for most of the meal. She would see his eyes drift downwards and then jerk upwards again, as if horrified at their own behaviour. He talked to her about capital costs, investment and the wage-price spiral, and seemed astonished when she understood what he was talking about. He told her about marketing policy, of what happened when a new food product was launched: how the product—in his case a noodle soup—would at first contain quality ingredients, while the market established itself: how then the cost—in other words the quality—of the ingredients would be reduced until minimum costs and maximum sales met on the graph he kept in his office.

It was advantageous to advertise, he said, and thus keep sales up, rather than maintain the quality of the product. Minimally. Advertising, he said coyly, with a glance at his host and hostess, and a daring one at Praxis' cleavage, was more fun.

He looked like a tailor's advertisement, Praxis concluded. This was the kind of man she should marry. Kind, good-looking, forward-thinking, conventional and respectable. She did not think that he should marry her, not that he would even think of it. He needed a conventional, well-spoken, well-bred girl, with a Cordon Bleu cookery course behind her, a knack for flower arrangements, and parents to provide her with a formal white wedding and grand reception after a year's engagement.

Mother, meet my fiancé, Ivor. Ivor, this is my mother, Lucy. Ivor, this is my sister, Hilda. Yes, she's very clever. In the administrative grade of the Civil Service. Why is she wearing a fur coat at dinner? It's the static, you see. Now they weave nylon into the carpets, it's everywhere. No, Ivor, don't bring the dog. It might be a bit tricky. There's rat poison down in the corners. And did you know the stars shine by day?

Hilda was going through a bad patch. Praxis met her for lunch occasionally. Her smile was a grimace. Or so Praxis thought. No one else noticed.

Hypatia, not Hilda. If you'd only go back, thought Praxis, find the real enemies, face demon truths, outstare them, you might feel better. My sister Hypatia.

Ivor took Praxis home to her flat in his M.G. sports car. He drove fast and well; she felt secure, exciting and excited, secure in his admiration.

He asked if he could come in for coffee and was hardly able to believe his luck when she said of course.

Praxis had made the flat as bright, comfortable and conventional as she could: buying from Irma, at exorbitant prices, the bits and pieces she was throwing out as she went up in the world.

"You're a bohemian, too," he said, glancing round. She made coffee: they kissed on the sofa. Daring, he parted her lips with his tongue and thrust it into her mouth. His tongue was cool, sweet and unaccustomed.

"That was a French kiss," he said.

"I know."

"I think you are a very daring young lady," said Ivor. "How do you know I'm to be trusted?"

His simplicity amazed her. She realized how easy it would be to manipulate his innocence: to offer herself as a forbidden delicacy, forever further and further out of reach, until he interpreted a frustrated appetite as love. She saw that he would believe whatever she told him about herself: that if she were more like Irma and less like herself she would construct an edifice of sweet smiles, reticences and false assertions around herself which he would happily mistake for her. She also knew that she could not do it, even if the prize was respectability, matrimony and motherhood—which it surely was. It would affront his dignity and her own. He was a good, kind, clever—if obtuse—man. She owed him honesty.

"I know you're to be trusted," she said. "The trouble is, I'm not." She pulled away from him and stood up.

"Don't," he said. "I'm sorry. I was carried away. You've no idea what you make me feel. How could you know? Men are such brutes. It won't happen again. Trust me."

She stared, open-mouthed. He mistook incredulity for moral censure.

"You shouldn't have asked me in for coffee," he said, like a small boy searching for excuses.

"Why not? You asked."

"I'm supposed to ask and you're supposed to refuse."

"Is it all games, then?"

"So far as I can see," he said desperately. "It's all games."

"I was never any good at games," said Praxis. She briskly took off her clothes. He seemed shaken and appalled.

"This is me," said Praxis, naked and herself. "Come to bed." He followed, fumbling with tie, and buttons, embarrassed, folding his clothes, putting shoes neatly together, delaying, turning out the light. He was disappointed. He had wanted romance, and all she would offer was sex.

"Leave the light on," she said, at which he looked even more wretched.

I will never see him again, thought Praxis, after this. And just as well: this Ivor, this advertisement for a clean-cut decent man is far more than I deserve, and certainly more than I want.

She named the parts of his body in medical and colloquial terms: as she did her own. She described to him coldly what he was doing to her, and she to him, in both technical and obscene terms. He seemed hardly to hear.

"You're so beautiful," he said. "It's so beautiful. I had no idea."

He seemed transfigured: she, to herself, merely animal.

When dawn was breaking he said, "I love you."

"That's ridiculous," she said. "This is not how people love each other."

"Yes it is," he said, determined. "Other people can do what they like. You can do what you like; I love you. Nothing's going to change that."

When dawn had fully broken, he said, "I have to get back to my flat now, and bath, and change. I don't want to leave you but I have to be at the office at eight forty-five. A lot of people depend on me. Will you have lunch with me?"

"All right," she said, baffled. He kissed her tenderly; it seemed difficult for him to withdraw his flesh from hers. He rang her during the morning, at her busiest time. Flowers arrived. The other girls envied her.

"How do you do it?" they asked. Praxis replied, with truth, that she had no idea.

Irma rang.

"What have you done to him?" she asked. "Or what didn't you do, for a change? He's been on the phone to me for half an hour and all he talked about was you. He didn't even mention dinner, after all the trouble I went to. Some men take too much for granted." Praxis didn't want to talk about it. There were four taxis available at reception, and five M.P.'s to be got home, all claiming priority of need, and she wished to give her attention to the problems this discrepancy posed. She was short of sleep and annoyed with herself.

"Ivor is rather boring," said Irma doubtfully. And then, more hopefully, "But you might change all that, Praxis."

Ivor collected Praxis from the BBC Centre at lunchtime. The envy of the other girls flattered her. He took her to an Italian restaurant at Shepherds Bush, watched the food disappear between her lips as if even that was blessed and held her hand under the table. She fell asleep over the crème chantilly. He did not mind. He met her out of work, escorted her home, looked away while she changed out of her work clothes, sat reverently by her while she slept. He did not seem to feel the need for sleep, himself.

"I can do with three hours a night," he said proudly, "like Napoleon."

When she woke, he ran his well-manicured hand over her breast, tentatively.

"You are everything I adore," he said. "You are an angel come down from heaven."

She could not believe him. She guided his hand down to her crotch, to dispose of his gentlemanliness.

He told her the story of his life, and informed her as to his principles. He believed in hard work, honesty, industry and firm but kindly discipline for children. He feared that since the war and the coming of the welfare state British workmen had turned into work-shy scroungers, who these days had to be bribed, by means of piecework, to work at all. Then they complain, he said bitterly, "because the belts move too fast. They don't seem to realize that their wages depend on our productivity. Where do they think the money comes from?"

He did not want to hear Praxis' life story, or Praxis' principles. He wanted her life to have begun the day he met her, and his opinions to be hers. She could see it might be restful. It was how most women lived.

"I'm a figment of your imagination," she complained, yawning, on the second evening of their acquaintance.

"Come here," he whispered, "I'll show you how much of a figment you are." He had learned his love-making vocabulary, she feared, from romantic novelettes: perhaps his mother had left them lying around when he was a lad. It never ceased to embarrass her.

Presently she felt she loved him. Her flesh called to his: learned to miss him: tingled with expectation at his approach. And he was always there. Before work, at lunchtime, after work. In the middle of the night. If work called him away, there were flowers and phone calls. Sometimes she wondered if the love she felt was a mental haziness induced by lack of sleep.

"Has he taken you to meet his mother?" asked Irma, and shook her head dubiously when Praxis said he had not. Sometimes Praxis wanted to be Ivor's wife; sometimes she did not.

"Anyway," said Irma, "it doesn't matter to us. Phillip's changed firms. He's making boring documentaries now, of a sociological nature: he's lost all interest in soup mixes. I think I preferred the old days. At least people laughed at the dinner table, and noticed what they ate. These days they just drone on, and use their soup spoons to eat the sweet."

Praxis was offered a job in the Research Department at the BBC. She accepted. Ivor was angry. It meant a small drop in her salary but good prospects of promotion.

"It's a waste of time," he said. "You'll have to work far too hard for not nearly enough money. They're only taking advantage of you. You must turn it down. You're happy where you are."

Ivor liked to have Praxis where he could see her; where he was accustomed to seeing her, flanked by girls on either side. In the Research Department she worked for men, amongst men.

"I'll do as I choose," said Praxis. "We're not married." He did not see her for two days. She cried in bed, and wondered where Colleen was, and whether she still cried at night, or whether she was happy water-skiing on Bondi Beach, amongst the sharks, and whether the Pacific winds had blown Michael's asthma clean away.

Ivor came back, as if nothing had happened; except that he slapped her once or twice during their love-making. Praxis had won, in a way: but she knew from the occasional sad expression on his face that he had considered asking her to marry him, and decided against it. She was not a suitable wife for a rising business executive. Suitable wives were virgins, or all but virgins; they did not have complex pasts and unhappy childhoods, best not spoken about; they did not take jobs which went against a prospective husband's grain.

Praxis liked her new job. She would do all the work required on this programme or that, quickly and easily, and her immediate superior would get his name on the screen. She did not mind. She thought that to have her name there would only upset Ivor the more.

Willie, on one of the few occasions that Praxis now visited Brighton—for Ivor liked to take her out to lunch on Saturdays, and to the pictures on Sunday—remarked that Praxis had become rather boring. She hoped that it was jealousy speaking, but feared that he was right. Certainly, when she was with Willie and Carla, she seemed to have nothing to say. She had lost her dread of Holden Road, but at the same time it no longer seemed like home. She had no rights in it. The whole house sparkled and gleamed: Carla sang as she serviced it. The garden was neat: the drive was weed-free. Willie's bike was oiled. The front door opened easily. All this Carla accomplished, as well as working in Willie's canteen. Willie bought Carla fabric in the markets, and she made it up into clothes for Mary, which lay properly ironed and neatly folded in the drawers. In Praxis' day Mary's drawers had been a jumble of mostly unwearable garments, shrunk vests and single socks.

Mary herself seemed friendly, but distant. She was Willie and Carla's child now, and so far removed—with her long, lean legs, and pleasant serious face—from the baby Praxis had rescued and tended that Praxis herself could scarcely make the connection.

"She doesn't have to wear school uniform," complained Carla. "But she insists. She says not to wear it makes it obvious which girls are poor and which aren't. I tell her her clothes are as good as anyone's, if not better, and she says, 'Exactly, that's the point.' I ask her if I've been wasting my time and my eyesight making her nice clothes, and she says, 'How can it, if it gives you pleasure?' I say, 'It's more work for me, keeping your school uniform in order,' and she says, 'I'll do it then,' and so she does. She doesn't seem like a child at all. She thinks before she speaks. Well, she's the only one I've got. Willie says we can't afford children of our own. I have to keep on working."

"You could always have an accident," observed Praxis, "and simply find yourself pregnant," at which Carla looked quite shocked.

Praxis missed the early train home, and took the opportunity of walking alone on the dark, pebbly beach, under the starry sky. Betelgeuse twinkled redly, and had nothing to say. There was no magic in the night. Some grace had been withdrawn from her.

"How long?" she asked, but there was no reply. And if the dark clouds which gathered over the horizon, bright-edged by the concealed moon, had any shape or significance for good or bad, it was not apparent, now, to Praxis.

Praxis presently decided that she did not love Ivor. She began to feel he blocked her vision: that there was something else to be seen if only he would get out of the way. He had to go to Stuttgart for two weeks, for his firm, to study German methods of soup production. She found she did not miss him at all; that the minute he was out of sight he was out of mind. One day before he was due to return she went to a party, had too much to drink and was taken home by a cameraman whose wife was in hospital having a baby.

She was in bed with him when Ivor returned. There was a fight: she herself felt in no particular danger, and the cameraman seemed in a way grateful for his bloody nose and cut eye, as if this was the penance he owed his wife. He left swearing and grasping his stomach where Ivor had kicked him. Ivor knelt by Praxis' bed and wept.

"I can do as I like," Praxis said. "We're not married."

This time she did not see him for a week, and did not cry once, but there was a flatness and emptiness in her life which frightened her. Then she had a letter from him, asking her to marry him, and she said yes, she would.

They were married presently in a registrar's office. Praxis invited only a few friends from work; Ivor invited a handful of grey-suited, crop-haired, suave business colleagues, and his parents, who were a good deal less grand than Praxis had supposed. She was glad that Hilda was not there, to detect the vulgarity behind the careful curls and floury face powder of Ivor's mother. Hilda was away on her annual holiday, touring the Greek islands. Irma and Phillip came. Praxis thought Phillip looked rather sad. When he kissed her in congratulation he held her rather hard and long, and Praxis knew she should not have married Ivor.

Praxis gave up her job: Ivor did not want a working wife: there was, in any case, plenty to do in the new house, some fifteen miles outside London on one of the new executive estates. The houses were neat and compact: built above and around garages, open plan and with large expanses of glass window. When trees and hedges had time to grow, as the estate agent explained, there would be more privacy: in the meantime there were lace curtains, and the knowledge that the other householders were of good business and social standing.

Praxis became pregnant almost at once. Ivor destroyed her rubber contraceptive on their wedding night, and that night and thereafter made love to her in the missionary position.

"That's marriage," he said, "isn't that better?" And Praxis, bemused, agreed that it was.

Praxis was, at last, respectable.

"Praxis," said Irma, much, much later, "you got so boring. You've no idea."

"Nothing ever happened," Praxis explained herself.

"Of course things happened," said Irma. "Things happen on an executive estate as much as anywhere else. The tragedies and triumphs of the aspiring middle classes, not to mention births, deaths, cancer and road accidents. No, your personality went into eclipse for five years. You should try and work out why."

"Perhaps I was married to the wrong man?"

"The entire female population is more or less married to the wrong man," remarked Irma, "but we are not for that reason a race of zombies."

"Then it was the children."

"More like it," said Irma, darkly.

"I had the wrong children?"

"Oh no," said Irma, "they had the wrong mother."

It was not that the children depressed her, so much as that they drained her of animation. They made demands on her, and offered no reward. She could take no pleasure in them, nor they in her: that, they reserved for their father. Robert and Claire. They would leap up as he came through the door, and hold his hands, and chatter; and Ivor's face would light up with the wonder of it all. They were more Ivor's children than her own: she felt they recognized her instinctively as the impostor she was, regarding her with Ivor's cool, brown eyes, but without the adoration that softened Ivor's gaze. A smooth-skinned, smooth-haired pigeon pair, born tidy and careful as their mother was born untidy and careless. She seldom had to tell them to put away their toys: they guarded them too well, in the politest possible way, from each other and from their mother's casual dustpan and brush. Her pregnancies were peaceful. Pregnant, she glowed and felt content. Ivor treated her with extra reverence, bringing her roses and delicacies, helping her over steps, supervising her diet. First Robert, then, a year later, Claire, were born quietly and decently, without causing their mother too much physical pain. But after the birth she would stare and stare at the little mewling creatures and feel only disappointment, not elation. She had hoped for so much, and so little had emerged. She preferred being pregnant to having babies.

"A love child," Ivor said, on each occasion, holding Praxis' hand and making her uncomfortable in both mind and body.

"A love child," she agreed, biting back the information that a love child means one born out of wedlock, not one born out of love.

She was protective towards the children, but they seemed to

need little protection. They were seldom ill, seldom naughty, never surprising. Robert and Claire, little strangers, foreign fruits of her womb. They got on well together. Too well, Praxis sometimes thought. If they had disliked each other, they might have liked their mother more. She had felt closer to Mary.

On summer evenings, Praxis could look out through the graceful folds of the net curtains which looped her wide drawing-room windows, and see the red dwarf Betelgeuse. But the affairs of heaven and the affairs of earth made no contact here. Little boxes of dwelling places covered the hill: stars, like ornaments devised by the estate agent, sprinkled the sky at night, and that was that. No one on the hill went to heaven or hell, Praxis thought. All dwelled in limbo, and were extinguished on their death.

Ivor was an attentive husband. Other estate wives envied her. He caught the same train every morning, and the same train back. He remembered wedding anniversaries, and birthdays. Sometimes problems at work made him bad-tempered at home, but he was efficient, straightforward, and unafraid, and more interested in what he was doing than in the status that accrued to doing it, and the problems did not remain unresolved for long. The events in Ivor's life—as Praxis came to realize—the sense of forward travelling, of progress and personal achievement, came from his work: at home with his family, he rested.

"You see the children growing strong and healthy," said Ivor. "Doesn't that give you a sense of achievement?"

"Of course," said Praxis. But it didn't. It seemed to her that if you let a growing thing alone, it would grow strong and healthy by itself, and no credit to her, or anyone.

Presently Ivor was obliged to spend less time at home. He travelled by air about the world: sometimes he would be away for days, sometimes for weeks. He developed a far-away, absent look in his eye: his teeth seemed whiter, his chin more cleanly shaved than ever: his shirts crisper. There was little to do in hotel rooms, after all, but pay attention to matters of grooming. He was promoted to group product manager, then junior management director—the youngest in the firm's history. The firm was taken over by an international company: Ivor went forward: it was his colleagues who were made redundant. No one begrudged him his success. He deserved it.

"Behind every great man," he'd say, laughing, his hand round

Praxis at the firm's annual ladies' night, "is the love of a good woman."

When he was away he would telephone frequently, every day if possible. The company paid for the calls, aware—for research had told them—of the value to an executive of a happy domestic life. Praxis wondered whether the calls were to check her fidelity, or to confirm his own, or merely because he wanted to talk to her, and decided that it was the latter.

Praxis now lived in the largest house on the estate. It had an attic floor, and a detached garage. Fewer wives dropped in to morning coffee: more came, on invitation, to tea. Praxis gave dinner parties: the same rotation of guests in ceaseless gavotte, in endless competition: company talk, recipe talk. Nothing was said that Praxis could not have said herself. Robert and Claire went to the little day preparatory school around the corner. They left the house in the morning clean, shiny and tranquil: and returned in the evening clean, shiny and tranquil. Sometimes, when she collected them, she found it hard to distinguish them from the other children; or herself, for that matter, from the other mothers. She learned to drive. Ivor bought her a car.

Praxis had a brief, secret affair with the estate agent who arranged the purchase of their various houses, but had lost the taste for sexual adventure, and it came to nothing, when she discovered she was one of many of his mistresses. She made artifacts, by the hundred, out of cardboard egg boxes for Robert and Claire's benefit, in the hope of developing their artistic talents. Robert and Claire cellotaped with finesse and painted cautiously.

"You do make a mess, Mummy," complained Claire.

"Fingerpainting is for babies," said Robert. They cleaned their brushes before putting them away.

"See," said Praxis. "It's a castle with a submarine moored in the moat."

"How would a submarine get into a castle moat? You are silly, Mummy."

She felt that her friends—the young wives of other rising executives—were both envious and critical. Their eyes would wander from hers as she talked, shifting and darting as they inspected the state of Praxis' home, not Praxis' soul, and finding it wanting. The scent of furniture polish and pine disinfectant wafted out from the open front doors: stand and sniff as you might outside Praxis' front door, you would never detect the pleasant aromas of conscientious housewifery.

"You're too sensitive," said Irma. "They weren't passing judgment: they were merely interested, and why not? You probably got it all wrong anyway. They hated your taste: loved your dusting."

Praxis developed backache and headaches: she sat with the other wives in the doctor's surgery, and was prescribed tranquillizers, which unlike the others she did not take. The doctor took to visiting her at home, and talking about his unhappy marriage, and she was flattered to have been thus selected, out of all the other women in the estate. Staring at herself in the mirror, at her doll's face, stiff doll's body, curly blonde doll's hair, she wondered what experience or wisdom it was that could possibly shine through the casing that Ivor had selected for her.

She did not blame Ivor: she knew that she had done it to herself: had preferred to live as a figment of Ivor's imagination, rather than put up with the confusion of being herself. The doctor laid his head upon the table and wept. She stroked his head with her doll's hand. They kissed.

"I'd better not come again," he said.

"No," said Praxis. "You'd better not."

Little doll voice, piping gently in the wilds!

Praxis asked Hilda to Christmas dinner one year, but Hilda, fortunately, could not come. She was going, she wrote, to spend Christmas with Willie, Carla and Mary. The names sounded unfamiliar to Praxis. She found it hard to believe that they still lived and breathed. She had long since ceased visiting Lucy. She had sprung to life ready-made on the day she met Ivor: it was what he wanted and what suited her.

Sometimes Ivor's mother would visit. Praxis would pour her long, gin-based drinks from the wheeled cocktail cabinet, and they would talk about Ivor's father, who had one lung and seldom left home, and Ivor's childhood in the small Northern town where they lived. Ivor was his parents' only child: their pride and achievement. Ivor's father was not, as Ivor had implied, the county surveyor, but a clerk invalided out of the surveyor's office. Praxis did not condemn Ivor for this mild deception: on the contrary, it made her feel soft and protective towards him. He lied for his father's sake, as much as for his own.

"You are happy?" Ivor would question her, relentlessly, bringing home gifts of duty-free scent, Swiss chocolates, Malaysian orchids.

"Perfectly happy." But the question puzzled her. How would she know if she were happy? She felt neither happiness nor unhappiness. She waited, for what she had no idea: she endured, why she could not tell.

Sometimes, when Ivor was away and the children were asleep and television palled, she would walk out under the stars, and remember her vision on Brighton Beach: a distant, ridiculous fancy, best forgotten. Loving husband, happy children, lovely home.

A letter came from Sister in Brighton to say that Lucy, thanks to new medication now available, could safely be cared for at home.

"I wish we could have her here," said Ivor. "But it wouldn't do. Think of the children."

"She doesn't rant or rave or break things," said Praxis. "She just sits and stares."

"We must think of the children," repeated Ivor, and Praxis was relieved to think of the children and tell herself that it was not practical to have Lucy installed in the spare room. What was Lucy, in any case, to the creature who had sprung ready-made from Ivor's imagination? She had no mother, no father: blonde curls, doll's eyes, doll's mind.

Praxis decided, with what glimmers of her old self remained, that Hilda should be given the opportunity of looking after Lucy, and wrote to her to that effect. She, Praxis, had husband and children to look after: Hilda, the implication was, had neither: had a career instead, which any right-minded woman would give up in order to look after an ill mother.

Hilda responded by sending an unsigned letter to Ivor, asking him if he knew what everyone else knew: that his wife had been a professional whore before he married her, working from the Raffles Esplanade Dive in Brighton?

It was unfortunate in a way that the letter arrived on one of the rare mornings when Ivor was at home, yet fortunate in another. Had Praxis been alone, she might well have steamed open the letter, read it and destroyed it, and gone on in her half-life for years more.

As it was, she watched Ivor's face grow pale with shock and

distress, and recognized that some kind of reality, however dreadful, was at last beginning to surface, and that she should be grateful.

"I don't understand," said Ivor. "Why should anyone send this?"

"It's Hilda," said Praxis. "I know her writing. She's mad. I told you she was mad. Anything to do with mother sets her off. She'll do anything to damage me."

"Your own sister?" He didn't believe her. In Ivor's world family offered mutual support; they were not natural destroyers of each other.

"If you'd let me have mother here," said Praxis, tears in her eyes, pain in her heart. But Ivor just stared at her as if he saw things in her that he had never seen before.

"You didn't cry before," he remarked. "You were only too glad not to have her. I knew that. I just provide the excuses. That's my function in your life. What's going on?" As if he had discovered the accountant cooking the company's books.

He left to catch his plane during the morning. He did not ask her to deny or confirm the contents of the letter, but neither did he kiss her before he left. When he returned, two weeks later, he was critical of Praxis; he found fault with the cooking, the house, the way she behaved with the children; was rude to her in front of them: insisted that she make love to him in the ways she had done when they first met. She felt degraded by it now. His eyes followed her wherever she went. She was almost afraid of him.

"What's the matter?" she kept asking. "What's the matter with you?"

"Nothing's the matter, what should be the matter?" he'd reply, setting out for his usual train, leaving her bruised, slightly shocked and sore, pecking her goodbye as if everything was normal.

"If it's my past," she volunteered, eventually, but he did not want to hear.

"You've never let me talk about it," she protested.

"I don't want to know," he said. "Let's leave it at that. You have a mad sister and a mad mother. Isn't that enough?" She could see that, in this particular world, it was more than enough. There were too many different worlds, it seemed to Praxis, with very little cross-reference from one to the other: each with its different ways and standards, its different framework of normality. Women crossed the barriers easily: were required to by marriage, moving house, changing status: men seldom crossed them, went on as they began, their lives under their own control.

"Perhaps I should get a job," she persisted. "When you're away I've nothing to do. When you're back all you do is find fault."

"There's plenty to do in the house," said Ivor. "If you did it, I wouldn't find fault."

He worried over the remark, as these days he worried over everything she said or did, chewing and tasting and discarding, only to scoop it up again, poor denatured thing, and start all over again.

"Why should you want to work?

"What sort of work?

"You mean I keep you short of money?

"You find the children boring?

"You want to work with men, I suppose? Find someone new?"

The wives on the estate did not work. Husbands, for the most part, had fought their way out of a world in which a working wife was a sign of family disaster, disgrace and humiliation. They reckoned their achievement in life by the leisure and comfort they could offer their families: the picture windows, the carpets, the air, the light, the safety.

"Forget it," said Praxis. "Just forget it."

But he didn't.

"You could always sell yourself," he said, starting up one night out of the insomnia which now plagued him. "Is that what you mean by work?"

"Let me tell you about it," she begged.

But he wouldn't have it. He had moulded her to his liking, but been mistaken in the clay he used. His whole life was like that, he felt. You achieved what you wanted, or rather what your parents wanted for you, and it tasted, not delicious, but sour and rancid on the tongue. He blamed the postwar Socialist government for a great many of his own and his company's misfortunes. When Praxis asked him what misfortunes, he merely shrugged.

Ah, she was to blame for so much: her past like a hideous millstone round his neck. The doctor prescribed sleeping tablets.

"But I think he's gone mad," she said. Ivor too! The doctor laughed.

"Shortage of sleep can make many a man seem mad," he said. "I should know."

He wouldn't take the pills. He suspected her motives in obtaining them. Presently he began to feel better. They returned, almost, to normal.

"What's the worst thing you ever did?" said Diana to Praxis one day. Diana was the nearest to a friend Praxis had on the estate. Her husband, Steve, had a drinking problem. Diana's pretty, child-like face was occasionally bruised, which she would explain away with one excuse or another: a lamp-post, a fall, a sudden braking in the car.

"The worst thing I ever did," volunteered Diana, "was pour two bottles of my husband's whiskey down the sink. What about you?"

"I slept with my father," said Praxis, the words leaping to her lips out of nowhere, as if they'd been lurking all this time, waiting to be said, preventing the formation of other words, other thoughts, other conclusions: keeping her in limbo, year after year.

"You're joking," said Diana.

"Yes, I was joking," said Praxis.

When she looked in the mirror that evening, she thought she looked older: more like some other person, less like a doll.

Ivor was away. She stretched out in bed alone that night, and allowed herself to remember; the pleasure, humiliation and shame. She had barely seen her mother since: had avoided the thought of her. Was her sense of sin, of having stolen something illicit, and of having damaged her mother by it, first by intent, then by actuality, the waves of shock and horror travelling backwards and forwards in time, before the event and after it, damaging, wounding, and traumatizing?

These hands, she thought, turning on the bedside light, looking at them. What they've done, where they've been! And it seemed to her that, as she looked, they lost their white powerlessness, the well-creamed pretty look they'd had of late, and became stronger, older, more her own.

In the morning her hands looked much as usual, sleep had smoothed over the gritty surface of her night-thoughts. Life went on as usual. Nearly but not quite.

A new couple moved into the estate: always a welcome event. New tastes, new faces, new clothes, new gossip. Rory was chief sales manager of a big paint firm, and had almost, but not quite, the same status as Ivor. He had the most powerful car on the estate, and spoke about his public school. Carol spoke genteelly,

dressed quietly, had once run a hairdressing salon, had a larger
refrigerator than anyone else, looked after her two children well
and held hands with Rory in public. They seemed a safe and respectable pair. They lived next door to Steve and Diana.

Rumours, however, soon began to fly. Rory and Steve, it was
said, had contrived together to exchange beds for the night, first
making their wives so insensible with drink that they would not
notice the difference. Carol had, and hadn't cared: Steve's wife,
Diana, hadn't, which everyone reckoned was just as well. Now
everyone knew except Diana. Rory and Carol were swingers: they
played strip poker: they wife-swapped: they took nude photographs.
Rory and Carol gave a party: everyone was invited: quite a few
went. Carol drank a whole half-bottle of whiskey, stripped to the
waist, and then altogether, and danced on a table. Rory, in the
meantime, while the men gaped at Carol, openly kissed and fon-
dled one of their wives after another. The lights went out. Unlikely
couples paired off. Presently sanity returned: someone turned on
the lights, couples sorted themselves out, and all returned home,
abashed, to quiet homes and sleeping children. In the morning
Rory and Carol were seen to kiss goodbye, affectionately. He even
brought home some bookshelves in the car that evening, and could
be heard hammering that night. A good and handy husband, walking evidence that sexual experimentation did not instantly bring
about the collapse of a community.

Everything seemed safe: only rather more interesting than before. Praxis had not been to the party: she seldom went out when
Ivor was away. He would question her too closely, afterwards, to
make it worth her while.

For a time a kind of sexual madness seemed to possess the estate.

Rory and Carol gave key parties. At the beginning of the evening
the men would throw their front-door keys into a central pool. At
the end of the evening the men would pick out a key, any key, and
escort home the wife whose own front-door key matched.

Carol rang Praxis.

"Do come," she said. "You and Ivor, do come! It's the third time
I've asked. I'm beginning to think you're avoiding us on purpose.
Of course, we all know you're so *grand*—"

Ivor said, to Praxis' astonishment, that they were going to accept
the invitation. She didn't want to go.

"I would have thought it was your style," said Ivor.

"It's not," said Praxis. "Why do you want to go?"

"Because I'm bored," said Ivor. "I'm as bored with you as you are with me."

It was a bad day, after all, and she had thought it was a good one. He had pruned the roses in the garden. She cried, which always affected Ivor.

"I do love you," he said, as if puzzled by himself. "None of this means I don't love you."

"What, like Rory loves Carol?"

That annoyed him. He didn't relent. They went to Rory and Carol's party.

"I love you," she said, before they went. When he was angry and she was miserable, she felt that it was true.

"I don't believe you," he said.

He read the children bedtime stories before they set out for the party. As he grew older he became even more handsome: his face less innocent, more stern. The other wives envied her. She was considered an intellectual, because she read the *Guardian*, and not the *Telegraph*, like everyone else: she was never quite totally accepted, she knew that.

They were, she thought, rather surprised to see her there that evening.

Ivor had insisted that she wear black underwear and suspender belt and stockings, instead of the tights that had lately become fashionable.

"It's what you used to wear," he said. "I prefer it." He had been irritable about her make-up, and made her draw crude black lines around her eyes and put heavy, sticky lipstick on her lips. It was no different from what the other wives wore, but unusual for Praxis. She had been to the hairdresser. It was crowded that day, and everyone had been excitable and rather bad-tempered. She stared at herself in the mirror: she was a doll again, to be pushed here and prodded there. All the same, she was not as young as she had been.

"I think I am a figment of your imagination," she said, as she had said before, a long time ago.

"Yes you are," was all he said, this time. "I am tired of having you in it."

She understood that he was trying to rid himself of something. Well, so had she, once, and succeeded.

"Since Hilda's letter," she said, "everything has changed."

"You imagine it," he said. "A mad letter from a mad woman."

Praxis drank too much at the party: she watched Ivor dance with, kiss and fondle in turn Beryl, Sandra, Sue and Raquelle. He watched to see if she were watching, and she obliged him by doing so. She looked and felt pained, which was as he wanted it to be. Ivor, usually so attentive, so discreet. She did not join the dancing, a kind of musical chairs, in which, whenever the music stopped, the women peeled off a further garment.

"Don't be such a wet blanket," said Carol, spitefully, as she passed, bare breasts pressed up against Ivor's suit. When the keys were given out, Ivor got Carol, and Rory got Praxis. Praxis had understood that she and Ivor were the prizes of the evening; the last to succumb to the communal madness.

She walked home with Rory. The moon shone. Nature was calm.

She could almost believe she was walking next to Ivor. She pretended that she was.

Dutifully, in bed, she performed her seductive tricks, summoning them out of memory. Had she once been, nightly, so generous?

"I knew you'd be hot stuff," Rory said, entranced. She shuddered. She really could not spend her life amongst these people.

Rory went and Ivor returned in the early hours, and lay still and sleepless beside her. Presently she heard him crying. I seem to have heard that for so long, she thought, from so many people. Women in relation to men: men to women. There must be something wrong. She slept and so did he.

In the morning Ivor was as he had been before the advent of Hilda's letter; he was kind, affectionate and uncritical. He made no mention of the previous night, and nor did she. They went to no more of Rory and Carol's parties; Rory came round once or twice to issue special invitations but soon gave up. Praxis recognized Carol's voice on the phone, asking for Ivor, but Ivor was brusque and unfriendly with her and the calls stopped.

The parties, to all accounts, grew yet wilder.

Someone procured a vibrator from the States, which was raffled, and publicly used. Things began to go wrong. A wife killed herself with an overdose: someone started divorce proceedings: one of Diana's children ran away: Rory was convicted of a drunken driving charge: the parties stopped as suddenly as they had begun. Madness ebbed and drained away. Rory and Carol moved to another estate. Roses were pruned; grass seed put down: everything was back to normal.

Except that Praxis knew she would not, could not, stay with Ivor: and that if she ruined his life, and destroyed his happiness, as he would surely claim she had—and Robert's and Claire's too—then it was just too bad.

21

You end up as you deserve. In old age you must put up with the face, the friends, the health and the children you have earned.

I used to say that when I was young. Now I am old, I don't recant. I am alone, deserted, ill, and my children don't speak to me. Very well. It's no more than I deserve.

I hobbled to the cooker this morning and made a cup of tea. The milk had gone sour, but I put in a slice of lemon, which looked old and dry on the outside, but was surprisingly juicy when cut. A shaft of sunlight found its way into the room. I saw the dust motes dance: I was elated by the wonder of creation, and my spirit seemed to join the motes and jig about for a time in cheerful worship. When the fit had passed I hobbled to the mirror, and recognized myself. Not Pattie the prisoner, but Praxis. My hair was thicker than I thought: my eyes were less rheumy. I saw that I might have a future, and I was afraid. Do I really have to put up with being Praxis?

Children!

When I was young it was rare for a mother to leave her children. It was considered an unspeakable thing to do—an unnatural crime. Bad enough not to love a husband—but for the misfortune of not loving a child, the penalties were, and still are, cruel.

I left my two children. I think perhaps if you want to leave a child, if you cannot love it, you should leave it before the look in your eye shrivels its life and its hopes. I would watch the expression in Robert's and Claire's eyes, fearing to see there a look of Lucy or Hilda: and I would see Ivor looking at me with a love I was incompetent to return. I did not really feel good enough or whole enough to have children and trust them to exist in the simplicity of their perfectly healthy, perfectly ordinary natures. I was a good mother: years, years I spent: first for Mary, then for the next two, keeping the structures of life steady around them, allowing them to grow: encouraging Willie's fondness for Mary: loosening Ivor's fear that children, simply left alone, will grow rampant and wild, like a well-bred rose reverting to briar; thorny; demonstrating to him time and time again that it is not discipline that is needed, but understanding, and an awareness that the world to a child is a dangerous place; and that fear of the dark needs not a slap and the lights out, but fear of the dark shared and acknowledged. By the time I left, Ivor would sing the children to sleep and think nothing of it.

He was better at it than I was.

After I left, his knowing look disappeared: the innocent one returned. He looked happier.

Perhaps it wasn't that I could not love the children: but that I loved myself too much. Certainly the neighbours thought so. Diana, Sandra, Beryl; wanton lot! Their children took to vandalism, motorbikes and drugs. Mine didn't: no thanks to me, they'd say. Thank Ivor. Good, decent Ivor.

Ivor, with Carol dancing up against his suit, bare-breasted. Good, decent Ivor. Have it your own way.

So I don't recant. If I am alone now, I deserve it. I set my Mary free by imprisoning myself: that is sufficient reward for the likes of me.

The cat's come back.

22

PRAXIS WAITED, a small immobile figure in an arid landscape: she waited for something to happen. The children had new shoes: Ivor had a new suit. She did not prune the roses, although Ivor kept reminding her to do so. Praxis knew she would not be there to watch them bloom.

Something happened. Irma telephoned. Praxis had not heard her friend's voice for two years, but recognized it at once. The tones were a little more commanding than before, as if Irma had stood once too often at a Harrod's counter; she was a little more petulant, a little less charming: but the pent-up, bitter, invigorating energy remained.

"I only ring when I want something," said Irma. "I want something now. I'm having a bloody baby. They're taking me into hospital early. Nanny's walked out, naturally: they only take these jobs for the pleasure of walking out at the worst possible moment—it's an art in itself. Will you come and look after things for me?"

"What about my own children?"

"Leave them with neighbours. I'm sure you've got neighbours," said Irma, as if the having of neighbours was a plebeian activity.

"Don't you have any friends, Irma?" enquired Praxis. There was a pause.

"That sounds more like the old Praxis," remarked Irma, hopeful. "No, I don't seem to have any friends, come to think of it."

Praxis left the children with Beryl next door, packed the few things she might possibly ever want to see again, and left home. Ivor was away for the week. He would telephone in the evening, and no one would answer. She could envisage his agitation, jealousy and distress, and it did not affect her. He would eventually, she imagined, ring Beryl and discover that the children, at least, were still his.

Irma sat on her stairs, monstrously pregnant. A taxi waited outside: she made no move to get into it, or put the driver out of his misery.

"The fare's ticking up," said Praxis, anxiously. "It's already over a pound. I looked at the clock."

"You have such a suburban mentality, Praxis," complained Irma. "Let him wait. It's Phillip's money anyway. Why should I care?" Her face was puffy and pink: her ankles swollen: her feet pushed ruthlessly into too-tight, bright pink, very high-heeled shoes. When she stood, she clearly found it difficult to balance. Her blood pressure was high. She was going to hospital to await the birth, due in a week.

The crescent had been gentrified since Praxis last saw it. Most of the houses were freshly painted, had window boxes on the sills and carriage-lamps in the porches. Victoria and Jason, indifferent to their mother's fate, played outside in the gutter.

"They don't care about anything," complained Irma. "I don't expect them to get upset about me, but they might at least have the grace to mind about Nanny leaving. I'm sure I do."

"Is it safe for them to be in the street?"

"I don't know," said Irma. "I left that kind of thing to Nanny. It's all Volvos and Rollses anyway, these days. A good class of car to die by. I am glad I'm not going to be around when you are, Praxis. Nag and fuss all the time. I can tell the sort of mother you are.

"At least I can trust you with Phillip," said Irma, wandering the house in search of a hair-dryer. "You're not his type.

"Phillip only likes important people," said Irma, "and let's face it, Praxis, you're not important.

"Of course Phillip's a voyeur," said Irma. "He sublimates with cameras, that's all.

"Now don't start cooking him little meals or anything," said Irma. "He'll only expect them when I get back." Now she had lost her tweezers.

"At least, I don't have any real worry about other women," said Irma. "Phillip's so undersexed. He's impotent. Did you know that?"

The taxi driver rang the doorbell.

"I don't know what he's worrying about," said Irma. "He's getting paid, isn't he? Do I look really awful?"

"I don't think it matters much," said Praxis, "at the moment."

"Yes it does," said Irma, "since Phillip's going to be filming the birth.

"Not to mention a full camera crew," said Irma. "With any luck they'll faint and slip their discs falling.

"You notice I have to get myself to the hospital," observed Irma. "When it's real life, and not images of life, he simply can't concentrate."

Irma by now seemed to have almost everything she needed packed into a dusty bag made of Persian carpeting. It seemed an old and shabby bag to Praxis, who had yet to acquire a liking for the artifacts of the past. There wasn't, so far as Praxis could see, a single new, dark, shiny, polishable surface in the house. Everything was old.

"I hate Phillip," said Irma, calmly, "and I hate this house. The stairs have enlarged my calf muscles. I hate all men, all children and the institution of marriage, and most of all I hate this baby. We won't go into that now. If I get excited my blood pressure goes up. Now look after everything, Praxis. Keep your hands off Phillip. And thank you very much," Irma added as an afterthought, remembering some childhood lesson.

Irma tottered on her high heels to the taxi, and engaged in conversation with the driver, who now seemed reluctant to have her as a fare, but presently drove off. Irma then remembered to turn and wave to her children, but they did not seem to see her. After the taxi had gone, however, they came inside, went up to their attic bedroom and sat close together on a bed watching television, eating fruit and sweets from the bowl, letting peel and wrappers lie where they fell. They were clearly not as tidy or biddable as Robert and Claire; they heard only what they wanted to hear, and did only what they wanted to do; but Praxis could see that Irma's children would do very well to sop up the overflow of her maternal affection, which still drained from her, like mother's milk in the presence of a weaned baby. It would get better with time. She knew it would.

Praxis sat beside them on the bed, and presently took a tissue to wipe Jason's running nose for him, but he turned his face sharply away, and said, in an irritable voice, "Don't *do* that. I like it running." Then he put out his tongue to investigate the pale trickle.

It would never have done on the estate. Praxis laughed. She felt she was home.

Phillip, returning that evening, seemed taken aback to find his wife gone and Praxis in her place. He had worked till past nine in the cutting room, and was tired. His hair was receding. He no longer had the look of a young man.

"She was meant to be going in tomorrow," said Phillip. "I was taking her in. It was all arranged. I was editing today. I couldn't leave it, how could I? She knew that perfectly well."

The children were in their nightclothes, in bed, still watching television, still munching through fruit and sweets. The nanny had left, apparently, in dispute about the propriety of the late hours they kept, their diet and their viewing habits. They were well-built, healthy children, on an altogether larger scale than Robert and Claire, with pale, mobile, fleshy faces, brown hair falling into their eyes, and each with a version of Phillip's full, curved mouth. Praxis' heart beat faster, observing him in them. They should have been her children. She knew it.

She was embarrassed, as ever, to be alone with Phillip. He wandered about the kitchen, finding bread and cheese. He opened a bottle of wine as if it was an everyday occurrence. On the estate wine was for birthdays and celebrations. He ate and drank standing up. Praxis, from long years of laying tables, first for Willie, then for Ivor, and setting before the home-coming male a plate of soup, followed by meat and two vegetables, and like as not a pudding too, was disconcerted. She sat on a stool and watched. Phillip pushed bread and cheese towards Praxis. The bread was a long French loaf: the cheese soft and rolled in black peppercorns. On the estate, bread was a sandwich loaf and the cheese cheddar or processed.

"Irma has good taste in cheese," he said, sadly. "Did she go off happily?"

"Not particularly."

"I don't make her happy," he said.

"People make themselves happy," said Praxis, disloyally.

"Are you happy?" he enquired.

"No."

"I should have married you," said Phillip.

An awkward silence fell.

"I know," said Praxis, eventually.

"On the other hand," said Phillip presently, "perhaps no one should marry anyone. There's so much to be done in the world, and the people best equipped to do it keep getting bogged down in these terrible partnerships."

"Where I've been living," said Praxis, "the question of partnership didn't arise. The women did what they were told, and no one tried to change anything."

"You speak about it in the past tense," said Phillip.

"That's right," said Praxis.

"Irma trusts you with me," observed Praxis.

"She's mad," said Phillip.

"I rather thought she was," said Praxis.

"I knew I should have married you," said Phillip, in the middle of the night. "You're so warm. You must be wonderful in the winter. Willie always said you were so warm."

"Willie had a very cool body. I might just have been a matter of comparison."

"I don't think so," said Phillip. "We should have got married. Saved ourselves all this trouble."

"I did always find you difficult to talk to," said Praxis. "I don't know why."

"I do. It was all so embarrassing," said Phillip, "from the very beginning. If I'd won the toss with Willie how different things would have been. Fancy tossing for a girlfriend."

"I thought you did win it."

"No. I lost."

"I feel bad about being in Irma's bed," said Praxis.

"Don't start all that," said Phillip. "Once you started that you'd never stop."

"I'm sorry," said Praxis. "Sheer hypocrisy, anyway."

"Quite," said Phillip. "In any case, she's never in it. Irma mostly sleeps in the spare bed. She uses sex as a controlling weapon."

"She seems to get pregnant, all the same."

"You know how it is," said Phillip, rolling on top of Praxis. She had never quite realized, before, that sexual satisfaction could result from the fulfilled desire for a whole person; she had seen it as the occasional outcome of local physical stimulation. She supposed that this was love. Whatever it was, it suffused her. She did not doubt that it was right to pursue it.

In the morning the hospital rang. Irma was in labour. Phillip rounded up the film crew.

"I wish she wouldn't," said Phillip. "I find it distasteful. It would be easier to film someone not one's wife: but as Irma says, it is two hundred pounds for her and five hundred for me. We do have to have the basement done out after the old lady: the film is sponsored by the Natural Childbirth Trust: the clouds of ignorance and fear shrouding the mysteries of birth have to be swept away, and so on, and so on: but frankly I wish she wouldn't."

"Ivor wouldn't do it for a thousand pounds."

"Go back to Ivor, then." He was angry.

"Never."

"Well," said Phillip, "there is no progress without sacrifice." And off he went to the hospital. It was a false alarm. The crew had to be paid for the day's nonwork.

"We'll never bring this film in on budget," said Phillip. "That's Irma's plan, no doubt."

"She can hardly help it," said Praxis, but wasn't so sure.

Victoria and Jason discovered Phillip and Praxis in bed.

"What are you doing in my mummy's bed?" asked Victoria.

"Keeping it warm," said Praxis.

"I'll tell Mummy," said Victoria crossly. "She doesn't allow anyone in her bed, not even me." Victoria was six. Jason got into bed beside Praxis.

"You're warmer than Mummy," he said.

"What are we going to do?" asked Phillip, helplessly.

"Perhaps you're lost without a story-line," suggested Praxis.

"I make documentaries, not features," he said. "There is no story-line. That's part of the trouble. I'm not doing what I want, or living as I want."

Irma was in labour again. The crew reassembled, set up their lights and got some decent footage on contractions, major and minor. After that they hung about, waiting. Twelve hours later,

the doctor turned the crew out, and Irma had an emergency Caesarean. It was a boy. She would be in hospital another ten days.

"The Trust is right," said Phillip. "There's far too much interfer-
ence in natural processes. If they'd left her alone she'd have had
the baby naturally, and we would have got our film. They should
never have given her that first injection. It slowed things up. I'm
not worrying for myself: we can get another volunteer easily
enough: it's just that Irma's going to be so furious at having to do
without her moment of filmic glory; not to mention her two
hundred pounds. I think she wants to be a film star. That's her
whole trouble. She doesn't understand why I can't make her one."

Praxis would have remonstrated and said "poor Irma" but feared,
rightly, that sympathy would appear hypocritical.

Phillip was agitated. He strode up and down the kitchen, when
he should have been visiting Irma.

Praxis had polished the copper saucepans, cleaned behind the
taps and scoured the butcher's block. Other women's kitchens are
easy to transform.

"I want to make my own films," he said, "not other people's."

"Then why don't you?"

"Because I have to keep all this going." He gestured to include
house, children, absent wife, missing nanny, present mistress,
rooms, insults, sulks, self-indulgences and disciplines and the
whole paraphernalia of middle-class life. "It takes money."

During the day Praxis had opened up the basement door so that
the council workmen would clear away the belongings of the deceased sitting tenant. The men threw everything into the street,
and from the street into the waiting dust-cart, where a churning
iron screw compacted everything. Chairs, sofa, bed, all sodden
with urine. Christmas cards; wedding photographs; old letters and
postcards, greasy and dusty; the newspaper she had kept as extra
blankets for cold nights; cracked crockery and tinny cutlery;
mousetraps; mouldy sliced bread. So much for a life. The workmen
finished, nodded, declined a tip and went away to the next address
on their list.

Even empty, the place stank. Praxis hated Irma.

"I'd have done better," thought Praxis. "I wouldn't have let her
rot." But would she?

"You mean you let them throw everything out?" Phillip was worried. "Irma was going to go through the old postcards. There might have been something interesting. People collect them, these days, you know.

"I'm sorry I missed it," he said later. "There might have been some interesting footage."

Another day passed, of love, tranquillity and reciprocated passion. Victoria and Jason had some friends to tea. The noise and mess were exhausting and exhaustive. Their parents, collecting them, looking coldly at Praxis. Her roots were growing out: she feared she looked hollow-eyed and sexually satiated. And poor Irma, she could hear them thinking, having such a terrible time in hospital!

Did anyone really think poor Irma, wondered Praxis? Or did they think, as she did, selfish, bad-tempered bitch of an Irma, better out of the way!

"You ought to go and visit Irma," said Praxis.

"It's not my child she's having," said Phillip, becoming, at least for a while, impotent. "Unless I conceived it in my sleep. You've no idea what life's been like."

"Irma's been going to poetry readings," he said. "She was having an affair with a hairy poet." Phillip was smooth-skinned, almost hairless.

"I find that rather hard to believe," said Praxis.

"He's an American," said Phillip. "A Pulitzer Prize winner," and Praxis had less trouble believing it.

"I can't let you go," said Phillip.

"Then don't," said Praxis.

"Irma told me she hated you," said Praxis.

"Irma said you were a voyeur, and used cameras as a sublimation," said Praxis.

"Irma said you were impotent and a social climber," said Praxis. And so on. Praxis was fighting for her life, her happiness and Irma's children.

"I love you," said Praxis. Not only did she say it, but it was true.

"I can't be married to a madwoman for the rest of my life," said Phillip.

"Then don't be," said Praxis.

Praxis telephoned Ivor, who wept. She marvelled at the telephone system. Every house in the country, physically linked by bits of wire to each other: the vibrations of distress passing so easily over distances.

"Where are you?" he wept. "What are you doing? Where have you been? Who are you with? Never come home! I'll kill you if you do, bitch, whore, slut. When are you coming back? The children need you. The cat is ill."

She put the telephone down and rang again later. He was calmer. No, she wasn't coming back. What about the house, he begged; their life together; the children?

"What about Carol?" enquired Praxis, unkindly. "What about you not letting my mother live with us?"

"You only asked once," he replied, astounded.

He was angry. He said he'd divorce her. She said she'd counter-petition. He said she wasn't fit to look after the children, anyway. She said she knew that. He said she was mad, monstrous, unnatural. She did not deny it. He said the children lay awake at night, crying: he could not go to work because of them: what was he to do? She said she did not know. He could always get Carol to help out, she supposed.

"It's all very vulgar," said Phillip, calmly, taking the receiver from her and putting it back in its cradle. Praxis cried for her children. Phillip said they'd soon get settled and she would see them again.

"How?"

"We'll manage," he said. "And your mother, too."

"But it will all be just the same for you, only more," she wept. "More people, more households, more obligations." What Praxis really meant was that she wanted just the two of them. Phillip and Praxis. They wrote to Irma to tell her so.

Irma was too weak and too stunned to say anything at all: or at any rate neither Praxis nor Phillip was there to hear it. Irma went straight from hospital, with the baby, to stay with cousins in the country.

"It isn't my baby," said Phillip. "This proves it. She must be feeling very guilty, or she wouldn't take it so quietly."

The Pulitzer Prize winner went to visit Irma in the country, and Praxis felt better about everything. The neighbours fell silent as she passed, all the same, and the shopkeepers looked at her with hostility. Praxis hoped that she just imagined it, that people were not really so prejudiced and unreasonable. She could not see that she had done Irma any great harm. Irma hated Phillip, her children and the house. She had said so.

Irma, in any case, suffered some internal complications and went back into hospital for three whole months. The cousins looked after the baby for her and called twice weekly to collect Victoria and Jason for the day. There could be no doubt that the cousins—he wearing a tweed cap, and she in horsey headscarf—regarded Praxis coldly, and positively gobbled at Phillip. Praxis and Phillip thought that quite amusing, except it was disconcerting to imagine how Irma had misrepresented the situation.

It was as if Praxis were blinkered: her focus limited to what was in front of her: everything else blurred, or black; she was unable to register the implications of what she had brought about, what she had done. She was dizzy with desire by day, weak with satiation by night.

Sometimes she lay awake grieving for Robert and Claire, but not often, not for long.

Victoria and Jason came back from their days with the cousins wild and noisy. Children were not allowed to visit in their mother's ward. Jason started to wet the bed. Stoically, daily, Praxis stripped the bed and washed the sheets. She thought Irma ought to be grateful. When she needed money she asked Phillip for it. He handed over banknotes blithely, in wodges, without counting first or asking Praxis to account for what she did with it. Praxis had kept careful budgeting books for Ivor.

Within weeks Phillip was sitting down to an evening meal, each one an extravaganza, of the choicest cuts of meat, the rarest vegetables, any error in cooking remedied by the addition of brandy or cream, or both.

"A real woman," said Phillip, gratefully. They sat together on the same side of the table, to be the closer, the better to be able to lean into each other.

One day when Phillip was away filming, and Victoria and Jason were off with the funny cousins, Praxis went to Brighton, to visit Willie and Carla.

The house on Holden Road seemed smaller, less set apart: it was just another house in a long, long road, rather old-fashioned and inconvenient, but no longer dark with nightmare. Willie and Carla seemed a mildly eccentric couple; small-town. Willie was no longer powerful; Carla was no longer a trump card pulled out of Willie's pack. Rather, she was a slight, tired, put-upon young woman with an unhealthy pallor and hollow eyes, and the manner of a servant. She scurried about in an apron, with damp cloths and steaming dishes, sulky, reminding Praxis of Judith, long ago. And Willie, moving sometimes above-stairs, sometimes below-stairs, unsure of his status, was a version of Henry the photographer, cut down to size. Praxis had the feeling that her life had lapsed out of colour and into black and white: as if she too were now some part of Phillip's imagination. What she saw lacked solidity, as if Phillip were making an eternal square with his two hands and framing her through them, able at will to cut to the next square, to edit and delete.

I'm going mad, thought Praxis.

Willie counted on his fingers.

"Well done, Pattie," he said. "That's seven people's lives ruined, at a minimum. Your two wretched children, your unbelievable Ivor; the impossible Irma and her two trendy brats. And, of course, Phillip."

"I love Phillip. He loves me."

"What kind of an excuse is that? He's just another bloody idiot, like the rest of us. No, not seven, eight. There's Irma's new baby."

"It isn't Phillip's."

"Who says so?"

"Phillip."

Willie laughed. Praxis wept. Carla heaved obvious sighs. Mary came home from playing tennis. She was in adolescence now: long-legged, long-haired, smooth-skinned.

"Auntie Pattie!" she cried, pleased. "Auntie Pattie! We haven't seen you for ever so long." She went to Brighton High School. There was no longer a school uniform, and the girls no longer jangled their achievements on metal bars over plump bosoms.

Sunday dinner was served.

Praxis talked brightly to Mary about chemistry exams and medical school, but the image was now clear in her mind, worming its way finally through the barriers put up to bar its way. Robert and

Claire, crying in bed. Crowding in, on the periphery of her consciousness, a cluster of others waiting for admission. Irma, her friend. Ivor, her husband. Jason, wetting the bed. Victoria, confused and pale. The cold cousins, the censorious neighbours, the shopkeepers.

"However, no doubt we all have a right to be happy," observed Willie.

"I'm not so sure," said Praxis, and went to the bathroom and brought up roast beef, Yorkshire pudding, roast potatoes, frozen peas, plum duff, custard and all.

She went back to London without visiting her mother. She rang Ivor, who refused to let her see the children. She was in no state to do so. Later, perhaps, he said. Had she seen a psychiatrist?

Phillip formed his two hands into a square and observed her grief.

"Irma never cried," he said.

"I'm sorry."

"Not at all," he said. "It waters the roots of my being." He consoled her. She loved him: though she could see that he was flawed. Seeing this, a kind of sanity returned.

Hilda came to visit Praxis.

"You're making a mess of your life," she complained. "You had everything a woman could want: loving husband, lovely children, nice little home, and you've thrown it all away."

Praxis regarded Hilda with more coldness and less fear than usual. Hilda was dressed in black and white, and had her hair piled high in a kind of lacquered beehive on top of her head. She wore a string of pearls, and moved briskly and competently.

"It's not what *you* want from life," observed Praxis.

"If you have a career," said Hilda, "you have to make sacrifices. We were always different, in any case. You were always more, well, physical, than me, and it's caused everyone a great deal of trouble."

"Has it?"

"Poor Willie," said Hilda. "He was prepared to stand by you. But that wasn't good enough for you either. And you realize it was because of you and that filthy incident with another girl when you were barely into your teens that mother had to spend the rest of her life in hospital?"

Praxis cried. She couldn't help it. Hilda relented somewhat, but not much.

"I suppose it's not your fault, Praxis. You have a kind of innate vulgarity of spirit. You must have inherited it from poor Mother's husband."

"He wasn't her husband."

"You see?" Hilda felt her point was proved. "You scrub around in the underside of life: and look at you! You look common, like a servant."

Indeed, with the roots of her yellow hair dark, and her sore eyes, red from weeping, and the cold in her nose which always accompanied any change in the manner of her living, Praxis did not look her best. Phillip did not seem to mind. He found it restful, he said, after Irma's lacquered perfection: and the slip-slop of Praxis' slovenly slippers preferable to the brisk and dangerous clatter of Irma's stiletto heels. They lay with their arms around each other in bed, Praxis snuffling and sighing, Phillip peacefully sleeping.

"Hilda," said Praxis. "I might be living with Ivor if someone hadn't sent him an anonymous letter telling him I'd been a whore before I married him."

Hilda looked blank.

"But no one would believe a disgusting thing like that," Hilda said, in all sincerity.

"You really hate me," said Praxis. "Ever since the beginning you've hated me."

"That's childish," said Hilda. "You're a mature woman in your thirties and you talk like a six-year-old. It would have been better for everyone if you'd never been born, but that's not your fault."

Praxis cried, mildly. Hilda observed her sister, coldly.

"What's the matter?" She sounded curious, rather than concerned.

"I've got no one," said Praxis. "I've never had anyone. Mother, father, you—nobody ever wanted me."

"Good heavens," said Hilda. "You were everyone's darling. You've had man after man ever since I could remember. You even have children. All you seem able to do is throw them away. Look at you! You're hysterical. I expect you're premenstrual. I'm afraid women are hopelessly handicapped by their biological natures."

Hilda was doing what she could at the ministry to block a scheme to introduce women trainee executives into the nationalized industries.

Hilda gathered her neat, spinsterish things together and went back to run the country. Praxis was crying when Phillip returned.

"She stands me on my head," Praxis complained, "and shakes every bit of my brain about until it's addled. She's always done it. She always will."

Praxis went to visit Irma; her hands trembled: she had difficulty in breathing: she stood on the wrong platform and missed the train, but she got there. Phillip hadn't wanted her to go, so she went without his knowledge. He would find out, but she would have to put up with that. The cousins lived in a Sussex farmhouse. He was a stockbroker and she bred horses. Irma was the worldly member of the family.

Praxis was coldly received: dogs barked and leapt up at her, and were barely restrained. She was not offered refreshment but taken round to where Irma lay stretched out in a deckchair, wearing dark glasses. The baby slept in a cot beside her.

"I'm sorry," said Praxis. "I think I've been mad. I'll move out at once."

"Don't bother," said Irma. "I've got cancer. I really don't want Phillip filming my death throes."

("Of course she hasn't got cancer," said Phillip, savagely. "She's been threatening me with cancer for as long as I can remember. She'll use anything. Nothing's sacred.")

"No," said Irma to Praxis, "you stay and be nanny, and wipe Phillip's nose for him while he plays make-believe. That house is really terribly hard work. And nothing changes except you have another child, or the ones you've got grow older, or some different boring people come to a dinner party you've got to wash up after.

"I tell you," said Irma, "unless you wake up in the morning wanting to be alive, there's no point in any of it. And waking up next to Phillip, I just want to be dead."

("The trouble with Irma," said Phillip, "is that she's an acute depressive. Can you imagine what it's been like, living with a depressive all these years? What it's been like for the children? What it's going to be like for the wretched Pulitzer baby? She ought to have been sterilized.")

"All the same," said Irma, "one would always rather leave than be left. He'll do the same to you, one day. Just watch out for his sense of timing, that's all. It's murderous. He nearly killed me. You nearly killed me, Praxis. I didn't trust him, but I trusted you. Didn't you have any sense of *me*, at all?"

"No," said Praxis. "Not when it came to it."

"When we were girls," said Irma, "it was all fair in love, I seem to remember. A date with a man always took priority over a date with a girl. But now there's property and children and whole lives at stake, Praxis. Are people speaking to you?"

"No."

"Good," said Irma. She didn't seem to have much strength. She began to cry.

"I thought you were my friend," said Irma. "I really did."

"I love him," said Praxis, "and you don't. I could make him happy."

Irma looked quite astounded, an expression Praxis had never before seen on her face. Irma took Praxis' hand and laid it against her own cheek.

"Well," she said. "Love!"

Praxis cleaned Irma's home, looked after Irma's children, slept with Irma's husband. She was overwhelmed by the notion that someone as malicious as Irma could bear so little malice: and surprised by the knowledge that Irma's feeling for her ran so much deeper than her own for Irma.

Presently Irma regained her health and strength, and ceased to be so forgiving.

Writs flew: from Irma, and from Ivor. Damages were claimed. Phillip was away making a film about poverty in the Third World, and came back, to his indignation, with some obscure and debilitating tropical virus. Praxis dealt with the solicitors.

Eventually Phillip was divorced by Irma; Praxis was divorced by Ivor. Phillip had custody of Victoria and Jason, a state of affairs which Irma did not contest. Ivor had custody of Robert and Claire: a state of affairs which Praxis wanted to contest but did not, under threat from Ivor that he would bring up the subject of the Raffles Esplanade Dive and her moral fitness to bring up children. She was, however, granted liberal access to them.

Phillip was required to buy Irma a flat and provide her with

maintenance, and was thus further weighed down by practical obligations. He began to count the notes in the wads he handed over
for housekeeping. Praxis would have to go out to work.

"I suppose it's all been worth it," said Praxis, on their wedding
night.

"Of course it has been," said Phillip. "I'd love to get some hand-
held cameras into the Registrar's Office. Those faces!"

He always kept his eyes open when they made love. Praxis, in
these days of love and modesty, rather wished he would not. When
the very soul left the body and flew to join in a cosmic ecstasy, the
details of the flesh seemed irrelevant. But not apparently to Phillip.
He had her enclosed by the square made by his two hands.

He was working for the BBC now: not on the staff, but free-
lance. His hair was thinning. He played startlingly rough games
with Victoria and Jason in the little garden: hurling garden stakes
like javelins: narrowly missing neighbours' cats and children. Victoria and Jason were surprised at, and slightly superior to, these
outbursts of boisterousness, but joined in, obligingly. Robert and
Claire, when they came for the weekends, were nervous and
frightened, and would not join in. Robert played with Lego, and
Claire stroked Irma's white cat. Praxis felt her children did not
really enjoy their time with her, in a house where meals came at
irregular hours, no one washed their hands before eating, or particularly said please and thank you. They stared at her wonder-
ingly, with Ivor's brown eyes, and she felt that she had little to
offer them. But they slept soundly at night and did not cry. She
would listen at their doors to make sure. Victoria and Jason put up
with their presence but found them boring. Phillip was happy to
have his empire spread.

Praxis' roots grew out. Phillip found her a job in an advertising
agency.

"I thought you despised advertising," said Praxis.

"I don't see what else a bright and totally untrained person can
do," said Phillip, "except be a school dinner lady."

"You didn't exactly get me the job," Praxis murmured, later. "I
had to do any number of tests." She worked in the Copy Department, writing pamphlets for the Electricity Board.

"They would never have given you the tests," said Philip, "if it
hadn't been for me."

Whether he was demanding credit or blame, Praxis could not be sure.

"Women are so fundamentally immoral," Phillip would complain, admiringly enough, at dinner parties. "They go after what they want, red in tooth and claw. Whether it's babies, or a man, or sex, or promotion, they let nothing stand in their way. They're barbarians."

That was in the days when men were prepared to generalize about women, and women would not argue, but would simper and be flattered by the attention paid.

It was difficult for Praxis to get to see her mother. There were four children at the weekends—since Irma seldom took her pair—the house to run, her job to do, the food to buy, the meals to serve, the clothes to keep washed, ironed and put away and so on. Phillip did not want her to engage a cleaner, let alone house an *au pair*.

"It's nicer without outsiders," he said, with truth. "Don't worry about standards. Let's just live."

Just living, all the same, was exhausting. And he had become accustomed to three-course meals in the evening, complete with cream and brandy.

"Why don't you have your mother here," asked Phillip, "if you worry about her?"

"Because I'd have to give up my job," said Praxis, shortly. She had begun to speak shortly, she felt, rather too often; with such breath as she had left while passing from one task to the next. "And your income is so erratic we have to depend on mine."

If she left the bills to be paid by Phillip, the services would be cut off, and debt collectors would ring the bell, so she paid them herself. It didn't matter.

"Don't worry about money," said Phillip. "That would be very boring and rather lower middle class."

She was happier than she ever had been. Or if not happy—it now seemed to her that actual, overflowing happiness was a function of extreme youth, and since she had missed it then, she was not likely to encounter it now: and love was a good deal, but not everything—if not happy, she was at least living an appropriate life, amongst people who did not look at her curiously but understood what she was saying, and responded to it.

She was promoted: she wrote headlines now, and not just body copy, and the small print. She found the work easy. She had an assistant and a little room with a carpet and pot plants on the window sill. She honed and fined sentences down to fill the brief and fit the space available. A daily, day-long crossword puzzle, with people clapping as she fitted the last clue.

"God made her a woman," she wrote blissfully. "Love made her a mother—with a little help from electricity!"

She found decisions about what to have for dinner more difficult than decisions regarding campaigns, typefaces, artwork and so on. Wrangles with the children upset her more than differences with art directors. She would sit at her desk reading recipe books, planning the evening's menu. Meals at home became more and more elaborate: Phillip came to expect them. He would bring home friends from the film world, and they expected them, too. She did not invite home anyone she met and liked in the advertising world. Phillip found them shallow and meretricious.

She remembered what Irma had said, departing, monstrous.

"Don't start serving him proper meals; he'll only come to expect them."

Too late.

She went to meetings. People listened seriously to what she had to say. Colleagues struggled to avoid blame: Praxis acknowledged her shortcomings impatiently, in order to get on with the work in hand, and home in good time to clean the stairs and get the dustbins out for the next morning. She gained a reputation for efficiency.

Phillip, when he wasn't working, sat at home and played records, prepared camera scripts, and worked towards a feature film.

"A house must be a background to one's life," he'd say. "Not a source of work and effort." But he'd complain when it was untidy. He didn't like to see Praxis busy about the house either.

"Sit down," he'd say. "Slow down. What does it matter? I've asked people for supper tomorrow. Shall we have *osso bucco?*"

To get *osso bucco* meant a journey into Soho in her lunch hour. She would accomplish it. Now that she had a reputation as a cook, she would not easily let it go.

"Women's highest calling," she wrote, "keeps a woman busy! Here's how electricity helps a working mother keep calm, keep cool, and the children kissing her goodnight." And so on. She was a real discovery in the agency world. Other agencies tried to poach her. She stayed loyal and got another rise. She was agreeably thin. Clothes looked good on her.

News came from the estate. Diana's husband had been killed in a car crash, on his way back from a night-club. His secretary was killed with him. His way back where? people asked. Diana was left with two children. Ivor married her within the month. Love or common sense? Did it matter? Robert and Claire came less often: when they did, Robert was dressed like a little man, in suit, collar and tie: Claire wore a blouse, pleated skirt, white ankle socks and red button shoes.

Victoria and Jason, in dirty jeans and sweaters, declined to play with them. Robert played with Lego and yawned: Claire stroked Irma's cat and missed Diana's older daughter, her best friend. Irma left her Justin, now just walking, with Praxis, and went off to America for three months.

"But I'm working," said Praxis.

"According to your advertisements," observed Irma, "mothers shouldn't go out to work."

She had changed her style. She wore sneakers, jeans and no make-up. Her hair was short and fell naturally. She looked more intelligent and less petulant. She had been sterilized.

"Now I can't have a baby," she said, "I feel like a person, not a cipher."

Praxis was shocked. Praxis was on the pill—as yet unrefined, massive doses of oestrogen and progestin mixed, causing acute depression, blood clots, oedoema, infertility and, in extreme cases, death. Doctors, for the most part, denied these side-effects vigorously, while refraining from prescribing it for their wives. Apart from severe midcycle pains, Praxis showed few ill effects. But her daily pill still seemed a daily denial of her femininity, and her femininity her most valuable attribute.

"Here's how electricity helps you keep feminine, and well and truly loved!" she wrote.

"The electric way to start the day!" That was one for men. Sweaty and muscly under the hot shower: soapy under open armpits.

Men had public armpits: women's, though more troublesome, were considered private.

"I can't take Justin," pleaded Praxis, "I really can't. He's lovely; but he's not even at school, and I can get temporary help in if ever Victoria and Jason are ill, and they don't seem to mind, but I do; I feel guilty, and that I'm neglecting them; so far I've been lucky, because when they're ill Phillip hasn't been working, and at least he's at home, but I don't like to ask him—"

"You must be mad," said Irma, enigmatically. And then: "Well, you wanted them. You got them. You wanted Phillip. You've got him, too."

"I don't think Phillip will want Justin."

"Why not? He's his child, after all."

"I thought he wasn't his child. He was some poet's child. That was the whole point."

For the second time Praxis saw Irma look astounded.

"Good God," said Irma, and left Justin with Praxis.

Justin was accustomed to being left here and there. Phillip took him on his knee calmly enough, said "The more the merrier," and handed him to Praxis when his nappies needed changing. Justin was not, as they said in the nursery world, "potty-trained," and she had difficulty finding him a nursery which would take him all day. When she did, it was some three miles and a bus ride away: Phillip needed the car: he was working with one of the BBC's major documentary units now, and large sums and many people's jobs were usually dependent upon his prompt arrival here and his even temper there.

People said how happy he looked. They had many friends. The husbands greatly admired Praxis. She seemed to have all the qualities needed in a wife. An excellent cook, a good earner, a lively conversationalist and a loving mother; a scarlet past and a virtuous present; she was a somewhat messy housekeeper, however, all agreed. She washed the dishes but seldom actually put them away. She paid the bills but never filed the receipts.

Praxis' blood pressure rose. She had to take a month off work, which was fortunate, since it coincided with, first, Justin's, then Jason's, then Victoria's, and then Robert's catching measles. Diana wrote crossly to say she should have been warned about the measles: she would not have let Robert come over had she known. As it was, half the estate were now down with the disease and it was, by implication, Praxis' fault. No, Claire wouldn't be coming over that weekend. She missed her friends when she came, and she loved to potter about the kitchen with Diana, in any case, icing chocolate cupcakes, and doing all the other things which Praxis somehow failed to do.

Praxis wept all night. She was tired.

"Perhaps we should have a baby," said Phillip.

"I'm just tired," said Praxis. Phillip, all concern, managed to take a holiday. They all went camping, to the Continent. Phillip sat under a Mediterranean palm and read books on film technique. Praxis saw to the family.

Praxis, after a spell in hospital on her return for mysterious stomach pains, developed a kind of second wind. Irma returned from the States, took Justin back, and things went better.

Irma paraded outside the Miss World contest with a banner saying such contests were humiliating to women. She threw a smoke bomb and was arrested. Nobody could understand her attitude, except Phillip.

"She's got so ugly lately," he said. "I expect she's jealous."

Years passed: flew past: where did they go? Jason wore the same size shoes as his father: Victoria borrowed Praxis' clothes, and Praxis was jealous.

"Growing up clean with electricity!" wrote Praxis.

Willie and Carla took Lucy to live with them. She was now a quiet, elderly woman, with few memories. Praxis sent money every month to pay for her support. She assumed that Willie must by now have tens of thousands of pounds saved, and consulted with Hilda as to the possibility of charging him rent, but Hilda would have none of it. Hilda did not contribute to Lucy's keep: nor to the upkeep of the fabric of Holden Road. Praxis did all that, and was happy to do so. It seemed to her that the roots of much of her misery had lain in lack of money. To provide money was so much simpler in the end, than providing love, companionship or understanding. To earn it, so much easier than asking for it.

Praxis grew bolder: she hired a cleaner and had a girl, Elspeth, to come in by day to help with the washing, shopping and so on. Phillip did not seem to mind. She had been foolish, she could see in retrospect, to regard his lightest word as law. If you pushed, Phillip gave. She did not enjoy the discovery. Her love for him did not exactly lessen, but it changed its form.

Colleen wrote from Sydney. She had divorced Michael—the family doctor remarking that he was so clinically depressed he would scarcely notice whether he was divorced or not—and now had a job with the life saving department on Bondi Beach. Praxis had a vision of her, hand in hand with some muscled Australian giant, bronzed and curly-headed, free at last, striding the sandy beaches, while the sharks snapped out to sea, and hoped that it was true. Sleeping such a healthy sleep at night, there would be no time left for crying.

"A woman's satisfactions," wrote Praxis, "are husband, child and home. And a new electric stove is one of her rewards."

Phillip went off to Vietnam to film the fighting and the dreadfulness. He came back in a state of shock and indignation because one of the camera crew had been shot by a stray bullet, and was paralysed.

"I don't understand you," said Praxis. "Did you think it was just a game? Didn't you know the bullets were real?" She shouldn't have said it. It seemed to her that afterwards his love diminished. He began to complain about the standard of her housekeeping.

Jason fell off a ladder, and Phillip was angry because the children were so badly supervised. Jason was concussed and grew worse instead of better. There was internal bleeding. Praxis waited at the hospital all night.

In the early hours Phillip turned up with a hand-held camera and filmed the casualties coming in. He took shots of Praxis' stunned face, too: and even of his son, still lying in the reception bay, wired up with drips, too acutely ill even to be moved.

Irma, summoned from some women's meeting (or, as Phillip described it, "She's gone all dykey, you know"), physically attacked Phillip. There was a scene in Outpatients: Irma screamed, Phillip shouted, Praxis wept, the camera was smashed. Jason, by some miracle, recovered. Afterwards, Phillip was obliging and kind for some time. He even tried to explain himself to Praxis, when they were in bed.

"I don't know what it is," he said. "I can only face real life if there's a camera between it and me. Perhaps I need some kind of treatment."

Phillip's mother had died when he was four. His father was an army officer; he had retired after his wife's death and started a fruit farm. Phillip had been sent to boarding school from an early age.

His father, he had always felt, was fonder of his fruit trees than of Phillip. He was a Methodist: a formal, disciplined and undemonstrative man.

"He never played with me," Phillip would complain. "I don't think I can remember playing as a child. I don't really know how to be spontaneous. I have to work out what I ought to feel, before I feel it."

"You play with your children," said Praxis, comfortingly. "You're spontaneous with them."

"I suppose so," he said, uncomfortably. "I always thought I was. Now I'm not so sure."

He rolled on top of her and the familiar magic reasserted itself.

Presently he felt better, justified. He had been transferred to the BBC's Drama Department. He felt their restrictions against the showing of female nudity were puritanical and absurd. He was irritated by the actresses' refusal to take their clothes off.

"There's nothing to be ashamed of," he kept saying. "A tit's a tit."

The political revolution had come and gone. Phillip had been at the barricades, filming. For a day or two it had seemed as if the world would change. Now they were back with the sexual revolution.

Phillip wanted to intercut telecine of Praxis' bare breasts, seen in the shower, into his latest play, since the leading actress declined to do the shots he needed.

"Yours are very similar," he said, and then clearly felt he had given himself away.

Praxis, shocked into stillness, wanted to ask how he knew, but dared not, for fear of finding out the truth. A good deal of the play had been made on location. The whole cast had gone off together.

She still saw the truth as a demon, bat-winged, hovering over her life.

"Are you showing the men nude?" she asked, absently.

"Who's interested in nude men?" asked Phillip. "Now don't get all coy, Praxis. You never used to be. Your tits won't be filmable forever: make the most of them while you can."

"No," said Praxis. "I won't. They're private."

Phillip felt insulted and betrayed: he rolled away from her at nights to the far edge of the bed. Praxis took to sleeping in the spare room: not because she wanted to, but because his cold and hostile back made her miserable and tearful, and she needed to sleep in order to function, and earn, and keep the household going. Phillip had bought a Maserati. It was exciting to drive in, but expensive to run. He would not talk about money. He found the subject tedious and depressing.

Mary wrote to ask if she could come and stay with Praxis and Phillip, while she did the final year of her medical training at a London hospital. She preferred to live out.

"What do you think?" asked Praxis of Phillip.

He didn't think. He shrugged. Hadn't she enough to do? She always claimed she had too much to do. She must make up her own mind. So long as Victoria and Jason didn't suffer.

Victoria and Jason seldom suffered, Praxis thought. They stayed in their rooms and played records, loudly: or stayed out late and, Praxis greatly feared, smoked pot.

Phillip belonged to a reform group who were trying to legalize the smoking of cannabis.

"No more harmful than alcohol," he'd say, downing whiskey of an evening, while Praxis agitated about what party they were at, or where, and why they were not home; envisaging Jason in the clutches of the police, Victoria driven incurably mad by LSD. She was glad Robert and Claire so seldom put in an appearance. Robert had joined the Army Corps at his grammar school, and Claire had become religious.

In the morning, eyeing her hung-over husband and Victoria and Jason, irritable and alienated at the breakfast table, Praxis suffered and said nothing. She wished Mary to stay: but she did not wish to have her own discomfiture witnessed. She attempted to trim her own nature a little more to suit Phillip's requirements and bring back peace to the household.

She drank a little whiskey, smoked a little pot, did not ask Phillip where he was going or where he had been, bought Jason a leather jacket and Victoria a guitar, and waited up in the evening for no one.

Money's easy, she thought. Nothing else is.

"I'll do the nude shots if you want me to," she finally said, one night in bed, to Phillip's turned back. He seemed surprised.

"I got someone to do them long ago," he said. "The world doesn't stand still and wait for you to get over your sulks." But he turned back towards her, and made love, and she felt that things were back to normal and that she could write to Mary and say, yes, of course, come and stay.

"Did you audition for suitable breasts?" she heard herself ask Phillip, but fortunately he had gone to sleep.

He had, in fact, as Praxis discovered later, and selected those of a girl called Serena out of some thirty available applicants. It was her first part.

Mary came to stay. She did not join in the life of the household: she went early to the hospital, and returned late, and tired, having lived through a day of dramas and decisions, other people's pains, reliefs and tragedies. She was friendly, but cool: a rather severe and unsmiling young woman. She made Praxis feel frivolous.

"So you are," said Phillip. "Zipping about over the surface of things!"

"What about you?" asked Praxis.

"Fiction does more to change the world," said Phillip, "than any amount of fact."

"A working mother," wrote Praxis in her office, in deference to the changing times, "needs extra love and extra electricity."

For once her copy was turned down.

"Too small a part of the market," said the deputy creative director. He took her out to lunch. He was a clever, softly spoken, gentle-eyed man who said he preferred gardening to advertising, but Praxis did not believe him. He liked Praxis, and Praxis liked him. "You haven't studied the research."

"I have," said Praxis. "And it may be small now, but it's growing."

"Then heaven help the nation's children," said the deputy creative director. "We do have some kind of social responsibility, Praxis, and if it is a trend the last thing we should do is encourage it."

"I'm a working mother," said Praxis.

"I know," he said, over his steak *au poivre*. They were both experienced expense account lunchers, and ate melon, steak, and salad and shared a frugal half-bottle of wine. "But are you happy?"

He reminded her of Ivor, sometimes, long ago, far away: married to Diana. Tears stood in her eyes.

"If I'm not happy," she said, "it's not because of what I do, but because of what I am."

Praxis went home and waited for something to happen.

Praxis presently received an invitation from Irma to evening coffee. She was surprised. Irma sometimes called at the house to check that Victoria and Jason were being properly cared for, but had shown no signs of wishing to pursue a friendship. Praxis was gratified, if tired. She was usually tired, these days. Phillip was away, allegedly taping a play. She no longer asked for details of his absences, or believed him if he offered explanations.

Praxis accepted, and went to visit Irma.

23

WHY DOES IT TAKE SO LONG? Why do we stay so stubbornly blind to our own condition, when our eyes are not only open, but frequently wet with grief and bewilderment?

I'll tell you, old woman that I am, without an old man to hold my hand, or call the ambulance. Don't disregard me on that account. Women outlive men: it is how most of us will end: and most of us, I sometimes think, misspend our youths in blind panic on that account. This man or that. Really! Willie, Ivor, Phillip: does it matter, in retrospect? No.

We are betrayed on all sides. Our bodies betray us, leading us to love where our interests do not lie. Our instincts betray us, inducing us to nest-build and procreate—but to follow instinct is not to achieve fulfillment, for we are more than animals. Our idleness betrays us, and our apathy—murmuring, oh, let him decide! Let him pay! Let him go out to work and battle in the terrible world! Our brains betray us, keeping one step, for the sake of convenience, to avoid hurt, behind the male. Our passivity betrays us, whispering in our ears, oh, it isn't worth a fight! He will only lie on the far side of the bed! or be angry and violent! or find someone else more agreeable! We cringe and placate, waiting for the master's smile. It is despicable. We are not even slaves.

We betray each other. We manipulate, through sex: we fight each other for possession of the male—snap, catch, swallow, gone! Where's the next? We prefer the company of men to women. We will quite deliberately make our sisters jealous and wretched. We will have other women's children. And all in the pursuit of our self-esteem, and so as not to end up old and alone.

I tell you, it is not so bad to be old and alone.

Well, no doubt men and women should walk through life hand in hand. There is enough to be done in the world, as Phillip once said, without all this trouble. And it does not take a man to make a woman cry. I think of Colleen, crying through the night: and I think of my all-women prison. It was not a pleasant place to be; yet I imagine the sum of emotion, good and bad, happy and unhappy, was pretty much the same inside as outside. A girl can cry all night because a woman has been unkind: it doesn't take a man to do it.

Outside my window old men and women shuffle by: their chins are whiskery: their slack mouths mutter: they are full of discontent and will die in the same state—I don't believe that life has dealt fairly with them.

It can't, as I used to say (usually wrongly), go on!

24

"DO YOU REALIZE," said Irma to Praxis, "that you are not only a personally misguided woman, but a danger to other women as well?"

"Well, no," replied Praxis, trying not to laugh, "actually I hadn't."

Four women regarded her with speculative and sombre eyes. They seemed to see nothing ridiculous in the situation, and Praxis' smile died. No one said anything. It was a hot evening. Irma, Bess, Raya and Tracey wore jeans and T-shirts, making no attempt to disguise the various unsuitabilities of the bodies beneath. There seemed to Praxis to be a great many brownish, sinewy, sweaty arms in the room: too many rather large, shiny noses, strong jaws, wild heads of hair, intense pairs of eyes, pale lips, and rather dirty sets of toes cramped, stockingless, into sandals. Praxis was wearing high-heeled shoes, black mesh stockings and a red-flowered Ossie Clark dress. Her hair was shorn, dark and neat against her face. She had the sudden feeling that she looked and behaved now as Irma had once done.

"You did say coffee," murmured Praxis into the silence, but Irma did not move. Cuttings of Praxis' advertisements for the Electricity

Board lay on the table before her, scored with red markings and indignant exclamation marks.

Irma's room seemed arranged for a permanent meeting. Hard chairs were placed around the walls. The central table was long and functional. Irma's bed was pushed against the wall: narrow, hard and used for sleeping not for sex. Praxis wondered what Irma could do with all the money that Phillip sent her, monthly. Or rather which Praxis now sent, for Phillip had no money to spare. The sources of his income, gradually but inexorably, were drying up. The BBC employed him less and less frequently. Now that naked women appeared quite happily and quite often on the television screen, the sources of his creativity seemed to be drying up. And he was expensive and temperamental, and a temperamental director was capable of bringing a whole studio out on strike. The race, these days, was to the adaptable, the economical and the polite—Phillip was none of these things: and there was a whole new young breed of television directors who were. Phillip, rightly, was gloomy about his future. He cancelled his banker's order to Irma, if not for the Maserati.

"You have to send it, by law," objected Praxis.

"If she has the audacity to sue," said Phillip, "let her." So Praxis sent the banker's order herself. What difference did it make—Phillip's money or hers?

She began to feel the first stirrings of anger against Irma. Perhaps Phillip was right, and she was Irma's victim, and not Irma hers.

Irma, besides, had taken to strange behaviour, eschewing the company of men and claiming that women were oppressed. She had paraded outside the Albert Hall in protest against the annual Miss World beauty contest, appeared on television to defend her conduct and been derided for her pains. The protestors, everyone agreed, were ugly, warped and jealous.

"She's a lesbian," said Phillip. "That was the whole trouble. Basically unfeminine. Look, I do believe she's growing a moustache! She certainly will if she goes on like this. And her voice was always raucous but it's getting worse. Switch her off, quick!"

And since to be lesbian was the worst insult Praxis could think of, second only to being rated unfeminine, she switched Irma off, and kept her mouth shut, deciding that what might be right for

Irma—or, at any rate, the best Irma could do, as a divorced woman without any status in the world—was certainly not right for Praxis, and the great majority of contented homemakers in the world. She was happy, she told herself, to be a wife and mother, who also had the added stimulation of going out to work. And if she were not happy, if she woke sometimes in the morning with a pain round her heart so severe it all but made her cry out, a great anguished unclassified scream into the world, it was surely nothing to do with the society in which she lived—which suited everyone else well enough—but surely had its roots in her own unhappy childhood, in her relationship with a mad mother, a loony sister and an absent father. Enough, after all, to upset anyone.

Phillip certainly thought so. He would regale dinner tables with amazed accounts of his wife's background and beginnings.

"Praxis is no ordinary person," he'd say. "No conventional home life for a wife of mine! A mother in a mental home and a father who, to all accounts, was no ordinary Jew, but a gambling, drinking, fornicating Jew."

It was all right, now, after the Six-Day War, for Praxis to have Jewish blood. It was, in fact, a point of advantage—not just in cultural and intellectual circles, as it always had been, but with more ordinary people. The Jews of the diaspora now basked in the reflected glory of Israel—no longer a cowering, pitiable, persecuted race licking their wounds in a donated desert, but a hard, tough, victorious, efficient nation, in danger, if anything, of being an oppressive and colonial power, rather than one oppressed and colonized.

All right to be Jewish. No need to hide. Less and less need to hide anything: unmarried couples came to dinner: people talked openly about cancer: mad relatives were talked about with relish: you could dine out on a visit to a mental hospital. Phillip made films about psychophrenic art.

Praxis held her head a little higher. Phillip noticed, and cut her down to size.

He thought she should, perhaps, give up her job. The children, he said, were suffering from her absence. Victoria had nits in her hair: Jason had scabies. Wasn't she being selfish?

At home Praxis pretended she did not go out to work: never took jobs home: never talked about her office day. It would have annoyed Phillip. In the office she pretended she did not have a family: never talked about her home: never took time off. It would have annoyed her employers. She juggled her life with amazing dexterity: always guilty, always in a hurry.

Running home from work to get the *boeuf bourguignon* into the oven: up in the morning, before anyone, to iron her smart white office blouse.

Happy, lucky Praxis. With a husband, a home, children and a job. Tired Praxis.

"Mother's love is everything in the first five years!" wrote Praxis. "And electricity helps her show it!"

"How to be loved and lovable!" wrote Praxis. "Let electricity take the strain."

Now Irma had asked her to coffee. Rashly, she had accepted, expecting what? Friendship, apology, the bridging of gaps for old times' sake? But here was the new Irma, firm and strong, demanding principle, in a masculine way, denying love. For that was what it amounted to.

"You must realize, Praxis," said Irma, "just how socially irresponsible you are."

"You," said Praxis, lightly, "are maternally irresponsible. I have looked after your two children for years. Have I complained? No."

"You were in no position to complain," said Tracey, sourly. She was barely twenty, and should not have been so sour, Praxis thought. "It was what you wanted. Someone else's husband, someone else's children."

"People aren't possessions," replied Praxis, smartly, but alarmed that these strangers should know so much about her affairs. She had expected, in spite of all, some kind of loyalty from Irma: some kind of return from the monthly money she had invested in Irma's welfare, Irma's silence and the lessening of her own guilt.

All sighed, unimpressed.

"It's no use criticizing her on a personal level," said Raya. "She's as much a victim as anyone else."

Praxis regarded Raya's bulging hips and reflected that it was imprudent of her to wear jeans.

"She doesn't half ask for it, though," said Bess. Bess would look at home in a cowshed, thought Praxis: sturdy bare arms up to their elbows in milk and mud. "Do you realize what you're doing, Praxis, when you write these advertisements?"

"Earning a living," said Praxis, rising to go. "Contributing to Irma's quite unnecessary alimony, keeping Irma's children in pot and guitars, and paying my taxes so you can get your social security allowances."

"Do you have no sense at all of the effect you have on women? 'God made her a woman, love made her a mother—with a little help from electricity.' Don't you see that it's debasing?"

"I see that there's no coffee," said Praxis, "and since I came for coffee, there seems no point in my staying."

Bess and Raya stood between Praxis and the door. They did not move. Praxis still smiled, but there was a frozen antagonism in her heart. Did they really believe that she would be a convert? That she could ever be as they were, ever think or act, let alone dress, as they did? They were the women she pitied: the women without men: the rejects. They should keep their voices low and not draw attention to themselves. Lucy without Benjamin: mad: retiring into her own head forever and ever. Hilda, who could be as much a success in the world as she liked, but who was a failure as a woman. Irma, defeated, finished. What did she, Praxis, have in common with any of them?

"Let her go," said Irma, in the tones of the victor. "She's too far gone. It's no use."

"I'm sorry, everyone," said Praxis vaguely and amiably. "I suppose you're Women's Libbers. I am sympathetic, actually, in principle."

"But not to the point of inconveniencing yourself." Tracey sneered so much Praxis almost supposed she had a harelip. Perhaps that accounted for her sourness.

"The trouble is," said Praxis, "I really can't take a roomful of women seriously."

Bess and Raya moved aside to let her go. Bess even opened the door for her. Still no one smiled.

On her way home Praxis caught sight of Betelgeuse in the night sky. She sat on a public bench and stared at the star, and wondered if the strange, tough, knowing person she now was had any connection with the wretched but hopeful Praxis she once had been. Perhaps it was everyone's fate, to harden without ripening, as she feared that she had done?

"What shall I do?" she asked aloud.

The night around her grew still: the street was empty: the brilliance of the stars increased in intensity, dazzling her. She felt that she had stopped breathing: she bowed her head away from the light, and the fingers of her right hand felt for the pulse of her left wrist, in an automatic but pointless gesture. Her hand stilled. Betelgeuse grew enormous, and brilliant, dulling the brilliance around him, and leaned out of heaven, with his spear.

"Wait."

She heard the word, enormous and deafening, inside her head, not outside it. The noise and the brilliance faded; the outside world started up again; she breathed; she heard: cars and pedestrians passed, noisy and ordinary.

Imagination, she told herself. Hysteria. Stress. The shock of the encounter with Irma, Bess, Raya and Tracey, setting up some kind of short circuit in her brain. For to encounter hostility when you have done nothing to deserve it must surely be a shock. To know that you are observed, and judged, and that you have secret enemies, is indeed shocking, and might well, Praxis thought, bring about a retreat from reality, back into childhood fantasy. It did not mean that she was mad.

Praxis turned the meeting with the Women's Libbers into a joke, into a dinner-table story, and presently could stop trembling when she thought about it.

She told no one about the visitation from the red dwarf Betelgeuse, however. Shock and hysteria it might have been, but it comforted her. More and more often now, she slept apart from Phillip. Whether it was her doing, or his, she could no longer make out. It was certainly not what she wanted. But though it grieved her, made a sombre background to her life, it no longer distressed her.

Phillip was part of a journey she was making: he was not the end of the journey. She must wait.

Praxis was asked to take on a cigarette account. Reports had been emerging from universities and medical foundations to the effect that cigarette smoking caused death by lung cancer, and ill health in those it did not kill. The validity of the research was hotly denied by heavy smokers and by those who profited, one way or another, by the manufacture and sale of cigarettes. The advertising agencies merely said blandly that since advertising did not increase the total sale of cigarettes but merely switched brand allegiance between the various makes, it was all nothing to do with them.

"Of course advertising increases total sales of cigarettes," said Praxis naively to the deputy creative director over melon and ginger. "We spend our time associating cigarettes with young love, virility, achievement and good living. I don't want to do this new account."

The deputy creative director's warm eyes grew noticeably less warm. "It's an all-or-nothing matter, Praxis," he said. "If you take a salary from an employer, he has a right to expect loyalty. If you don't approve of what we're doing, then hand in your resignation. Anything else would be hypocrisy."

Praxis put the matter to Phillip.

"The way things are going," he said, "you can't possibly give up your job."

Phillip had been six months without work. He felt, obscurely, that it was Praxis' fault. Victoria had a boyfriend with long blonde hair, who was discovered in her bed. Long-haired girls called at the door for Jason, and were uninterested in Phillip. Hard times.

Praxis kept her job and took on the cigarette account.

Government regulations were introduced, forbidding the association of cigarettes, in advertising, with sex, sport, youth or healthy activity of any kind. She contorted her mind to get round the new restrictions, and managed a subtle connection between airlines and cigarettes, which was applauded.

"It's not," said Phillip, "as if you told lies. Nothing you say is untrue."

"But nothing I say is true," complained Praxis. "Truth lies in the gaps between sentences. That's what copy-writing is."

"No one takes any notice of advertising anyway," said Phillip. "They recognize it for what it is."

Phillip was employed to make a documentary about a new hydroelectric scheme in the Scottish Highlands. It was not fiction, but it was work. He cheered up.

Hilda had become a negotiator for the Industrial Relations Board. She and Praxis rarely met. They seemed to have little in common. Praxis dealt with the surfaces of living, the material things of life: Hilda with the deeper significances. Praxis supposed that it had always, really, been so. Hilda had escorts, not lovers. Her jaw retreated more as she grew older. When Praxis did see her, she was reminded vividly of Hilda as a plain little girl, playing on the beach. She was respected by both management and unions:

Praxis suspected that she intimidated both. If either side walked out swearing that she was mad, at least the other side could presently be relied upon to do the same, and the situation, at least, made for a certain community of interest and attitude. Hilda's success as a negotiator was established.

"I'm not like a woman, you see," said Hilda to Praxis, when they did meet once, for lunch. "They forget I'm a woman." She spoke as if she had solved her problems, and Praxis felt sorry for her.

"What's for dinner?" said Phillip, coming home from the Highlands, where the eating had been frugal. "Who can we ask round?"

Who indeed? The sixties were over.

The friends who had thronged to the house during the sixties, eating, drinking, enthusing, profligate of money, health, time and life, had gone their various ways—some to the country, some to new marriages, a few, even, to their deaths, remembered only by a scored-out line in a telephone book. Phillip and Praxis seemed to make few new friends. Phillip did not like Praxis to invite her colleagues home, and his contemporaries in the film world seemed either absurdly rich and successful—too much so for easy conversation—or else too shamefully left behind to comfortably ask round.

"It would only be embarrassing," Phillip would say. "He'd be envious and I'd feel awkward, and how could they ever ask us back? You're a very flashy hostess, Praxis, all cream and brandy. I rather think you've driven our friends away. This is the age of austerity, and fear of cholesterol."

And so it was. Petrol prices and inflation soared, long faces and recriminations. Architect friends went bankrupt; a friend in the building industry went to prison. Their wives just melted away. Too embarrassing to ask them round: besides, since a wife basked in the glory of her husband's success, so must she share his fall.

In the meantime, whom to ask for dinner? Praxis looked through the telephone book and found there was no one to ask.

Victoria and Jason were out. They usually were. Praxis and Phillip ate alone, facing each other. There seemed little to say. Phillip brooded.

"It's not my fault there's no one to ask round," said Praxis, picking at her take-away kebab. But Phillip clearly thought it was.

"Everything must change," said Praxis. "We must just change with it."

"You've certainly changed," said Phillip, pushing back his chair, and leaving his kebab half-eaten. "You don't even bother to cook properly anymore. No wonder we don't have any friends."

Praxis was less easily made to feel guilty. She finished her kebab, and then ate Phillip's.

She was, astonishingly, forty. She knew, because men no longer whistled at her in the street, but otherwise she felt the same as usual. She felt rejected, and discarded, and humiliated when men at work or at home made lecherous remarks about other, younger, sexier women.

"If you live by your looks," said Irma to her over the phone, "you die by your looks. Come to a meeting."

But Praxis wouldn't. A meeting of all women! She felt she would be finally relegated, down among the women. A woman past her prime, taking comfort from the company of other rejected, ageing women. There was to her something blackly depressing in the notion of any all-female group, which must lack the excitement and pleasure of mixed company.

But the company of men was not what it had been. The deputy creative director took up with his young secretary, and Praxis suffered pangs of unreasoning jealousy. Phillip complained about her looks and her increasing lack of bosom. He would not do it directly; rather he let the implication be felt.

"I think you should stop using so much make-up. It's beginning to get in the cracks." Or he'd point out a passing girl.

"God, what a figure. Look at those knockers!"

Praxis, while pained, felt a vague, rising indignation in herself. She could no longer quite take his attitudes for granted. They were those of most other men she knew, although expressed more cruelly, and with an increasing desire to hurt.

Irma appeared more and more on television, and what she said seemed to Praxis less and less bizarre.

"If only women would realize," said Irma to the world, "that their miseries are political, not personal."

"What poor Irma needs," said Phillip, "is a good lay. But where's she going to find that? Look at the way she dresses! Christ, what happens to frustrated women."

Praxis thought Irma looked rather good, with short hair and no make-up. Praxis, on Phillip's insistence, still went to the hairdresser twice a week and sat under the drier with her hair in rollers, hot and bored.

"Let's face it," said Phillip, "it's all right for Victoria to go about al fresco, but hardly you, darling, at your age."

It occurred to Praxis that Phillip, too, was not as young as he had been. He was certainly going through a hard time. He suffered from insomnia and fits of depression. He would brood and sulk for days over imagined slights: he had indigestion. All Praxis' fault, his manner implied, even when his words did not.

Phillip complained, as once Ivor had complained. He complained about the grease in the ox-tail soup, about the dryness of the duck, about the way she handled the children, about the untidiness of the house, about the rate she spent money. He could not work, write or think while the cleaner was in the house. The cleaner left and was not replaced. Then he complained about the state of Praxis' hands and the meanness of her temper.

"What have I done?" she asked, rashly.

"You haven't done anything. You just *are*," he complained. She knew what he meant. She had begun to feel, herself, that her very existence was an affront to him.

Her enigmatic stomach pains returned.

"Menopausal," said Phillip.

Things will get better again, thought Praxis. Things do. And so indeed they did, from time to time. When Phillip was working he would be enthusiastic, loving and friendly, and she would move back out of the spare room and into the double bed, and all would be as it had been.

"I love you," he'd say. "Don't get too fed up with me. Don't ever leave."

"Of course not. Why should I leave?" She had a wonderful, useful gift for forgetting the events of the past. Useful, at any rate, to everyone except herself.

Then work would dry up, and the difficulties begin again.

"Things only get better," wrote Colleen from Sydney, "if you do something to make them better." Her little girl, not so little now, was backstroke champion of New South Wales. The shelves were covered with her silver trophies. Colleen had lost three stone through diet and exercise. She had been to a matrimonial agency, and was marrying a swimming coach. "Do write," begged Colleen.

Praxis wrote, a cheerful, bouncy account of her life with Phillip. A tale of progress, achievement and good cheer. She tore it up. Phillip was out of work and she back in the spare bed.

At the firm's Christmas party Praxis drank a great many champagne cocktails and ended up under the boardroom table, coupling with the deputy creative director.

"I've always wanted to do that," he said.

"So have I," she said.

"All those half-bottles of wine!" he complained. "If you only knew how much I always want to get drunk."

But it did not develop into an affair. She was too conscious of the photograph of his wife and children on his desk. All the same, the incident cheered her up.

She exercised half-forgotten and neglected skills on Phillip, and he responded well enough. Things will get better, she thought, yet again: as she sprawled on a chair, naked and ungainly, and he pumped away, and excitement rose: but it was of the flesh, not of the spirit. Useless.

Victoria and Jason were both increasingly troublesome. Victoria chose to see more and more of her mother, and spoke more and more curtly to Praxis—whom she affected to despise—and talked in a patronizing fashion to her father. She had given up boys. Presently she announced that she was a lesbian, and brought home a friend to prove it—a pretty girl with curly hair and dimples, who prided herself on her likeness to Shirley Temple in *The Little Colonel*. The friend stayed the night and in the morning Praxis found them sleeping in bed together, arms wrapped round each other's necks. She crept away, horrified, woke Phillip and told him.

"Why shouldn't they?" asked Phillip. "If it gives them pleasure. Safer than boys."

He pulled Praxis down to the bed and made love to her, buggering her, something he seldom did. She cried, from pain and shock. She thought perhaps he was mad: perhaps he was in love with his daughter: perhaps anything.

"I hear you are a lesbian," he said to Victoria at breakfast time.

"That's right," said Victoria.

"You must tell me what you do," he said to the curly-headed friend, who turned pale at his crudity. "If you do it under my roof," he said, "I think it's the least you can do." Victoria left the table, offended. Her friend followed. Phillip laughed.

Victoria packed, and stayed with Irma for a month, but presently returned—or so Praxis suspected—for the sake of comfort, good dinners and ironed clothes.

"It must be difficult being a stepmother," said Victoria on her return, and kissed Praxis' cheek. Praxis cried, with relief.

"You should never have gone off with Phillip in the first place," said Victoria, "but I'm glad it was you and no one else. When I think of the women it could have been!"

But she showed no further interest in boys: only in girls. Praxis felt that she had failed with her stepdaughter. Victoria assured her that lesbianism was a higher state than heterosexuality: that there was affection, comfort, consolation to be found in girls; and only war with boys. Praxis remembered Louise Gaynor; long, long ago. Perhaps if they had slept together, spent nights together, discovered each other, so much since might have been different?

"I wish it didn't turn Daddy on, that's all," Victoria said, bitterly. "Men!"

Jason was increasingly rude and defiant, and left girlie magazines about for Praxis to see. Phillip, discovering them, became hysterical, took his belt off and hit his son. Jason hit back and went to stay with Irma.

"You talk so much about sexual freedom," said Praxis, mildly, "I find this display of prudery quite surprising."

"It's not prudery," said Phillip. "It's decency. How dare he behave like that to you? Unless, of course, you provoke him?"

Nightmare times.

Mary passed her finals, and emerged from her room glowing and confident. She was to take up a hospital job in the New Year. She walked about the house like a good dream, chatting here, tidying there, interested in Phillip's work, in Praxis, in the problems of Victoria and Jason, which she assured Praxis would soon pass.

"It's only their *age*," she kept saying. "They're both so nice. They'll be back to themselves, presently. Why do you doubt yourself? What you put into children is never wasted."

But Praxis doubted. On the other side of London, Robert now

played obsessive rugby, and Claire was a Girl Guide leader. They were going to live good, orderly lives. They were their father's children, not hers. They thought their mother strange.

Certainly, she was unhappy.

At Christmas Mary went home to Willie and Carla, and came back with a boyfriend, a trainee estate agent. He was strikingly handsome: he and Mary joked and chatted easily; they held hands. It seemed a simple relationship, if not profound. Mary explained the world to her Edward, and he listened, happily enough, because he loved her, but he had no opinions of his own to return. He liked sailing. He knew about winds and tides and boats, and house prices, but that was all.

In January Mary started work, junior member of a group medical practice. In February she announced that she was pregnant, and in March that she was going to marry Edward, have the baby and stop work. Praxis wept.

"It was bound to happen," said Phillip. "But just think of the waste of tax-payers' money. All that training, and what's at the end of it? Babies!"

Willie shrugged, Carla sighed. Praxis risked Mary's upset by suggesting an abortion and more time to think.

"Abortion is all right in theory," said Mary. "But I've seen the reality of them, in practice. By the dozen. It's carnage. A woman's got a right to her own body, and all that: she's not got the right to ask anyone else to make her unpregnant. If I could do my own abortion, I might consider it. But I'm not asking anyone else to do it for me. I'd rather wait for it to be born, and then kill it myself."

"That would be murder," said Praxis, shocked.

"It's murder at any stage," said Mary. "In any case, I love Edward and I want his child. I'll be able to go back to work sooner or later."

"You don't understand," said Praxis. "You'll shrivel up and die, mentally and emotionally. Women do."

"Not me," said Mary, and laughed. "In any case, I rather fancy the domestic life. It's woman's highest calling, according to you. 'God made her a woman, love made her a mother; electricity made it easier.' "

Praxis shuddered, but went to work as usual the next day.

Praxis went to visit Willie and Carla.

"She loves him," said Willie. "Why, what did you hope for her? That she wouldn't love anyone?"

Willie's beard was grey. The hairs on his thin chest curled white and wiry.

"Of course not," said Praxis. But perhaps she had.

"She reminds me of you," said Willie, "at her age. But she's not your flesh and blood. Perhaps it's just that all girls are the same?"

"Perhaps," said Praxis.

"I'm going to be a grandmother," complained Carla, "without ever really being a mother. Mary's been like a daughter, but it's not the same as your own flesh and blood." She was superintendent manageress of the canteen, now. She drove a little car.

She took Praxis in to see Lucy. Lucy sat in an old chair in the dank master bedroom and stared out over the drive, and tut-tutted vaguely at the behaviour of the common children on their way to school, although the school had long since been closed.

"Who are you?" she asked Praxis, and drew Carla towards her and said, "I only like to see family."

Carla, upset for Praxis, hurried her out of the room.

"Don't worry," said Praxis, weeping. "I understand."

"But she knows who you are, I'm sure she does!"

"I don't," said Praxis, sniffing.

"You will come to the wedding, won't you?" begged Carla. "Mary will be so upset if you don't."

Willie walked her to the gate.

"You don't look like yourself at all," said Willie. "When you were a whore you looked most like yourself."

He had never forgiven her.

Mary was married in Brighton in a becoming white dress which did not even attempt to conceal the bump in her tummy.

Edward's parents were there. Praxis thought she recognized the father from the old Raffles days, but did not study him too closely in case she was right. It was a good outing. They all went. Phillip, Victoria and Jason; Robert and Claire, too. Everyone laughed: nobody said anything unkind. Praxis had the feeling they were all supporting her, bolstering her against misfortune. And so they were. Even when they were stuck in the traffic jam on the way back to London—it was one of the first fine spring weekends, and

Brighton a pleasant day's outing for Londoners—they sang, and did not grumble.

Praxis resigned herself to the futility—or so it appeared—of human effort. Phillip seemed happier: he did not ask her to sleep in the spare bed: he had a feature film to direct: a disaster movie about the great flood. (His documentary on the hydroelectric scheme had won two awards.) The commission meant spending much time away on location. When he was not home she served fish fingers and chips straight from the pan, instead of filet of sole *véronique*, potato *duchesse* and *mange-tout* from Wedgwood serving dishes, and had time to recover her strength and energy.

There was, finally, trouble at work.

Advertising budgets had been slashed. Staff were fired, on a last-in, first-out basis, which at least left Praxis protected. But now the cigarette account was lost altogether. She did the work of three people. The value of money diminished, the annual rise was not forthcoming. She felt her work was under scrutiny. The research department, increasingly powerful, seemed to feel the need to explain things to her.

"Sixty percent of women go out to work," they said. "And it's not interesting work like yours. They have boring, repetitive, tedious jobs. The work that men won't do, but women don't mind."

"I know," she'd say. "I know all that."

"You mustn't lose touch with the market." Had she?

Lucy had a stroke and lay still and silent in the damp, dank bed where she had lain with Benjamin long ago, and later, sporadically, with the photographer. Praxis sat at her bedside, but when Lucy stirred, or turned, she made the movement towards Carla. Carla, after all, had looked after her: Praxis had provided the money—but what was money? Easy. Days passed. Praxis did not go to work. Lucy's condition remained unaltered. Her breathing was difficult: it would seem to stop altogether from time to time; then it would restart.

Hilda was sent for. She peered at her mother. She sat by the bed, opposite Praxis, and fidgeted with her gloves, and occasionally spoke.

"She should never have left father," said Hilda.

"What sort of mother was she anyway?" asked Hilda.

"I hate this house," said Hilda. "You can smell the rats.

"We'd better sell it, now she's gone," said Hilda, hopefully.

"Hilda!" beseeched Praxis. "For God's sake be quiet. She'll hear you."

"She never could hear anything," said Hilda, and cried. Praxis could not remember Hilda having ever cried before.

Hilda and Praxis went round the house, looking at damp, peeling wallpaper, rotten plaster, crumbling woodwork.

"Really," said Hilda, "Willie is the meanest man in the world. He'll have to go. It would be a kindness to Carla."

It was as if, with her tears, at least some of the madness had drained away.

"We don't need the house for Mary and Carla," said Hilda, "do we?" The "we" touched Praxis.

"Miss Leonard was so kind to you," said Hilda. "We owed Mary something."

Hilda looked out of her old bedroom window.

"How wonderful the night sky used to be," she said. "With the searchlights and the flak and the guns. Nothing's been the same since."

Hilda went back to London. In the night Lucy died. Her breathing stopped, and did not reassert itself.

"A peaceful end," said the doctor.

"A peaceful life," said Carla.

"With a few struggles," said Praxis, remembering the distant past.

Praxis took more time off work; she organized the funeral and disposed of Lucy's belongings. Carla wept, and was helpless. So long as somebody is rendered helpless, thought Praxis, that's all right. Blood ties don't matter, not as I thought they did. Now Carla is my dead mother's daughter; Mary is Willie's child; Victoria and Jason are mine; Robert and Claire are Diana's. We claim as much or as little as we want, through the degree of responsibility which we offer.

Phillip rang through just before Lucy's death, and asked if Praxis would mind if he came down and filmed her end for the disaster movie. Aged actresses were always difficult to locate and employ, and tended to get upset if asked to simulate the brink of death.

Praxis refused.

Phillip was hurt: wasn't Praxis being selfish and unfeeling? Did she really want to put some old actress through inevitable pain, when Lucy would neither know nor care? And the fee could go towards the funeral; or, if Praxis preferred, to any charity for the aged she cared to name.

"Why don't you just cut the scene altogether," enquired Praxis, "if it's so difficult?"

"If I was to cut out all the deaths," said Phillip, "there wouldn't be a film at all. This is a disaster movie." He put the phone down.

After Lucy's funeral, Praxis thought she would call at the hotel in Sussex where the film unit was based, and make her peace with Phillip. There was nothing he could do to Lucy now.

"Room 22," said the desk clerk.

Praxis went into room 22 and found Phillip in bed with Serena Walker, whose breasts he had auditioned long ago. She had done well since then. Praxis recognized her long, thick red hair from publicity stills. She was not yet thirty and was renowned not just for her looks but for her acting ability, and for the scandal, now six years old, of the birth of a baby with an allegedly royal father.

"I've nothing to be ashamed of," she had said. "No, we're not married. And not getting married. I'll be mother and father to my baby. It's all right." She had been one of the first: now there were many others following her footsteps, and Serena was reduced to disaster movies. Her mother looked after the baby.

Phillip and Serena did not hear Praxis come in. Praxis watched them for a while. Serena's red hair spread like a modesty veil over Phillip's loins. Her smooth, plump behind arched delicately over his face. It was a strangely decent sight. There was a Polaroid camera on the end of the bed. Phillip had been taking photographs of her: Serena like this; Serena like that: of Serena and Phillip together, using the delay buzzer. Praxis shuffled through the cards.

"I love you," she heard Phillip say. Praxis laughed aloud. Phillip and Serena twisted themselves about and stared at her; not shocked, not guilty: secure in the conviction that what they were doing was right, beautiful and natural, as it probably was.

Praxis felt an intruder, foolish for having turned up uninvited, foolish for making claims. She went and sat downstairs in the lobby.

"You in the cast?" asked the desk man.

"Yes," she said. "A bit-part player."

Oh, I'm cool, she thought. Like Irma. Like Irma, once.

"A great movie," he said. "Not a thing left standing at the end."

Serena came downstairs, presently. Apart from her spectacular hair, she looked more plain and ordinary than she did in her publicity photographs. Praxis even thought she looked quite nice. Victoria and Jason would like her: would enjoy the sensation of fame, of something special about the house: something supremely filmable.

"I'm sorry," Serena said. She had a little, high, piping voice.

"You're welcome," said Praxis. "Of course, he's a voyeur; he only uses the camera as a sublimation."

She wished she hadn't said it. It seemed, these days, an unnecessary comment. It made Serena cross, moreover.

"I love Phillip," Serena said, her voice rising. "I make him happy. You've never understood him, never appreciated him. You don't look after his house: you won't sleep in his bed: you've driven his children away. He lives in a kind of desert of nonappreciation. You've all but ruined his career. He's a fabulous director; fabulous. You made him nearly destroy himself in television; do those dreadful series: those boring commercials: you're completely superficial: you believe that advertising is real life."

"Go slowly," said Praxis. "My mother's just died. My mind isn't quite functioning yet."

"Listen to you," said Serena. "You're cold. So cold. You don't care about anything; not even your mother dying. You find your husband in bed with me and you just stand there and watch and then melt away—God, you must be guilty. You're sleeping with your boss, anyway. Everyone knows. You've no right to object: you drove him to it. Now we love each other and it's too late. We want to get married!"

"I told you you were welcome," said Praxis. "Take it all. I hope you have some money. You'll need it."

"And I'm having his baby. All these years you've refused him a baby, one excuse or another. You were too tired, you had pains, you couldn't give up your job. You're just so competitive. Prudish and old-fashioned: that's why his children are in the mess they are."

She cried, all the same, anxiously. Praxis took Serena's hand and laid it on her own cheek.

"Oh well," she said. "Love."

"You are a bitch," said Phillip to Praxis later, "upsetting Serena like that."

Praxis couldn't do anything right: nor did she try. She developed a cold in the nose and bronchitis and took to her bed.

"Don't cough over everything," said Phillip, "or you'll infect Serena."

Whether he was worried for the film or the baby, Praxis neither knew nor cared.

Praxis moved out of the house such few things as she thought she could bear to see again, and left the rest for Serena. Friends advised her not to: saying she would lose what few legal rights she had. The house was in Phillip's name. Praxis had no savings of her own: they had been spent during his periods of unemployment; the earnings of the past years had gone into the running of the home, not its fabric. The fee for the new film was safely in Phillip's account. They had no children between them: Phillip would not be obliged to keep her, or pay her alimony since she was earning.

"Well, why should he?" enquired Irma. Praxis spent a good deal of time, now, with Irma. "I took his money because I was angry with you both and I was ill. I gave it straight to the Women's Movement. But you're able-bodied and healthy. Why expect him to keep you? It's humiliating."

"Because of the years of service," said Praxis, angrily. "Doing the washing up and the cleaning and the children while he played records and criticized."

"More fool you," said Irma, unkindly. "Nobody made you do it, you volunteered."

"I've just evaporated from Phillip's life," Praxis wept.

"You evaporated from Willie's, and Ivor's," said Irma. She allowed Praxis no way out, turning her round to face herself, whenever self-pity or indignation threatened to overwhelm her.

"Victoria and Jason don't seem to care," she moaned.

"I know the feeling," said Irma, sprightly.

She would have gone anywhere else, but there was nowhere to go. She had few friends: well, she had hardly looked after them. They were mostly Phillip's, in any case. It was as if, over the years, he had been planning her downfall, her total misery.

"Of course he wasn't," said Irma. "You were merely sharing his life, that's all, edging over and over into it. Your fault."

"I hate you," said Praxis to Irma, eventually.

For a time, she did. It seemed that Irma required from her a whole new view of the world, and one which, while liberating her from the sense of personal failure which so afflicted her, would also free Phillip from the guilt she wished him to bear.

What, see Phillip not as villain, but as a victim of a crazy culture? No; she needed his villainy in order to survive. Anger was better than misery.

Phillip was bad, bad. He was selfish, wicked, cruel and shallow.

"You would have him," said Irma. "Nothing would stop you. Now you're being done to as you did."

"You're condoning him," complained Praxis.

"He is as much a victim as you are. He has his image of himself to maintain, as you have yours. You weren't happy living with Phillip, Praxis. You were thoroughly wretched. You're well out of it. You're just piqued because you can't act the earth mother anymore."

"Irma, my whole life is finished."

"Your life is just beginning, if you learn to live it among women. I know you have a low opinion of your own sex: it is inevitable; our inferiority is written into the language: but you must be aware, you must know what's happening: it's half the battle. Come to a meeting. Bess, Raya and Tracey want to see you again."

"They want to see me defeated, and brought down to their level. Manless."

"No. They want you to speak bitterness, and share it, so it stops destroying you. They're your sisters."

"They'll try and make me give up work."

"And so you should. It's immoral and antisocial. You can't still believe it."

"Yes, I do," said Praxis defiantly. "I believe that to be a wife and mother is the highest purpose of a woman."

"Fine mother you made," jeered Irma. "Running out on your children. Fine wife—letting your husband slip through your fingers."

Praxis cried, like a little girl.

But she went to Irma's consciousness-raising group, all the same. Otherwise, after work, there was only her bed-sitting room to return to, and loneliness. She viewed Bess, Raya and Tracey more fondly now. Bess's husband was a mental patient, Raya's husband had killed himself, Tracey, unmarried, was twenty-two and had six-year-old twins.

She did not give up her job. It was all she had. But she was less good at it than before. Her lack of conviction showed through: the words on the page rang false.

"You and Phillip will be back together soon," said the deputy creative director, comfortingly. "I expect he's going through the male menopause. Times will get better."

But his prophecies were not what they had been. The rules of advertising, as of living, had changed. What had worked in the sixties did not work in the seventies. He was not as young as he had been. He was fired in the afternoon of the morning in which he spoke to Praxis.

Hilda put 109 Holden Road on the market. The demand for houses at the time was brisk, and a buyer was found at once. Willie expressed some indignation at being obliged to move: Carla none at all. They bought a modern bungalow outright, for cash. Willie was assistant director of the institute.

Praxis went down to see them. Carla was out.

"You should never have married Phillip," said Willie. "You look much better now you're not."

"You always liked me in dusty black," observed Praxis.

"Yes, I did," said Willie. "It suited you. You were always in mourning for something or other."

He looked round the new gleaming walls of the bungalow, the smooth cool surfaces of built-in wardrobes and furniture. Carla had a taste for crimson velour.

"It's all too unused for me," he said. "I like dark places where people have been before."

He lifted Praxis' jersey and put his chilly hands on her breasts. Both fingers and breasts felt less resilient than they had in earlier years. He undid her jeans and pushed and nudged her back against the marble of a modern fireplace.

"It's all got to be used," he said. "It's all got to be made warmer and darker."

She wriggled away from him and rearranged her clothes. He did not seem to mind.

"You're married to Carla," said Praxis.

"You never used to think like that. All those husbands down at the Raffles."

"I do now."

"I don't see what difference it can make," protested Willie. "It's my wanting to is the offence to Carla, if any: not the actual doing. That's the harmless part."

"That's your truth. Mine is different."

"You must miss sex, now you're not married. Isn't it hard?"

He was inquisitive: he always had been inquisitive: his body as well as his mind. It had gone searching into hers, anxious to know the exact state of play within, at any given minute, trying to catch something elusive, as if something might be missed between this penetration and that: quick! Catch it as it flew!

No, she didn't miss sex. Yes, it was hard. She missed the establishment and warmth of the household: she missed a pattern of obligations, the fulfilling of other people's needs, no matter how badly she had, latterly, fulfilled them. She missed the telephone ringing, the laying of the table, the sharing of the day's events, the lack of time to think: she missed the exhaustion and the sense of self-righteousness. She was left with silence and herself and it was hard.

"I told you so," said Ivor, satisfied. She even went to visit Ivor, in search of herself. "You were always too rackety. People round here live perfectly happy, stable lives. If only you'd settle down, Praxis."

He still lived in the biggest house on the estate, which had grown in grandeur since she left. Diana had brilliant white Terylene curtains looped across the windows: her taste ran to chintz and little lamps. There was a handsome chrome cocktail cabinet. Diana clearly didn't wish Praxis to visit, so Praxis only went there once. Ivor regretted her: Praxis knew he did. She had been the excitement in his life: the opportunity for change and enrichment. It had gone sour: over a vision of Carol's bare breasts against his dark suit. Praxis felt that if she tried, if she pursued, if she seduced, it could all have begun again: but to what end?

When the money from the sale of the Holden Road house came through, Praxis gave up her job. She would have liked to give it up earlier, as a moral gesture, but the habits of prudence remained.

Irma shrugged, kind for once.

"I don't know that motives matter," she said. "It's not why people do things, it's what they do that has its effect."

Praxis considered suicide, but kindness of heart, not to mention the sheer habit of being alive and doing one's best to stay so, stood between her and the actuality of the deed. Someone would have to find the body and endure nastiness: others would have to put up with remorse, regret and, if not grief—for she could think of no one who would long or sincerely grieve for her—at any rate, the shock, dismay and disagreeable nostalgia which attends any untimely and violent death. Ah, better times, long past, when we were young, vigorous, and hope came in equal measure with despair! By dying, Praxis could see, she would be more closely connected with others than she was when living, and that, of course, was the main temptation. To brush aside, tear down, the blanket of unreality between herself and the rest of the world was indeed inviting. But she did not do it.

"What am I going to do with the second half of my life?" Praxis asked Irma. "I don't really want to live through it. I don't seem to have any function."

"Find one," said Irma, brusquely.

Praxis left her bed-sitting room and bought a small flat in Camden Town. She furnished it cosily and seductively, out of habit.

"A man trap," said Irma unkindly, looking round at soft sofas, deep carpets and little lamps.

"There don't seem to be any men to trap," said Praxis.

"All that means," said Irma, "is that you're not looking for one. Good for you."

But it seemed to Praxis to be a matter of sorry inadvertence, not resolution.

Serena had her baby—a little girl. Her picture appeared in the newspapers, the baby in her arms and Phillip smiling behind her. An unflattering snapshot of Praxis, as the ousted wife, also appeared, with a caption saying that she was seeking a divorce. Presumably Serena had raked through the family photograph album and provided the worst likeness she could. Or it might, of course, have been Phillip who obliged. Serena's little boy, the one with the allegedly royal genes, now lived with Phillip and Serena. A Sunday supplement presently ran a feature on the new young family as part of the prepublicity for Phillip's disaster movie. Serena,

Praxis observed, had made considerable improvement in the kitchen.

"It was nicer in my day," said Irma, "simpler and more functional." And Praxis, who had her mouth open in dismay, distress and indignation, had to close it again.

Praxis' mind could accept and condone Phillip's sexual relationship with Serena: her body could not. A sense of loss, of being usurped, of being in the wrong place while something dreadful happened elsewhere which she ought to be there to stop, kept her awake and tormented at night.

"I know the feeling," said Irma. "Try sleeping pills." Praxis tried them, and slept heavily at night. The feelings faded: broke through from time to time in dreams, and that was all.

"It's all no big deal," said Irma. "Really, it is all so unimportant. Regard the pain of rejection as an illness. It passes. It's a pain in the heart, in the mind, instead of in the stomach. Think yourself lucky not to have both, like me."

"You don't still care about Phillip?" asked Praxis, startled.

"He's beneath you, and me. We're worth ten of him and always were."

"What difference did that ever make?" asked Praxis, sadly.

Hilda's name appeared in the New Year's Honours List. She went to Buckingham Palace to receive the award from the Queen, wearing a grey suit and white blouse, with her hair piled high into a bristly beehive topped with a floppy emerald-green ribbon. She had found favour in high places by quietly and quickly settling a series of strikes before news of them appeared in the newspapers. She gave a small cocktail party to celebrate the event and even asked Praxis.

"You will wear something ordinary," she pleaded with Praxis. "And have your hair done."

Praxis obliged, and mingled happily enough with grey-suited civil servants and their pleasant wives. She stayed behind to help Hilda wash up the sherry glasses and the ashtrays. There were not many of the latter; fewer people smoked, these days, than had done in the past.

"You must be very pleased," said Praxis.

"The OBE? It is an acknowledgment. It's something."

"It's a great deal."

"I could never have got married," said Hilda. "I couldn't have coped with that and a career. Women can't. Besides, madness is hereditary. I didn't want to pass it on."

"That never worried me," said Praxis, surprised.

"I was always the responsible one," said Hilda. She washed and rewashed the same glass, with disdainful red-tipped fingers. She had done very little washing up in her life.

"I looked after children and had a career as well," said Praxis.

"You mean you managed, for a time," said Hilda. "And then everything broke down and now you have nothing."

"And you have the OBE." Another bar to hang on Hilda's chest, along with Latin, Geography and Deportment.

"Yes," said Hilda. "People fail you, children disappoint you, thieves break in, moths corrupt, but an OBE goes on forever. I shall write and tell Father."

Praxis said nothing. She polished and repolished a glass and waited.

"He's in a nursing home in Deal," said Hilda. "He's an alcoholic. Mother drove him to drink when she left him. He's very old now, of course. I write to him quite often."

Perhaps it was true. Perhaps it was not.

"I didn't know you were in touch with him," said Praxis, as casually as she could.

"I have been for years," said Hilda. "Since I was at school. Butt and Son put the wrong letter in an envelope and I found out where he was. I write to him once in a while."

"Does he write back?"

"That's not the point."

"How do you know he's in a nursing home?"

"I telephone from the ministry, sometimes. I keep up with his changes of address, one way or another. He's moved about quite a lot."

"What do you tell him, when you write?"

"Family news," said Hilda, blithely.

"Why didn't you tell me?"

"I'm the elder sister. I'm in charge."

"Did you write to him when I was living with Willie?"

"Of course."

"What did you say?" enquired Praxis.

"The truth."

"How did you know what that was?"

"Willie told me. Willie was very fond of me."

Hilda was both smug and evasive.

Praxis did not pursue the matter. Yes, Willie had been fond of Hilda: how fond, she did not wish to know. She remembered, or thought she remembered, Hilda dancing naked in front of Willie in the night. In the same way she remembered lying with her father in Elaine's summerhouse. But perhaps these things had not happened at all: perhaps they were fantasies, manifestations of inner fears and desires, which came to her with the strength of memories? How was she to know? And why should she want to know? There was no obligation, after all, to know the truth, let alone face it. And if Benjamin had not appeared by chance, but had come looking for his daughter in Raffles Esplanade Dive in response to a letter from Hilda, what did it matter now?

Old man in a nursing home—that part sounded true enough—with his memories to sustain him. If Praxis had contributed in any way to the richness of his memories, then she was glad. She had liked her father. The realization cheered her up, made some kind of rent in the mist between herself and other people. She leaned forward and kissed Hilda on the cheek.

"What did you do that for?" asked Hilda, startled.

"Because you're my sister," said Praxis. "Don't worry about it: about what I did, or what you did. Everything's quite all right, and you've got the OBE, and I'm glad."

She put away the glasses in Hilda's bow-fronted mahogany corner cabinet—Hilda collected antiques, of a dark and shiny nature—and went home, far happier than she had arrived.

As if in recognition of her new state of mind, Victoria and Jason came and sat in her flat, bringing their records with them, until she wished they would leave her in peace. Robert wrote to her, in avuncular terms, from Kenya, where he was doing a year's Voluntary Service Overseas, and Claire wrote, enclosing a photograph of her fiancé, who looked remarkably like Ivor and who was a trainee executive for a pharmaceutical firm.

Irma, Raya and Tracey were bringing out a weekly broadsheet, devoted to the wrongs done to women by society. Bess rode round on a bicycle and pushed the paper through letterboxes. Praxis, shocked by its grammar and the general inefficiency of its production, offered to edit the broadsheet. The offer was reluctantly accepted, by a group decision.

"We're not writing propaganda," said Irma. "We don't want any of your selling copy or slogans. But since you have more time than the rest of us, I suppose it would be silly for us to refuse."

The broadsheet grew into a newspaper. Praxis was its editor. She wrote rousing editorials, which she half believed, and half did not, in the same way as she had half believed, half not, her own advertisements for the Electricity Board. But she felt she was righting some kind of balance. She still occasionally thought of suicide, but knew it could never be done before the next issue, and there was always a next issue to be thought of.

"When did you become a convert to the Women's Movement?" someone asked her, eventually, and Praxis realized that this was what she had, in fact, become. Ideas which once had seemed strange now seemed commonplace, and so much to her advantage that she was surprised to remember how, in the past, she had resisted them.

She was a convert: she wished to proselytize. She wished all the women in the world to think as she thought, do as she did, to join in sisterhood in a happier family than the world had ever known.

"I can't really say," she replied. "It comes to some as a flash of light. For me it was a gradual thing." And she laughed, but nervously. She saw it as a religious experience: she stood divested of the trappings of the past, naked (with a body no longer proud and beautiful), humble before a new altar, in the knowledge that she was the Daughter of God, reborn.

Wherever she went she saw women betrayed, exploited and oppressed. She saw that women were the cleaners, the fetchers, the carriers, the humble of the earth, and that they were truly blessed.

She saw that men's lives were without importance and that only the lives of women were significant. She lost her belief in the man-made myths of history—great civilizations, great art, great empire. The male version of events.

She was, for a time, elated. (And in her writings, being elated, attracted no little attention. The women in the office, the women in the wider world, listened to what she had to say, and believed her.)

Praxis thought that perhaps now she was safe: that having lost her little loves, her shoddy griefs and pointless troubles—lost them all in the vast communal sea of women's tears—that she was immune, saved by her faith from more distress.

Follow me, the Daughter of God, and you shall be saved.

But she was wrong. She had a faith, but she was not divine. Human lives travel through time like the waves of the sea, rising to peaks of experience, falling again, gathering new strength, to rise once more. There is no finite point at which we can say, ah, I have arrived: I am saved: I am rich, successful, happy. We wake the next morning and see that we are not.

And there is perhaps a force abroad—or in ourselves—which demands that sacrifice is a part of faith. That Abraham must sacrifice Isaac, to prove that God exists.

Mary turned up at the newspaper office. She had a small child on either hand. She wore a neat, inexpensive suit, and looked what she was, a housewife up to London for the day. Praxis took her to lunch at a department store, where highchairs were provided for the children, and a special fish-finger and chips lunch was served at reasonable prices.

"Edward's left me," said Mary.

"He just sailed off one day," said Mary. "Took a crewing job on a yacht going to Madeira, and went with the evening tide.

"Sailing was all he ever cared about," said Mary. "And of course once I had the children I couldn't go out with him and he resented that.

"I don't blame him," said Mary. "He was in love with boats. We must have been very boring, in comparison. He wasn't a very clever man, so I used to keep the conversation down to a certain level, for his sake. So I daresay I never showed at my best.

"He hankered so after distant oceans and far-off harbours," said Mary, "and of course in Brighton you can always hear the sea. Even in bed at night.

"We were always all right in bed," said Mary. "You think that must mean something, but it doesn't.

"In retrospect," said Mary, "I can't really think why I married him. I think it might have been so the children could be born. They are very special children."

She looked fondly at their two quite ordinary faces, smeared with tomato sauce and chocolate ice-cream, and leaned over to wipe their mouths with the tissues provided by the management.

"The universe isn't magic," said Praxis, crossly, but even as she said it, knew that she was wrong.

"When the children are at school," said Mary, "I'll try and get back into medicine. It will be difficult, because of course I've lost six years. But I don't regret them. The children, that is: or the years.

"I might try and go to America," said Mary. "My father was an American, wasn't he?"

Mary leaned forward and arranged a straighter parting in her daughter's hair. She did not meet Praxis' eye. Praxis knew that she wanted information. Well, why not? The world had changed around them both. Causes for shame, disgrace, embarrassment and shock were not what they were.

"He might have been," said Praxis. "Your mother certainly hoped he was. She wanted you to be open and free, and so you are."

"When I was thirteen," said Mary, "I had an anonymous letter. It said my mother was a prostitute and so were you."

"Of course she wasn't. She was a respectable teacher of English literature. She was forty-five. She went out one night and slept with three men. A middle-aged and intelligent schoolteacher, his son and a passing G.I. of pleasant demeanour and aspect."

"Did she do it for money?"

"Of course not." Enough was enough.

"It might have happened to anyone," said the cool, clear young voice of the seventies. "Of course in those days it was a problem getting contraceptives."

"Yes."

"Did she try to get rid of me?"

"Not very hard."

"I'm a clear argument against abortion, but then I was plucked living, like Caesar," said Mary, "from my dead mother's womb."

"Yes." Praxis felt tears pressing against her eyelids.

"It must all mean something," said Mary.

"I expect so," but what it was, Praxis could not remember.

"And then you rescued me from a wicked clergyman's wife."

"They weren't wicked. Just neglectful."

"You were very young. You gave up a lot to do it."

"How do you know?"

"Willie told me."

"It wasn't all that much," said Praxis diffidently, "to give up."

"Just your life," said Mary. "Well, never mind. Good actions are never wasted." She spoke firmly, as if she knew. Praxis paid the bill. Mary sorted out her children and scooped them up. They went up and down in the lift, Mary holding the children so they could press the buttons.

"I seem to have difficulty," said Praxis, out of nothing, into nowhere, "in actually loving a man, in any permanent sense."

"Some do," said Mary, blithely. "Most, I daresay."

"What can I do about it?" Mary was half Praxis' age. Why she enquired, she did not know.

"What you're doing, I expect," said Mary. "You learn to love the world enough to want to change it."

Mary went back to Brighton, and Praxis to her office, where she viewed rather differently the women who came and went. Those whom she had privately regarded as rejected, humiliated, obsessive, angry and ridiculous, she began to see as brave, noble and attempting, at any rate, to live their lives by principle rather than by convenience. All kinds of women—young and old, clever, slow, pretty, plain; the halt and the lame, the sexually confused, or fulfilled, or indifferent, battered wives, raped girls, vicious virgins, underpaid shop assistants, frustrated captains of industry, violent school girls, women exploited and exploiting—but all turning away from their inner preoccupations and wretchedness, to regard the outside world and see that it could be changed, if not for themselves, it being too late for themselves, then at least for others.

Praxis smarted and fumed on Mary's account. Irma merely shrugged.

"That's what it's like," she said. Irma was grey and drawn in the face. She had been to the hospital for tests.

"They want to take my womb out," said Irma. "It's the current preoccupation of male surgeons. If they can only remove the whole thing, lock, stock and barrel, take away what women have and they don't, then that must be an improvement."

"But Irma—" said Praxis.

"Individual life is not so important," said Irma. "What are we?

Little centres of identity winking in and winking out! It's the manner of living that matters: not the length of the life. I don't want to drag on and on. Do you?"

"Yes," said Praxis.

Phillip's film, *Flood*, released after more than two years of delays, was not a success. It lacked, critics complained, grandeur of concept and scale. He was a television director at heart, and it showed. What would do on the living-room box was not enough for the big screen. Working in television had, they alleged, cut him down to mannikin size, and worse, had made him mean. If millions had been spent, as alleged, it simply did not show. Serena, they complained, was getting fat, and was red-rimmed about the nostrils in several scenes. If the leading lady had a cold in the nose, then shooting should be delayed. It would have been in the old days. Modern films, declared the critics, clustering round Phillip's film like blowflies around a god-given joint of meat inadvertently left out of the fridge, were not what they had been. In the old days camera crews and technicians had risked death to obtain their desired effects—had not an entire film crew been decapitated by the knives on the chariot wheels in the original *Ben Hur?*—but it was obvious that the team working on Phillip's film hadn't even risked getting their feet wet.

And so on.

Praxis was pleased to be able to say "poor Phillip." Victoria moved out of her father's house and slept alternately on Irma's sofa or Praxis' floor. Serena had become fanatical about yoga and refused to serve meat, or have cigarettes or alcohol consumed in the house. Jason took a job as a gardener in one of the royal parks and declined to give it up when the time came to go back to university. The majority of the other gardeners, he alleged, were honours graduates, and he found the conversation in the potting sheds more illuminating than any he had encountered at college.

Phillip, listening to this nonsense, hit his son, and Jason hit back.

"Next time," said Jason, "I'll use a shovel and that will be the end of you." But he apologized the next day.

The household was under considerable strain. Serena's baby had infantile eczema, and cried and cried, and scratched and scratched, and had to be fed on goat's milk and dressed in muslin and receive Serena's full attention. Phillip could not sleep. Work dried up again. Serena and the baby spent most of their nights in the spare room. The royal child, confused by the ups and downs in his life, wet his bed and soiled his pants.

Serena, her eyes wide with strain and dismay, did her breathing exercises, started each day with a glassful of wine vinegar and honey and achieved the lotus position, but little else.

She called to see Praxis in her editorial office. She held her thin baby with its skull-like head and staring, anguished eyes, against her bosom.

"I'm sorry," she said. "I realize now what I did to you. I didn't then."

Together they studied the baby: its scaly face, its raw limbs.

"I think she'll be all right in the end," said Serena. "They say she may grow out of it when she's three. In the meantime, I have to watch her suffer. I think I'd rather be dead, and I know she would, but they don't let you. Everyone has to go on trying."

"She's your child, not theirs," said Praxis, mildly.

"Yours to pay for," said Serena, "not yours for deciding what's best."

Serena went home and Praxis went off to a television studio to take part in a discussion on the reform of the abortion laws. She was recognized in the street these days. Some smiled and nudged each other; a few came up to her and abused her as a mass murderer, killer of unborn children.

"I saw you on telly last night," wrote Mary from Brighton. "I expect you're right but I feel you're wrong. I spent most part of a year on a gyne ward. I was the one who got blood on my surgical gloves, remember, actually doing abortions. I'd do it happily for the older women, who at least knew what was going on and were as distressed as I was, but I resented having to do it for the girls who used me as a kind of last-ditch contraceptive, because they didn't want their holiday interfered with. Or am I being like one of those people from South Africa who, when you say something about apartheid, say, 'Listen, I live there, I know what it's like'?

"I have a job!" wrote Mary from Brighton. "It's in Toronto. Not quite the States but getting near. In a big general hospital. There's a crèche for the children; they actually seem to want me, kids and all! So, you see, my life wasn't finished, merely postponed, by my marriage. I'm doing better than you!

"Trouble, I'm afraid," wrote Mary from Brighton. "The job's off. I'm pregnant. I met this married man at a party—"

Praxis took the train to Brighton. Mary was pale, thin, and suffering from bouts of vomiting. Carla came in daily to help with the children. The house was cold and sparsely furnished.

Mary lived on Social Security benefits.

"You're a qualified doctor," said Praxis, white with fury. "You must know about contraceptives."

"I don't like contraceptives," said Mary, calmly. "They're anti-life. I associate sex with procreation, and that's that. I'm not a Catholic; I don't go for the Jesus stuff; but I do understand what the pope is going on about. Life is either sacred, or it's not. People are either meant, or they're not. I believe I am sacred, and that my existence has some purpose. And I'm sorry, but I have been more convinced of it ever since you told me about my mother."

"You can't possibly go through with the pregnancy," said Praxis. "It's absurd. If you don't even know the father's name."

"Neither did my mother."

"If you don't have a termination, you're finished. Everything thrown away."

"Except the baby. And I'm not asking another person to abort it for me. I don't have the right. If I could do it myself, I might. But I can't, so that is that. I run my life on principle, not convenience, and that is that."

"If you don't believe in contraception, or abortion," said Praxis, "you might at least abstain from sexual activity."

"I like sex," said Mary, blandly. "And it's much more exciting without contraceptives."

Praxis slapped Mary's smooth cheek, and left. Mary did not see her out. Carla walked with her to the station.

"I offered to adopt it," said Carla. "But she won't have that, either. She's very stubborn. Sweet as pie just so long as she's doing exactly what she wants.

"Like Willie, I suppose," said Carla. "Like most people, come to that.

"Willie's run out of exams to take," complained Carla. "He simply doesn't know what to do with himself. Of course, he's director of the institute now."

Carla was still wearing dusty brown.

"He mends his shoes with cellotape," said Carla, "instead of tying the sole on with string. I suppose that's an advance."

Eventually Mary telephoned Praxis. Praxis had thought of apologizing but had felt too dispirited to do so.

"You shouldn't invest so much in individuals," said Irma. "It's always been your mistake. Stick to movements: wide sweeps of existence and experience. Ignore detail. It's how men get by."

"I'm sorry," said Mary. "I was behaving badly. In fact, everything's going to be all right. The Toronto hospital is holding the job open for another year; they say they'll stretch a point and take a small baby. It's a hotbed of feminism. So you see my life isn't over; it's merely postponed for a year. Come and see me in hospital, when the baby's born, when it's too late for you to wish it out of existence."

But there was a certain coolness in her voice.

"Of course there is," said Irma. "You can't safely suggest terminations to women who are consumed by mother lust."

Praxis devoted herself to the many, rather than the few. She wrote editorials of such power and vehemence—finding a certainty in writing which she certainly did not find in real life—that readers cut them out, stuck them on walls and quoted them in arguments.

"My diatribes," Praxis called them, diffidently. But others found in them the stuff of revolution: the focusing of a real discontent, and with that focusing the capacity for alteration.

Next time Mary telephoned, it was to say that she was in hospital and that she had a three-day-old son. There was no pleasure in her voice. Praxis went again to Brighton, stood yet once more on the railway platform and remembered Hilda's curse. "Wherever you go, you take yourself with you." She took the bus to the hospital.

Mary had a room to herself: she looked thin and grey, and moved with difficulty. The baby lay in a wheeled cot by the bed, swathed in blankets, lying on its side like a doll, still and silent.

"I had to have a Caesarean," said Mary. "Everything seemed to go wrong. It wasn't very nice.

"The baby nearly died," said Mary. "He's been in the special care unit, wired up to this and that. But they pulled him through.

"I fell in love with my other two babies," she said. "It took a day with the eldest, and the next was love at first sight. It's called the bonding process, I believe. It hasn't happened with this one. I suppose it still might."

But she did not sound hopeful.

"Don't look at him too closely," said Mary. "He's mongoloid. He's got a chromosome missing. I could have had tests done at four months but I didn't. They can detect mongolism as early as that. Or spina bifida. Then they terminate; but you know my beliefs. I would just have known five months earlier and had five months more misery in my life, that's all.

"It is the end of my life, isn't it?" said Mary. "I'll never get to Toronto now. Never get to the States. Never get anywhere. Why didn't they let him die? I wasn't asking anyone to do anything: just to do nothing. But institutions are incapable of doing nothing, I suppose."

"You can put it in a home," said Praxis.

"Him," said Mary, "not it. No, I can't do that. We all have to take responsibility for ourselves; we can't hand our troubles over. Besides, he might suffer. And what would the other two think? No. God sent him. He must have meant it.

"He's very low-grade, I think," said Mary. "He will sit in a chair and dribble and wear nappies when he's a grown man. Well, some people reach personal salvation through such events, I'm told. A life of dedication. And there's nothing wrong, to a mongol, with being a mongol. One of the doctors told me so. A Dr. Gibb. A woman. I liked her. And I seem to remember saying that, myself, to a woman in my position. When I was in obstetrics, and had a future."

"I'll look after it," said Praxis.

"No you won't," said Mary. "You call him 'it.' You're not fit. Other women have worse to put up with. I watched them in the special care unit. They sit by the incubators, staring at their children, little babies, taped to electrodes, fastened to drips, ill, in pain, possibly dying, possibly living: possibly deformed for life, possibly not. There is an animal look in their eyes; in the mothers, and in the babies. It shouldn't be there. We are spirits, not animals. They should let the babies die, when they get to that stage, and the mothers too. Life itself is not important. Only the manner of living.

"I thought I might kill it," said Mary. "Then I realized it was him."

Mary got out of bed, stiffly and painfully, to go to the bathroom. Praxis tried to help her, but Mary shook her off.

"I can manage all right," she said.

While Mary was out of the room Praxis took a pillow from the bed, turned the baby onto its back and pressed the white mass over its face. No movement came from beneath; before, or during, or after. It scarcely seemed like the extinguishing of a life: more like the rectifying of a mistake, which had to be done, in the same way that an inflamed appendix has to be removed, before it kills the entire body. Nature's weak point. Nature's error, not God's purpose.

Praxis put the pillow back on the bed and rang the bell. A nurse came.

"I think there's something wrong with the baby," said Praxis. The nurse ran the baby, cot and all, down the corridor. Red lights flashed, footsteps echoed. Mary came slowly back from the bathroom.

"Where's the baby?" asked Mary, and fainted.

Soon Dr. Gibb came. She was Pakistani, dark-eyed and frail, but had about her the same look of resolution which Mary had had, in better days, and which Praxis trusted would now presently return.

"I'm sorry," said Dr. Gibb. "Your baby did have breathing difficulties, as you know. Perhaps we took him from the incubator too soon? I'm not saying it isn't a tragedy—of course it is—but in the circumstances, I have seen worse things happen."

Dr. Gibb wanted no further discussion. Mary turned her back on Praxis and cried, but whether from physical weakness and shock, or from real distress, Praxis did not know.

Praxis left the hospital and walked down Holden Road and to the beach. 109 had been painted, and newly fenced. The garden bloomed. Two little boys, companionable, swung on the gate. It was getting dark. A woman came out of the front door and called them in to tea. The door, Praxis noticed, opened easily. It had finally been taken off its hinges, and planed.

Praxis walked along the seashore. The sky darkened, and one by one the stars emerged. The sea rustled the pebbles on the beach. The world became still: breathing stopped. Betelgeuse leaned down, in his fiery shaft, towards her: tears of flame dripped down around her. Betelgeuse spoke. The roaring faded her ears: the noise of the sea and the shore reasserted itself. The pebbles dragged up and back, up and back, soothing and reassuring. Her feet sank, as she walked back to the hospital, into the loose piled sand and stones of the upper beach. It held her back and made her the more determined.

She found Dr. Gibb sitting in the sisters' room of the postnatal ward, white-coated, filling up forms; an exotic creature, passing through, out of place.

"It wasn't natural causes," said Praxis. "I did it, and I think I was right to do so."

"And I think you are overwrought," said Dr. Gibb, "and should think carefully about what you say, in case you upset the mother more than she is upset already."

"We can't think about individuals all the time," said Praxis.

"I do," said Dr. Gibb.

"Well, I'm sorry," said Praxis, "if I'm a nuisance. But the fact is that the baby was alive and good for another forty years of semi-vegetable living, but because of something I did, deliberately, it is now dead. That is the truth. I offer it to you, Dr. Gibb."

Black bat wings hovered, and pounced even as she spoke. Claws of doubt dug into her skull. But for once Praxis was not unsure as to what was reality and what was not. What she remembered and what had happened were identical. She had passed into the real world, where feelings were sharp and clear, however painful.

"The death certificate is signed," said Dr. Gibb, sadly. "I suppose I will have to tear it up."

"Yes," said Praxis.

"Good for you," said Dr. Gibb, surprisingly. Dr. Gibb was back from Bangladesh, floods, famine, war and plague. She had seen hundreds die, and thousands dead. "Good for you."

It was not a view, it seemed to Praxis, that was held by many, first at the inquest, then at the trial. Praxis was held in custody between the two events, and only echoes of the row in the outside world reached her. The prison itself was newly built and bleak, but in no way horrific. Praxis had a small room with a window in the door, a comfortable enough bed, shelves, Home-Office-issue prints on the wall, and she was allowed one photograph from home, but chose to go without.

The diet was nostalgia enough—a daily reminder through lumpy

mashed potato and soggy greens of Willie and her distracted youth:
almost she felt the weight of Baby Mary on her arm, and the
constant jab of Willie into her. Her body as much as her mind she
felt—was allowed for once to feel, in the boring tranquillity of
prison routine—was the sum of its experience: even now it was
recording the smell of boiled cabbage, institution toilets, disinfectant, female bodies at close quarters, and so on, and would play
them back to her, in a wistful tune, in later years.

Praxis might get a life term, or a two-year suspended sentence,
said her lawyer, on one of his weekly visits. There was no knowing.
He was a young, nervous, busy man. He ran into the room, wiped
his bald, round head with an unironed handkerchief, asked questions, took notes and ran out again to see—or so Praxis felt—to
some other, more pressing business. He shook his head busily
when Praxis declined to plead temporary mental imbalance.

"What do you want? Martyrdom? To get your name in the papers? Isn't it there enough already?"

"I don't know," said Praxis. "They don't let me have newspapers
while I'm on remand."

"It's for your own protection," said the lawyer. "They're not
saying very nice things."

"I wouldn't expect them to," said Praxis. "I don't say very nice
things to myself."

Nor she did. But the sense of relief remained; lurking beneath
the self-laceration, as if she had finally faced and survived the
worst which could happen: which was not, it turned out, being
killed, but rather, killing. And now it was done, and over. And
along with the relief, consoling her, was the visionary notion that
the act of killing had not been petty, sordid, ordinary and mad, but
that she had been the instrument of some higher will.

Praxis could, and would, rationalize the deed away: she would
say that logically there was no difference between contraception
and abortion: that the termination of pregnancy at any stage,
whether the foetus was minus nine months, six months, three
months or plus one day, must be the mother's decision. That pregnant women must somehow be relieved of the fear they felt, now
that one baby in every twenty was born with some defect or other;
and so on, and so on: and half believe it, and half know that all
this was irrelevant.

She would cry for Mary's baby, moan with horror in the night because of what she had done, but something proud and implacable remained. She had been right.

The prison staff and her fellow prisoners discussed the matter with her.

"It's not as if you were the baby's mother," said the librarian. She had a degree in English literature and was in for baby battering. "What right did you have?"

"She was my sister," said Praxis. "All women are my sister," and sadly interpreted it, even as she spoke. "Hilda failed me, so I have claimed in her place all the women in the world."

"If my baby had been born handicapped," said the prison chaplain, who reminded Praxis of Mr. Allbright and who had a new young wife and baby, "we would have loved it the more."

"You're nice good people," said Praxis. "Not everyone is. You don't live at the limits of your endurance. Many do." But she knew he was right, and that others would have taken Mary's baby and looked after it. As the helpless were looked after—cruelty alternating with kindness. As others had looked after Lucy.

"One thing leads to another," said a prostitute, in for attacking a colleague with a knife. "First abortion, then euthanasia, then genocide. Well, that was Hitler's way, wasn't it? I just don't understand how people can harm little children. Let alone kill them."

"Life is not always preferable to death," said Praxis, and wondered how much of herself she had been killing, when she smothered Mary's baby. Putting herself, by proxy, out of her misery.

"You were quite right," said a grey-faced shoplifter. "They did their tests and told me at five months I was carrying a spina bifida baby. I had a termination. It was twins. I'd rather they'd waited the full nine months and then done it, when we all knew for sure. What's the difference, really?"

"Thank you," said Praxis.

A letter was passed to Praxis. It came from a film company with which Phillip was involved. It asked her to sign enclosed release forms, so that footage of Praxis in earlier days could be used in a documentary, *The Right to Choose*, which Phillip was making for the Women's Movement. Praxis signed, as requested. Motivation no longer seemed of much consequence. Results were what mattered.

"If the child's mother says she asked you to do it," said the lawyer, "we'll stand some kind of chance."

"She didn't," said Praxis. "I don't want her to say it."

"I don't think she will," said the lawyer. "She's very bitter."

Praxis cried at that, and the lawyer looked relieved, as if at last something he understood had happened.

The day before the trial opened, the governor sent for Praxis and handed her a file of letters.

"We thought you ought to see these," she said. She reminded Praxis of Hilda, but perhaps that was merely the capacity she had for writing adverse reports, and circulating them. "They might cheer you up. They're letters of support, from women saying they wish they'd had the courage to do what you did. Mothers, mostly, mind you: but grandmothers, relatives, friends, as well, who have watched the disintegration of households, as the years pass."

"I don't want to read them," said Praxis. "I want a rest from other people's misery. Thank you very much, all the same."

"Ah, well," said the governor, disappointed. "I suppose we can't be saints all the time."

As it was a murder charge, Praxis was handcuffed to a wardress on the way to the court. Through the side window she caught glimpses of groups of women with banners, and the sound of cheers, shouts and boos. As she stepped from the car she was dazzled by flashlights.

"People get hysterical," she remarked to the wardress, more in the spirit of apology than anything else.

"Better than being cold-blooded," said the wardress, who had a backward brother, could see the convenience of his elimination, despised herself for it and felt the more antagonism towards Praxis because of it.

"I'm not," said Praxis. "I'm not." But by whose standards did she judge?

"Yes," said Mary, loud and clear across the court. "I asked her to do it for me. She was my friend." But she did not meet Praxis' eye. She would tell a lie on her account, but not forgive her.

"No," said Praxis. "Of course I was not the proper person to do it. But who else was there?"

"No," said Praxis, "I did not have the right, but the mother did. I was her agent."

Thus far she would lie to get herself out of trouble.

"No," said Praxis, "I see nothing worse in killing a four-day-old imperfect baby than in killing a four-month-old perfect foetus. Except that it's more disagreeable to do."

"No," said Praxis. "I am not mad, am not receiving psychiatric treatment."

"Yes," said Praxis, "it is perfectly possible that my life to date is indicative of a damaged personality: but most of us are emotionally damaged in some degree or another. We do the best we can with what we have."

The judge was not unsympathetic. The abortion laws, he said, had confused both the moral and the legal issues.

The father of ancient Rome (he had a classical education) exercised the right of life and death over a newborn baby. If the living would suffer as a result of its birth—by reason of famine, war or danger—it was not allowed to live. Nor was a defective child: nor a female, in a family already overcrowded with girls. The decision was taken by the father: the deed performed by a servant. That was in the great days of the Empire.

The jury was out for two days and brought back a verdict of guilty, the judge finally consenting to accept a majority verdict.

Praxis was sentenced to two years' imprisonment.

Women crowded round the black Maria as she left the court, tapping at the windows.

"We'll be waiting."

"Don't give up."

"Don't give in."

If there were others—as there surely were—wishing to spit and abuse, or weep and reproach, they did not get near.

Mary went to Toronto, with the children.

Irma came to visit, and brought Praxis news of the outside world. Serena had left Phillip. Claire married her business executive: it had been a big wedding and Diana had played the mother of the bride very well, in a blue hat with feathers, as surely she was entitled to do. Mary's job was going well: she was to specialize in pediatrics. Irma herself was looking ill: she had cancer: she would not have treatment for it. Jason had given in, given up park keeping, and gone back to university. The winter weather drove him to it, he said, and not his father. Though now Serena had left, and

Phillip was plainly wretched, he felt more kindly inclined towards him. Robert had decided to stay on in Africa.

"To shoot Africans, I suppose," said Praxis, sadly.

"You should never have left them," said Irma. "As you sow, Praxis, so you reap."

Her own younger son lived with her country cousins. He rode horses, drove tractors and despised city life. Irma did not feel she had to keep alive on his account.

"As you sow," repeated Praxis, "so you reap."

It was, in the end, a comforting doctrine.

"Do call me Pattie," she said. "I've given up Praxis. It's a very pretentious name."

"Funny," said Irma, "your sister has started calling herself Hypatia."

When Pattie Fletcher left prison there was no one to meet her. She had, she assumed, been forgotten by a fickle world. She had very little money, and nowhere to live. Irma was in hospital, in a coma. Bess, Tracey and Raya had started a commune in Wales. Pattie could not, without effort, trace their address. She developed a cold, which turned into bronchitis. The Discharged Prisoners' Aid Association found her a basement room in a familiar neighbourhood: the Social Security people paid her a small weekly sum.

She fell, getting from the bath, cracked her elbow on the floor, tried to go to hospital, had her toe stamped on by the kind of young woman she had helped create, and came home.

She wrote, she raged, grieved and laughed, she thought she nearly died; then, presently, she began to feel better.

25

TODAY I MANAGED to get a slipper onto my foot and a coat onto my back. I left my basement, boarded the bus, was helped to my seat by the conductor and, when I reached my destination, out of it by a handsome young African with curly hair who did not seem in the least averse to taking my uninjured arm.

I arrived at the hospital at half past two and waited for attention in the Outpatient Department until three fifty-five. A handful of patients, who arrived after me but were dripping blood or gasping for air, were seen out of turn, but it was not, all the same, as long a wait as I had expected. Who wants to look at an old woman's toes when the lives of the young and virile are at stake, and the red blood spurting free? But I was not actively discriminated against. And the tea, offered by kindly volunteers, was of good quality and served in unchipped mugs and with unlimited sugar. (The young despise sugar, these days, seeing it as the root of many evils, both physical and moral, which leaves plenty for the likes of me.)

When I was shown into the treatment cubicle by the nurse, the young woman doctor had her back to me, and was studying my notes, as is their custom. I eased my foot from its slipper, my elbow from my coat. I was dizzy with mingled pain and relief. The doctor turned. She had a pretty, alert face. She wore no make-up. She reminded me of Mary. She seemed puzzled, as Mary seldom was. Mary's fault, if she had one, was a surfeit of certainty.

"Pattie Fletcher?" she enquired, staring at my card, then at me. "But I know your face from somewhere."

I wished she would concentrate on my injuries.

"You're Praxis Duveen," she said. "That's who you are."

I had the impression that she fell on her knees, but it can hardly have been so. At any rate, there were tears in her eyes.

"We didn't know where you were," she said. "We thought you must be dead."

"Who's we?"

"Everyone," she said. "Oh, everyone. Anyone who saw the film." Phillip's film: his apology; his justification.

"But what have they done to you?" she demanded, all ready to be angry.

"Nothing," I said, "I did it all to myself."

She said I was not fit to go home and had me wheeled along corridors and up in lifts into a small room off a man's ward, and the last I saw of her that day was pink-faced and gesticulating to the ward sister, who seemed aggrieved.

I do not want special treatment, but I see that I shall get it. I am not suffering from senility, it seems, but malnutrition. They feed me with spoonfuls of scrambled egg, which I hate. My skin is already better, my eyes are brighter, my hair is almost thick. I am not nearly so old as I had assumed. I remember Lucy's old trick of pretending extreme old age, as if madness was not enough, and she needed that protection too. My manuscript is carefully sorted and safely between plastic folders. There are flowers everywhere.

I do not want any of this: it is not what I meant. The pain in my soul, my heart, my mind, is not assuaged, as are my bodily aches and pains, by recognition and attention. I am surrounded, at too frequent intervals, by a babel of people, mostly women, either embarrassingly servile or self-consciously unimpressed. Cameras click and whirr. I have been elected heroine. In the meantime, I worry in case they are neglecting my toe. If it is broken, why don't they put it in plaster? All they have done is lay it, rather carelessly, in a bed of sticky tape, and say that will do.

Dear God, do I have to go on living?

It occurs to me that when I address the deity in these terms, it is in the conviction that he exists: or, if not a deity, some kind of force which turns the wheels of action and reaction, and gives meaning and purpose to our lives: if not in our own eyes, at least in those of other people.

And there, you see, I've done it. I have thrown away my life, and gained it. The wall which surrounded me is quite broken down. I can touch, feel, see my fellow human beings.

That is quite enough.